HOR
STORIES

Gayle Bunney

HORSE STORIES

The Publisher: Lone Pine Publishing

10145 – 81 Ave.   1901 Raymond Ave. SW, Suite C
Edmonton, AB T6E 1W9   Renton, WA 98055
Canada   USA

Canadian Cataloguing in Publication Data
Bunney, Gayle, 1954–
    Horse Stories

ISBN 1-55105-124-9

    1. Bunney, Gayle, 1954– —Anecdotes. 2. Horses—Anecdotes.
3. Horsemanship—Anecdotes. I. Title.
SF301.B85 1998   636.1'0092   C98-910741-8

Senior Editor: Nancy Foulds
Production Manager: David Dodge
Layout & Production: Michelle Bynoe
Book Design: Michelle Bynoe
Cover Design: Michelle Bynoe
Cover Photo: Wild horse by Michael H. Francis
Printing: Webcom Limited, Toronto, Ontario, Canada

The publisher gratefully acknowledges the support of the Department of Canadian Heritage.

I Wish to Thank

My grandfather, Mr. Frank Cartwright (deceased) for telling me to always follow my dreams. My parents, Ralph and Rebecca Caskey, who love me even though I never got off a horse long enough to dress like a lady. And most of all, the horses who have enriched my life with their own special way of accepting me not as their master, but as their friend.

Contents

Preface

This story is not about how to train or ride horses, although perhaps the average horse person will be able to pick up some handy hints on how to handle and how not to handle certain horses. Instead it is a story about the horses themselves: the good old boys and the rough broncs who can show up anywhere; the ones who nicker a greeting to their owner every morning, happy to see their master; the ones who would rather place a well-aimed kick to your ribs if given half a chance; the ones who, regardless of their thoughtless, uncaring owners who ride them mile after mile until exhaustion, will the next day still come to the fence to greet those people; and the ones who out of desperation learn to become unwilling partners in the game of cowboy and horse.

It is a story about birth and about death. There are few animals in our great kingdom as beautiful as horses in their newness as they struggle to their feet for that first suck of life-sustaining milk and only hours later run, buck, leap and play beside their dams. Their death, whether through old age or injury, or simply because their masters no longer wish to keep and care for them, is always a great sadness.

Just as no two people in the entire universe are the same, no two horses can ever be raised, trained, ridden or cared for the exact same. Each horse is exactly that, a horse, one of a kind.

Lost Freedom

It circles his neck, choking him,
He lunges, fighting the snake–like line
Chances of escape look afar and dim
His sweat–covered hide no longer looks fine.

The great chest filled with power
Surges and heaves against this enemy,
Trampling beneath mighty hooves, the prairie flower
Still he fights the dreadful thing.

His nostrils wide, his wind cut off
Fear shows plain in white–rimmed eyes
His breath a sobbing, racking cough
With a shudder he falls, his spirit dies.

His freedom gone, his freedom lost,
The gallant stallion lies in defeat
The wild one succumbs at nature's cost,
And finally rises, mild and meek.

ROAD APPLES

If a horse person knows what a road apple is, then he or she knows all about cleaning barns. Road apples love barns and especially box stalls inside barns. Once a couple of road apples take up residence inside a barn, they multiply like mad. Before you know it, there are hundreds of them, scattered here and there, with the latest arrivals still clinging to each other for support, in neat piles. Road apples are notorious for being smelly little varmints, so eventually you must take a pitchfork and escort them off the premises. This work can be back-breaking, for they do not co-operate with their removal. They prefer to jump or roll off the pitchfork and hide in the back corners, farthest from the doorway. It's a dirty job, but some-body has to do it.

Any older horse person who has many years of experience with road apples also knows they go where horses go. If a horse is anywhere in the country, these quaint little critters will also be present.

I once was neighbours with a horseman of great experience. He was past his prime, long ago giving up riding snorty broncs for a living. He was some crippled up with arthritis and horse-related injuries, so he pretty much drove his rickety pickup truck wherever he needed to go. Just moseying down those back-country roads for an afternoon drive, he was able to tell what the local horse population was doing. Most of his infor-mation came from road apples.

I had an afternoon off for a change and when Homer came along to see if I wanted to go for a ride with him in his pickup truck, I accepted. There we were, chugging along, when Homer gave a snort, "See them road apples lying around in the sun, in the corner of Pete's field, next to that stand of willow and poplar trees?" I assured him I did. "Well that means he never paid the rent money to old Mrs. Smurff, on that pasture land of hers he was running his horses on, and he ended up having to bring them home." As I had already heard that from Mrs. Smurff, I knew what Homer had said was the truth. It wasn't long before Homer spotted some piles of road apples in the ditch, next to a pasture fence. He shook his head. "See them apples in the ditch? Clarence never closed his gate to the pasture again when he checked his cows, and his old mare, Hazel, got loose. She was standing around the fence line there, wanting to get back in because she was thirsty and the dugout full of water is right across the fence there." I stared at him in amazement because he was right on target again. I knew because it was I who had passed by the evening before and let her back into the pasture.

Homer was good at reading road apples all right, and soon proved to me he was even better than I already thought he was. A little further down the road, low and behold, were some more road apples. But this time we drove right by lots of them, sprinkled down the edge of the road. Homer just grunted and muttered under his breath. I wasn't taking his lack of communication sitting still. I sized up those apples and said, "Looks like someone was out for an afternoon ride a couple of days ago." I figured a couple of days ago because some of the poor apples had already been run over and were as flat as pancakes, drying in the sun. He gave me a cross–eyed look. "Nope," he said, "that was young Ferguson riding his sorrel mare with her baby colt tagging along early this morning when he was chasing his Holstein milk cow back home for milking. He still hasn't got around to fixing those busted boards on his corral and that cow is going to keep getting out until he does."

I never said a word, but the second Homer dropped me off at home, I jumped in my own pickup truck and went back to them road apples. After stopping and getting out, I examined them with great care. By golly, Homer could be right again. Most of the apples were adult size but a few were from a very small colt. The ones I thought were squashed flat could just possibly have something to do with a cow, not a horse. About then young Ferguson drove up and stopped to chat. I made out I was check-ing a front tire I thought might be low on air, not wanting to be caught making a fuss over road apples. I asked him how his day was going and he said not badly except first thing this morning he had to find his missing milk cow, and chase her back home with his mare. He had let her colt tag along as there wasn't much for traffic that early in the morning. Homer had done it again, correct in all accounts, by spending years getting to know road apples.

A lot of people think that once apples have been disposed of and left in heaps out behind the barn for a long, long, time, they are only good for fertilizer on the garden or out in the fields. This is not true. If you collect them while they are still in good shape and air dry them until light in weight but very hard and firm, they can be varnished or painted, then dried again. Then you can tack them onto wooden bases, in different sizes and numbers. Then label your creation "Mr. and Mrs. Road Apple and Son." Or tack two on a wooden base and paint eyes, noses and mean–looking mouths on them. Then label them "My ex–Mother–in–Law and ex–Father–in–Law." Don't stop there; get creative and make giant hood ornaments for your car or truck. Wait, how about hanging bunches of them from your front doorknob on your house, to keep unwanted guests from walk-ing straight into your home without knocking first. The possi-bilities are endless. Enjoy your road apples any way you can!

THINGS A PERSON SHOULD NEVER DO

There are certain things even a crazy, horse–loving girl should never do in this lifetime. After every silly stunt I pulled, I always sat down and said, "Why? Why must I do these things?" I never did come up with an answer, but thank heavens as I get older I no longer have any desire to be recognized as half crazy by other members of society.

Take my graveyard stunt. My neighbours had a lanky grey gelding that with age appeared to be almost white. I thought it would be a real hoot to put holes in an old sheet, drape it over myself, paint my face white, borrow the gelding after dark, and ride him bareback around the graves in the local cemetery at midnight. Maybe, with any luck, I could throw a real chill into some motorists on the nearby highway. When everyone was asleep–meaning my grandfather, with whom I was living as a mid–teenager, and the neighbours, who did not know I was borrowing their horse–I dressed, snuck out and nabbed the horse from his corral. Jumping up on Spiker, I loped across the fields to the back entrance of the cemetery where I put on my sheet and whitened my face. Spiker and I moseyed along the pathways in the dead of night (get the pun there), careful of where we stepped. A few late–night drivers sped by without even noticing us, let alone getting a chill out of our perform–ance. It didn't take me long to figure out who I was really scaring. Me. I had never been in a cemetery after hours before, and my imagination was running wild. About the second time I thought I saw something move amongst the headstones, I tensed up as rigid as a stone statue. The big grey could feel my fear through the seat of my pants and started to panic himself.

Right about then, a weird moaning noise came from behind us. Half my brain said it's only the wind, the other half said run for your life. Spiker didn't need any urging from me. He burst into a mad gallop for home. We shot out the front entrance gate toward the highway and Spiker made a turn to the right in the ditch toward home. I had a faint glimpse of a terrified motorist, swerving crazily down the highway at the ghostly sight of us, when the sheet blew up over my head and blocked my vision entirely. I clung to the gelding's bare back as he beat all speed records getting home. We skidded into his owners' yard, making a terrible racket of pounding hooves and flying gravel. I was off him in an instant, pulling his bridle off and turning him loose in the corral. Then, still surrounded by inky darkness, I peddled myself home to Granddad's and up to the safety of my room. I huddled under the covers on my bed, not sure who was going to get me first, Granddad, the neighbours or the creepy crea–tures who may have followed me home.

I survived the night, and not a word was said to me about it during the next couple of days. Maybe I hadn't woke Granddad up or the neighbours with all the racket I made escaping from the haunted graveyard. On the third day, while having supper, Granddad mentioned how some elderly people got the fright of their lives when some idiot galloped a horse out of the grave–yard the other night in the dark. I hung my head in shame, but the only thing he said to me was, "If I ever find out you're riding after dark, I will personally give you the worst licking of your life." End of story.

The Buck Stops Here

I purchased a pretty black mare at a horse sale, even though she was fairly rank in the sale ring, spooking at everything and looking for a way out with determination. She appeared to be a four- or five-year-old, not even halter broke, but the price was right. Black horses always have brought a good price at resale time and she was in foal, a two-in-one package. I loaded her loose in the stock trailer, hauled her home and kicked her out on pasture to have her foal. She foaled an equally pretty black filly and I left them alone for another couple of months. Finally, the time came when I had to get her halter broke and started under saddle if I was going to sell her that year as a potential saddle mare with 30 days' riding on her already. A lot of people won't start a horse, but will certainly pay good money for one with a few hours of riding on them.

Blackie, as I called her, had other ideas. I had to chase the whole herd in at a dead run, so she would stick with the bunch and go into the main corral. Then I was the rest of the morning separating her and getting her in the breaking pen. The filly was as wild as her mother, and tore around the pen with the whites of her eyes showing too. I left them an hour or so to settle down, then eased the filly into a small holding pen, so I could rope the mare and work with her without the baby getting trampled.

Low and behold, I actually caught her on the first throw of the lariat. The fight was on. Blackie fought like a tiger, putting me right out of the pen once. I didn't really want to choke her down by snubbing hard and fast to a post, so the battle raged on longer than usual. Suddenly, she just quit fighting completely and stood absolutely still. She never moved a muscle as I worked my way up the rope and put a halter and long lead on her, taking off the lariat. Staying back out of her way, I pulled her head first to the left, then to the right, until she started to follow the pull and lead some. Finally I snubbed her so she could learn

20

that once tied, freedom was no longer an option. She fought the tied rope for only a couple of minutes then wisely gave up the battle. Within minutes she was leading around like a well-broke horse. I worked her the next day on her leading, then because I was going to be gone for a couple of days hauling horses, I turned her and her foal back out on pasture. Wrong thing to do. For most of the summer, I tried to chase her back into the corral, but she wasn't going to get trapped in there again. Finally, I asked another pair of horsemen to help me and the three of us out-manoeuvred her and got the pair of them into the corral. Her filly was old enough to wean off her now, and one of the men bought the young one, loaded her up with their saddle horses and went home.

It was already late in the season for making good money on green broke horses, so I decided to sell her without bothering to start her under saddle. If she fought anything like she did being roped when she was being ridden, she wasn't going to make me money anyway. The next day was a horse sale at Rocky Mountain House, so I loaded her with the other sale horses and went to town. I unloaded her and managed to get a halter on her in a confined pen and took her to my pen of horses, leaving her tied to a corner post. Well, you can't believe the people who were interested in her, as she was about the prettiest horse there. Every person out back at the auction had to stop and look at her.

Money signs started to flash before my eyes. Why hadn't I started her under saddle? Heck, she hadn't been that bad to halter break. If I had at least ridden her a dozen times, I could have tripled my profit, maybe more! Look at all the potential buyers!

Now, I like a lot of things in life, money being one of them. A crazy idea came to me (that happens now and then). I led the mare out of the pen, and took her away around back of a shed out of sight. Then I looped and tied the lead rope around her neck to form a single rein and jumped up on her bareback. I think she was too shocked to do much of anything. I pulled her around some, then opened the gate latch and rode her back, down through the crowds of people gathered in the aisles. Seeing me riding her guaranteed me a dozen more interested bidders.

When her number was called and I rode her into the sale ring, the bidding was fast and furious. Even though I had the auctioneer state that this was her first time ever ridden, the bidding never let up. Blackie topped the sale price for a horse, not just that day, but of all the sales held that year. What a way to go!

So, why shouldn't I have done this? Because she was in the Innisfail sale ring the following week. Apparently the buyer had not believed she was only ridden that one time and when he went to throw a saddle on her, she kicked him hard enough to break his pelvic bone. His older brother then managed to get her saddled and get on her. She reared over backwards with him, putting him in the hospital for what ended up to be two solid months. She was advertised at Innisfail as having been ridden by a young woman (me) with ease. The woman who bought her there ended up in the hospital with severe concussion after she was thrown. I next spotted her at a spring sale in Stettler, being advertised as broke, but needing an experienced rider. I hate to think what happened to the person who bought her there. I should never have started this chain reaction with a pretty black mare, who, when I sold her, actually only had two days of halter break training on her, nothing else.

Let 'er Rip

I may ride broncs, but never in my life have I been a bronc rider. The only way I can last on top of a bucking horse is to use all my strength to pull their heads up and around. Without controlling them to some extent, I end up on the ground, picking dirt out of my front teeth and feeling sorry for myself. I know I can't last two seconds on a real rodeo bronc so why do I try? I think I must have got rattled by some mean old cow when I was young.

Friends of mine had faith in my ability to ride broncs, I guess because I only told them about the times I stayed on, not about the majority of the times when I did not. So one day, they talked me into getting on a green bronc at the yearly Daines Bucking Horse Sale at Innisfail. You're supposed to let these horses buck after you come out of the chute, not try to hold their heads up and around. I didn't much like the thought of doing it, but I knew the ride wouldn't last very long anyway, so out of the chute I came. I was riding bareback on a mean little cuss. I lasted my usual two seconds, so I was happy. My friends' faith in my abilities was undaunted though, and a month later they had me advertised at a small local rodeo as an exhibition rider on a saddle bronc for the enjoyment of the crowd. Of course, they never told me this until we were already there. They had a bronc saddle all lined up for me and everything. I don't like an association, real-life bronc saddle because the darn things don't have a horn on them for me to hold. After all the saddle bronc riders were done, it was my turn. While the announcer gave his speech about cowgirls riding like cowboys (how else are we supposed to ride?), I settled myself down on a bay gelding in the chute and said my prayers. I nodded my head to open the gate.

Nothing happened. Nothing. The horse just stood there. Finally, a cowboy leaned down over top the chute and pushed the horse's head towards freedom. The horse sort of yawned and moseyed out into the arena in front of a thousand people. There he stopped, me with one arm in the air, leaning way back so I had a chance of lasting my normal two seconds. I wasn't wearing spurs, but I raked him a couple of times with the heels of my boots. Nothing happened. We just stood there. The crowd of spectators were on their feet, roaring with laughter, when along came the clowns. They joined hands behind the horse and pretended to boost him into bucking. I must have looked awful silly sitting there on that plug, in my let-'er-rip position. Finally the clowns led the horse and me out of the arena. I was so embarrassed that I actually felt terrible that I wasn't picking dirt out from between my front teeth. Later, when I found out my wild saddle bronc was some kid's twenty-four-year-old gentle horse used to set me up for some good fun and laughs, I wanted to kill my friends. After all, no self-respecting cowgirl wants to be caught riding some gentle old plug in public, and a thousand people is a lot of public.

No Dude Horse

I'm the type who hates to walk anywhere. If I'm not able to drive my pickup trick or ride a horse, I don't make it very far. If I'm forced to walk a block or two in town, I moan and groan something fierce. My theory is that the good Lord gave us two legs, not for walking, but to straddle a horse or at least work the gas and brake pedals in a vehicle. I also believe walking burns up calories, and if that happened I would end up thin, and that would be just terrible.

I was working for an outfitter one summer when I could have been killed because I hate walking. He and I had seven dudes in a camp high up on a mountain river. It was an isolated region, basically untouched by humans. After a supper of fresh-caught brook trout and some of my famous homemade crab-apple pie, the three couples and one single man made themselves comfortable around a big fire. Out came the bottles of rye and vodka from their packs, and they started into swapping tales and drowning their Adam's apples. After dark I made my goodnight speech and went to bed in my pup tent, set up a ways from camp.

Maybe two hours later the outfitter roused me from my sleep. The single man had taken on a tank full of booze, and got talking about his ex-wife to the three happy couples. As the evening continued, the three couples got even more happy, making this dude feel plumb left out. So he up and charged off in the bush, wailing something about killing himself. We couldn't have a dude running around in the darkness, just in case he did get himself killed, so we had to look for him. Now, remember I hate walking, so here I am, prowling through the black timber calling this idiot's name and hoping to stumble across him. Off to my right, I here the jingle of some of our horses' chain hobbles. A light bulb goes off in my brain, and I follow the sound of the horses until I practically fall over top of one in the dark. Until I flick my lighter and hold it up to the horse's face, I don't know which one is before me. Aahh, the blaze looks familiar, it must be the sorrel that is such a gentle dude horse for women and children. My lighter won't stay lit, so I pocket it, and going by feel, remove the chain hobbles from his front legs and do them up around his throat. I step up on a log lying there, and once on his back, boot him forward to continue the search for the missing dude. To turn and stop him, I reach forward on his neck, and pull on his chain collar. I worked my way back and forth around camp for quite a spell, before I hear the pre-arranged shout from camp saying the other searcher has found him. I trotted into camp on the dude horse, only to see the outfitter's jaw drop to the ground as I came into the firelight. Looking down at the horse's back, I see why. This ain't no dude horse! This is Levi I'm riding, kicking him in the ribs every couple of feet. I'm off Levi in a second, my knees already starting to shake.

See, Levi was a bit of a problem horse. I didn't even like riding him with a good bit in his mouth and a saddle on his back, because he would buck you off, run away with you or take a chunk out of your hide rather than be ridden. He wasn't even a completely reliable pack horse he was such an outlaw, let alone be ridden bareback, with no control on his head. Levi stood up to his bad reputation the next day by crashing through the timber and bucking off his rider, who was a far better horseman than me. The dear Lord must have been visiting the mountains that night and took care of me. Thank you Lord, and thank you Levi, for sparing my life and limb that night.

RIDING BAREBACK

With my first horse, Patches, I had to use a saddle. He was not trustworthy enough to ride without stirrups and a horn, put there on a saddle just so I could wrap my fingers around it. He was small enough that I could boost my lightweight kid's saddle up on him. If Patches was good for anything it was that he taught me how to ride well. He figured, I think, that he was put on God's green earth to not teach kids how to ride, but to teach them to hate riding. It worked with my two older brothers because neither of them can be talked into getting up on a horse's back. It was either my stubborn streak, which my mother claims I was born with, or a true love of riding, which made me keep picking myself up and getting back on him. I'm sure the saddle horn on my first saddle had deep grooves in it from me clutching it so hard with Patches and his bag full of Let's Dump the Rider tricks.

Queen Lady was my next horse and the bond between this mare and myself ran soul–deep. Patches taught me how to ride and Lady taught me to love riding. They were as different as night and day in temperament. Lady and I were a team from day one. She wasn't pretty and she was as slow as molasses, but she was all heart. She came out of the Caroline–Sundre country in Alberta, out of a school teacher's mare and a wild stallion who came visiting one day. She was three years old and well broke, and she even knew several fancy tricks her previous owner had taught her.

Now, she was also a lot taller than Patches. Patches' little saddle didn't fit her either, meaning I had to use Dad's heavy one. In those days I was as wide as I was tall. I really wasn't that terribly wide, but I wasn't terribly tall, either.

It was a lot of trouble every day trying to lift that big saddle up high onto her broad back. As you might guess, I soon learned to ride bareback. I was a determined cuss, and set on becoming excellent at riding Lady bareback. When she sailed over a ditch, I sailed over her head. When she galloped down a steep hill, I rode up right behind her ears. When she galloped up a steep hill, her bushy tail tickled my rump. When she shied at something on the ground, I landed on the ground for a closer look at what spooked her. But I kept riding, and then one day I realized I hadn't fallen off for weeks. Then the day came when we were not two separate creatures, but one.

Riding Lady without a saddle wasn't good enough for me. Lots of other kids rode bareback too. I had to be better than them. So I learned to ride her with only a halter, then with only a piece of twine, then with nothing. Just her and I, running with the wind, nothing to control her but my voice and hands on her neck. She learned to turn with only my hand pressing on her neck. She would usually stop the second I grabbed her long mane in both hands and pulled back, while saying whoa. If she wouldn't stop this way I knew a secret way to get her to stop. Leaning far ahead on her racing back, I would slap her hard on the side of her jaw. Lady hated this and would immediately slide to a halt, with her head down. It took all the strength in my legs wrapped around her to hold on when she did stop like this, but it was a thrilling experience.

Barrel Back

Back twenty years ago or so, Shetlands and other ponies were much in demand for children. They had to be trained first, though. I would buy the varmints at sales, take them home and break them to ride, and then sell them, often tripling my money. A person can do only so much ground work with any horse and then you have to ride it. Well, a Shetland pony can't pack an adult and big saddle, so I rode them bareback. The most amazing thing with such a diminutive equine is that to get rid of you, all they have to do is put their heads down to buck. They don't really have to buck, because you just naturally fall off over the ears when they put their heads down. One second there is a neck and head in front of you; the next, nothing.

I have always loved the sense of freedom a person gets riding bareback, without a clunky chunk of leather between you and the horse's skin. All of the horses I've trained were not sold until they could be ridden bareback also. At some time, some where, every horse person may find himself needing to ride his faithful companion without a saddle in sight. What a shock to some people to jump up on that quiet horse without that saddle and find out he won't tolerate being ridden bareback. Without knowing it, they find out that Old Dobbin can buck pretty good.

There's been a couple of times I had to ride this way, like it or not. One time I was trailing some horses home down the road in the winter time when the filly I was riding pulled up lame. She was too lame to keep packing me and it was too cold out to slow down the journey by walking and leading her. Looking the bunch of horses over in front of me, I realized the only other halfways broke horse around was a huge Percheron draft horse cross mare named Sally. She was really meant to be harnessed to a plough, but her previous owners had also broke her to ride. I managed to sweet talk her into letting me catch her. My bridle was far too small to fit her, but no problem, I fashioned a rough hackamore out of my lariat rope. Even with the cinch straps extended to the last hole, the cinch would not go all the way around her large girth. So much for using my saddle on her. So I put the saddle and bridle back on the lame filly for her to pack home, and stood Sally in the ditch by a culvert. After about a dozen tries I managed to jump up on her broad back. We were on our way again. She was the first and last gigantic draft horse I rode bareback. Only my ankles hung over her sides. I felt like I was squatting on top of a rolling barrel. Sally's gait was so rough to ride, my teeth ached from being pounded together. The only way I stayed on her was to madly clutch her mane in both hands. I had no control over her riding this way, and for every mile of straight road, she made ten miles wandering back and forth all over it. When I reached home, I slid slowly down off her to find my legs warped in a spread–eagled position. I could only hope it wasn't going to be permanent. Never again!

RIDING ANYTHING WITH HAIR

I rode bulls a long time before I ever straddled a horse. I think I was born to ride, that it was meant to be. I hadn't even seen the inside of a classroom the first time my Granddad's brother, Uncle Walter, lifted me up onto the broad back of a show bull at the spring bull sale. Uncle Walter worked the sale rings at different bull sales and to show that some of these Horned Hereford bulls were gentle as kittens, what better way than for the buyers and spectators to see a knee-high girl happily riding around on them.

Dad had a couple of mares on the place when I was little but one was unbroken, and the other was a far cry from being safe for a child, so no riding. I was nine years old before my constant begging for a pony of my own worked. What's a budding cow-girl going to do with no horse to ride? Well, ride cows, what else. Since there were no cows hanging around waiting to be an-noyed, well then, ride bulls. Dad usually had yearling or two-year-old Registered Horned Hereford bulls in the corrals for buyers to purchase. I loved these bulls and spent the majority of my time with them. I had no fear of them. Dad bred not only for size and conformation but also temperament, never keeping back anything except the level-headed ones. They all got used to me being in their pens, scratching them and feeding them wisps of freshly pulled green grass.

Now for the riding part. Now, there's no way a little squirt is going to put a halter on a bull that towers over her, and there's no way to take a running leap and get on, so this is where I had to be patient. You hang around the pen until one of them decides to take a nap in the down position. Once he is comfort-able, relaxed and chewing his cud, you sneak up on him, scratch his back like mad, and crawl on. At that size, I was about as bothersome to a bull as a bird perched on his back. It was fun just sitting on him, playing cowboys and Indians with a crowd of imaginary friends, but it was even better if the bull would get up and stroll around some. This is where I had to be very care-ful to sit perfectly still and not annoy the bull, because if he broke into a trot, my short legs couldn't grasp his sides, and any swift movement at all meant I fell off. I do not remember any of those bulls attempting to buck.

My mother didn't look too fondly at her only wee baby girl riding bulls. So for the most part, I was careful to not get caught in the act. I think it was my persistence that made my mother help talk Dad into getting me a pony. Even when I now had a horse to ride, I still loved cattle, and still spent a great deal of time in the bull pens, scratching them, talking to them and taking the occasional ride. As I got older and my legs got longer, I was able to kick them into a trot with a half jump or two thrown in, and last at least once around the pen before falling off. These bulls were never quite as tame as the ones when I was so little, probably because of kicking them to get them up and get a jump or two out of them.

Take Pigs

Now, take pigs. They don't really have hair and they don't smell all that good either, but you can ride them when you are still little enough. Once in a while, I would go home with a friend of mine, to her parent's farm for the weekend. Rosemary

31

wasn't the tomboy–type like I was, but she did get a kick out of the time or two we figured out how to ride her dad's pigs. You ride a pig a whole lot different from a horse or bull. You don't last very far in the upright position; instead, you have to lie on that old pig's back and hold on with legs, arms, anyway you can, and you still don't last all that long. Because you're not supposed to ride the pigs, you have to tell parents little white lies at the supper table too. Like, why do we both smell like pig manure? Well, it's sort of like this, we tell them. It seems that every time we pass through the pig pen, we both fall down a lot, but no way were we riding the pigs. Nope, no way, because we know we aren't allowed to.

Hard Lessons

Take my cow, old Pete, for instance. I rode old Pete out in the pasture many times. If friends dropped in and there weren't enough gentle ponies for the kids to go around, I would throw them up on Pete and she would mosey around the lawn, munching on green grass and doing one heck of a good job of babysitting those kids. In fact, you could just go sit in the house and leave Pete to babysit. It worked so well because them kids couldn't get in any trouble up on top of Pete, and most times they were afraid to get down off her by themselves. Besides babysitting, Pete had a dual purpose. She gave more milk than any other milk cow I ever owned. When old Pete went to cow heaven in the sky, I felt so bad I never ate hamburger or bologna for a month.

I remember one time when another young hellion named Brian and I got in an argument about riding cows at rodeos. I maintained those young potential bull riders should ride those cows with saddles on them because it would make it easier. Brian said I was crazy. So to settle the argument, we needed my bronc saddle, and a cow. Out to his dad's pasture we go. We managed to get a rope on a quiet old roan that must have been somebody's pet at one time, because she didn't kill us as we saddled her up. I had quite a time with the back cinch going around that cow's belly, but a few adjustments and we were ready. I screwed the saddle down tighter while Brian held on to the halter and lead rope. I figured I should be the one to go first because it was my idea in the first place. Brian figured he should go first because it was his dad's cow. I won first ride because it was my saddle too. Brian kept a death grip on her head while I stepped up. I had about four seconds to figure out that the saddle fit a cow a whole lot different from a horse before he turned her loose. About the same time I was beginning to think that the saddle had a bit of a roll to it, he nailed that cow across the side of her head with his hat. That roan did as good a job as any bronc coming unglued at the hinges. I lasted about, oh say, three bucks before I kicked loose from the saddle and rolled out of her way, because that saddle was sideways and under her belly, just about that quick.

She headed for the tall timber, bucking and bawling protests all the way. Once she got into the bush and trees, we couldn't rope her again to retrieve my equipment. We followed her until dark, hoping to grab the end of the trailing lead rope but she had learned her lesson and wasn't having us anywhere near her. Just as dark fell, she managed to kick right out of my saddle, which looked as if a cougar had worked it over by then, from being kicked and drug through the bush. We left her with the halter and lead, planning on coming back the next day with a couple of my horses to retrieve them, but as luck goes, Brian's dad checked cows first thing in the morning and found her tangled up in some willows. He was some mad about someone trying to steal one of his best cows. He had himself worked into a gun-totin' rage at whoever messed with that cow, so Brian and I decided it would be wiser to just keep our mouths closed. I not only had to agree that I had lost the argument that cows were best rode in rodeos without saddles, I also lost a good halter and lead rope because I didn't know how to ask for it back from the irate father. Lessons in life can be so hard.

SWIMMING HORSES

I am scared silly of water. At some time when I was only knee high to a jack rabbit, I convinced myself I was going to be drowned if I attempted to swim by myself, or even learn to swim. The school swimming classes were fun for all the kids in my class, but to me, they were on the agenda to get me drowned. The instructor tried for two years to teach me to swim and get me over my fear of water. Not a chance! He finally gave up. To this very day, if someone talks me into getting in a small boat or even on a giant tourist ship, I'm immediately convinced the craft is going to sink, and I'm going to perish. I break out in a nervous sweat, tremble right down to my toes and make myself sick.

Don't ask me how, with such a fear of water, that I learned to love swimming horses. Could it be that I am not alone in the water, as my hands are always connected to a horse somehow?

The only horse I hated to take anywhere near water was Patches. No swimming involved here, just a deep slough that he always thought he should lie down and roll in. At least when he pulled this stunt, out in a summer fallow field, I didn't have to worry about being drowned. He knew how much it scared me, and I am convinced he did it on purpose to punish me for some unknown crime against him.

With Linda on Patty, and me on Spiker, swimming horses became the only thing to do on a hot summer day. Linda's father had a deep slough that he had further deepened to ensure a good supply of water for his cattle. The horses only had to walk a short ways out before they hit the drop–off into swimming water. Then, with only their heads and necks break–ing the surface, they would swim for all they were worth. Linda and I would cling like mad to their long, floating manes, and let our bodies float free of their bare backs. It was exhilarating. The combination of fear and pleasure sent waves of excitement through my mind and body. Next, we discovered even more fun by sliding off their submerged rumps as they swam and holding on to their tails so they pulled us along, water skiing on our bellies. After each swim, we would rest the horses, then back in we would go, the horses appearing to enjoy it as much as we did.

One day on the ranch where I was working, the crew boss came up with a way to keep the horses from getting out of the home pasture. Their fence line ended at the edge of a creek, and the horses had all learned to enter the water, walk around the fence and escape to freedom on the other side. Almost every day they had to be rounded up and chased back home, which was very annoying. So the man devised a plan to thwart their escapes. In line with the end of the fence was a sandbar formed right in the middle of the creek. I would swim a horse out to it, pulling a thin rope with me, with a post and strand of wire attached to the end of it. Once safely on the sand bar, I could then drag across the post, push it down deep into the soft silt, then the wire could be stretched across to the anchored post from the end of the existing fence. I choose to ride Rainbow, as he was trained to carry a rider bareback.

Everything went as planned until Rainbow reached the small island. As soon as I slid off his back, he wrenched the reins out of my hand, and struck out swimming for the opposite shore, scrambled up the steep bank and trotted away. I pulled the rope in and sure enough the post was easy to sink into the sand. Then I attached the barbed wire to it, and went to stretch it tight. Then I could hold onto it and pull myself hand over hand through the deep water to safety as I still could not and would not swim across on my own. Wouldn't you know it, I had forgotten to tie the wire to the other post on shore. I was stuck on a tiny mass of sand in the middle of a whole lot of swimming water. I felt like bawling, but cowgirls don't do that so I sat down to wait to be rescued. Surely someone would soon come to check on me. Well, nobody came. Not after one hour, not after two hours, and the dark of night was creeping up on me. I was going to have to swim or sit there forever, so cursing crew bosses, horses, and life in general, I worked myself into a self-righteous rage and plunged in. I was young and strong and made it with ease, if you can call dog-paddling easy. I had felt no fear crossing on Rainbow, but my heart sure beat a different tune going back on my own.

Swimming Lesson

Not all horses know how to swim, which I did not know one day when I decided to go for a little swim with Rusty in Dad's huge manmade dam a few miles from the house. Rusty sure did not want to enter the water, and I had to force him in. He had barely taken two steps into the water when the bottom fell away from under him, plunging us into several feet of swimming water. By now I was an old hand at swimming horses, and this way was not the way it was supposed to be done. The frantic gelding appeared to be trying to maybe swim with his hind legs, and rear up out of the water at the same time with his entire front end. I instantly knew we were in serious trouble, and tried to turn him to the right to make it to the steep bank, which was the head of the dam. He sank out from under me completely and I kicked free from the stirrups, still clutching one rein, and flopped in some sort of fish paddle to the bank. Only then did I realize how steep and high the bank was to get to safety at the top. I managed to grab a sturdy bush with my right hand, and struggled to pull Rusty's head towards me and out of the water with my left. His head finally broke the surface almost on top of me, his white–rimmed eyes glazed over with terror. I released the first hand hold on the plant, and reached up and took a hold of the next one. I kept his head pulled up this way to keep him from drowning. He was mostly submerged in the water, not even trying to save himself. Again I inched my way upwards on my belly, taking a hold of an even higher plant. With all my remaining strength I pulled on that rein until he skidded into the bank with his front legs. Feeling ground again, he came alive and regained his feet to plunge awkwardly up the bank to safety. I was so exhausted from the strain that I must have laid flat on the steep earth for half an hour, until I felt strong enough to scramble up it. After that I never purposely swam a horse unless I had to in the mountains or to cross a creek or river that absolutely had to be crossed.

Attempted Suicide

While working for an outfitter in the mountains, I watched a sullen, mean–dispositioned stallion try at least twice to drown himself on purpose. He was a five–year–old, born and bred by a stock contractor to be a rodeo bronc. He had become a very pretty dappled palomino, and he had the nature to be a bronc but was lousy at bucking. So his owner decided he would like this savage horse trained instead for a saddle horse. The man who took the job on was the outfitter I worked for, and boy am I glad he took the job and not me. He figured to pack the sucker one day, ride him the next, and play him out enough to teach him some manners. No five–year–old, rough–raised stallion wants to be taught good manners. After eight or nine days of hard work, the horse was played out all right, but the more tired he got, the more sulky he got. The first time he tried to drown himself was something else. He was being ridden across a river that was not quite deep enough for swimming, but close. Suddenly he stopped, plunged his whole head and neck under water, then slowly folded up like a collapsed accordion. His shocked rider thought he must be having a heart attack and bailed off him in the river. As soon as he got his own way by the rider getting off him, that big palomino sprang back to his feet, water streaming out of his ears. None of us had ever heard of a horse trying to drown himself, but none of us rode man–hating horses like him either. The next day he did it again. Crossing the river yet again, he pulled the same stunt. This time the horseman stayed on him, and it didn't take long for the angry horse to explode up and out of the water, his sense of survival stronger than his desire to either drown himself or get rid of his rider. He wasn't ever going to make a trustworthy saddle horse, so his owner gave up on that idea and gave him a few bucking mares of his own to see if he would at least sire some good rodeo stock. He turned out to be a top sire of wicked broncs and lived for many more years instead of becoming dogfood.

IT'S SPRINGTIME, LET THE FOALING BEGIN

No foal should have to be born in an early March blizzard. But then, no newly purchased yearling stallion, locked in a neighbour's barn for a couple of days until the vet can get there to geld him, should jump a six–foot high fence or two and breed one of my mares either. Figuring Pokey was in foal, but at this time not knowing when or how, I still had her running out on pasture with the dry mares and young stock. They were on full feed with a stand of heavy timber for shelter. My intentions were to wait until the last week or two before her due date and then bring her into the main barn to foal. I like to get a mare in, in lots of time to let her get used to her new surroundings. Previous to this day, she showed none of the classic signs of being close to foaling. She had a small udder, still not full, definitely no waxing, nothing the day before. Although slightly relaxed in the muscles on either side of her tail head, it was on closer inspection nothing to indicate her time was due.

I was at work when the landowner I was renting from phoned to say my personal saddle mare, Whiskey, had foaled. Impossible, I say. Yes, he says, there's a scrawny, wet foal stand-ing on her off side, trying to get out of the blowing snow of a temperamental March storm. In fact, he says, it was nursing when he first spotted it.

I booked off work in one big hurry and headed for that pasture. Sure enough, the shivering baby was nursing my cranky, barren, unable to conceive, saddle mare. Now I was stumped. Due to cysts on her ovaries, Whiskey couldn't get in foal, and for Pete's sake, if she had, how? When? And why hadn't I spotted this before?

Opening the gate, I hollered at the horses, knowing they would head a half mile home to the buildings for shelter and grain. Well, that saddle mare broke trail all the way home, nickering to that foal and stepping plumb gentle. As soon as they hit the big cattle shed, out of the blizzard, I went to get blankets to dry that baby off. When I got back, Whisky had the foal in the corner of the shed, and like a good momma was out to kill any horse that came near her baby. The rest of those horses were staying clear of her too. I eased up to her and bent down to check her milk supply. Nothing! Talking nice I checked the rear of the mare. Nothing! This mare had no more had a colt, than I had. Pokey! Over in the other corner, Pokey was content-edly munching hay. I checked her; she had just foaled.

I hustled Pokey into the main barn, into a box stall. When I went to get her foal, Whiskey looked an awful lot like a ten-foot high tigress for a while. Once I had the baby separated and into the box stall, Pokey came alive. She talked to her baby, she turned around so her baby could have a real meal, she loved her baby.

How did it happen? My old saddle mare was Pokey's boss. She was every horse's boss. When Pokey's foal hit the ground, that barren mare fought the mother off and stole the colt. Being a passive mare, Pokey let her. Over the next years, Pokey raised me some fine colts. She was the best mother ever, but even after a month or two, if Whiskey was pastured with her and her foal, Whiskey took the colt. No fighting, she just persuaded the colts to go with her. Oh, they always went back to their real momma for lunch, but they lived beside and with Whiskey. They all learned Whiskey's good and bad habits. Their personalities were more like Whiskey's than their real mother's.

This showed me four things. The foal was full-term, showing not all mares follow the usual textbook signs that the mare's due date is on hand. Be prepared! Second, a dominant mare will and can steal a mare's newborn foal. Third, this does not necessarily say that the foaling mare isn't a good mother. Fourth, many primary traits and habits are learned from a foal's most constant companion and are not always hereditary.

Miracle Foal

I do not know of anything more special than a newborn animal. The mewling of a nest full of newborn kittens. Puppies, not yet completely dry, lined up at their mother's breasts, suckling contentedly. The baby calf, so new in this world, already bouncing around his mother, getting the feel of the earth beneath his feet. Most of all, the newborn foal, peeking out from behind his dam, eyes big and bright at his first glimpses of things yet to come.

Over the years, there have been so many foals in my life that I feel truly blessed to have been there over and over again to welcome them into this world. Each and every one of them holds a special place in my heart. I only have to close my eyes and I can picture them all over again, their warm fuzzy noses, their impossibly long, gangly legs, and their soft, new hides, every colour in the book, waiting to be rubbed and stroked by a kind hand.

Some hold an even more special place in my heart, for they are the ones who touched me with their will to survive, or perhaps had to overcome a poor start in life.

At an early spring horse sale, I purchased a brown and white pinto mare heavy in foal. She was so thin: except for the bulge of her belly, she was little more than hide and hair stretched over a rack of bones. She was only at my place two days when she gave birth. The newborn filly foal was not only slightly premature, but because her mother did not receive enough feed to nurture her foal properly in her womb, the filly was the smallest I had ever seen born from a mare that size. She lay on her bed of straw, every bone in her tiny body outlined beneath her skin. Her legs could not have been much bigger around than a man's middle finger. As weak as a kitten, she could not stand on her own and needed her first meal badly if she was to survive. I propped her up into a sitting position, and then boosted her to her feet. Matchstick legs trembling, she fought to stay on her feet. When she had some balance to her, I nudged her to her mother's side. Clumsily, she sought the teat that could give her strength through its nourishment. Weak as she was, she still managed to grab hold and suck for all she was worth. Once satisfied, she collapsed in a heap and soon dozed off. Every two hours, those first couple of days, I was at her side, helping her up and pointing her in the right direction. I named her Miracle, and marvelled at her strong will to survive. She was soon bucking and playing around her mother, like a mischievous child, seeing how far she could push her mother's patience. Her fine coat of hair, almost cream and white at birth, soon dark-ened into a brown and white pattern, like the mare's. By wean-ing time in the autumn, she was practically as big and sturdy as the other foals, except her hair, which still remained as soft as silk. When someone bought her, I felt an emptiness inside like I had lost my own child, having truly been touched by a miracle.

Abnormal

The man who cared for my foaling mares while I was at work phoned me to say that I had had another colt but things weren't quite right with him. It seemed he was struggling around in the corral with his dam, still attached to the placenta by his umbilical cord. When I told the man where to cut the cord and to dip the stump in an iodine solution, he seemed hesitant to do it. Then with a burst of unusual excitement for a man of his quiet, soft–spoken nature, he proceeded to tell me the umbilical cord was as big around as his forearm. Of course I scoffed at this, and told him I would be there as quickly as possible to take care of the problem myself.

He had not exaggerated in the least. Never before or since have I seen an umbilical cord that thick around. It was truly the size of a man's arm. The colt was perfectly normal in every other way as to size and strength, doing his best to follow his momma around with this huge cord and dragging lump of afterbirth tripping him up at every turn. Cutting the cord after this amount of time was not dangerous to the foal, but it was grue–some to me, like sawing through a length of gristle and sinew. After finishing the operation, I sat back and took another look at him. He was nursing with much enthusiasm, butting the mare's udder and whisking his stumpy tail back and forth. Just a normal foal, except for the huge end of the umbilical cord protruding from his belly. Wait, just a second, there was some–thing else odd about him. Now I had time to take a closer look. His colour was a light, smoky grey all over and covering that, were stripes of black, like a zebra. On his back, over his rump, around and up and down his legs were these unhorse–like stripes. In the first week after his unusual birth, the black stripes darkened still further, giving me no choice but to bring dozens of non–believers to see him. I think he was the most photo–graphed foal in the country. Right about the time I was having visions of making millions of dollars off the one and only zebra horse ever seen around those parts, his grey coat started to darken up also. By two months old or so, he was an even black-ish colour from head to toe, without a single stripe left. The next spring, he shed out his winter hair, and was one of the shiniest pure black horses I ever owned. There was not a trace on his belly to show that at birth, he had been born a bit of a freak in another way besides his original colour.

Pretty As Can Be

When one of my best quarter horse brood mares foaled at a stable in charge of foaling out some mares for me while I was away at work, yet another phone call came, telling me of some-thing that was not normal with the foal. Again it was something I had never seen or heard about before or since. The bay filly foal was normal in every way, except she arrived in this world with both hind legs swollen to unbelievable size. According to the experienced man on the phone, who had foaled dozens and dozens of mares in his lifetime, he had also never seen anything like it. He had immediately called his veterinarian, who had also never seen it, nor did he know what had caused it or what to do about it. This time I was mega miles away, where planes only come and go once a week for the company I worked for, so it would be at least five days before I could fly down and decide what to do with her. I advised him over the phone to have her put down humanely if she should appear to be suffering in any way. He said that she was up, had nursed and was frisking around on her swollen pins just like a normal foal.

As soon as the plane landed, I picked up my truck from the company parking lot and headed for the stable on the outskirts of the city, not even knowing if the foal was alive or dead. I had not communicated with the stable owner since that first call. Perhaps he had done as I said and had destroyed her for her own sake. Stepping into the mare's box stall, I was greeted by the friendliest foal I had ever known. She was all over me like a dirty shirt, demanding I pet her and scratch her ears. Her hind legs were grotesque, distorted and swollen to the size of five-gallon buckets with accumulated fluid. They didn't appear to bother her in the least, maybe making her a bit clumsy but nothing serious, so I agreed with the stable owner that she should have a chance to heal up, rather than put her down.

On the third day, when I was home on a week off from work, the skin split on the outside of both hocks, probably from rubbing on the floor of the box stall when she stood up and laid back down. Pint after pint of clear serum poured out of her legs. The legs continued to drain for two whole days, helped along by her bursts of energetic activity, until they were normal sized. I left her at the end of my week's leave of absence to fly back up north to work, knowing she was going to be fine. She is a mother now, all grown up and pretty as can be. Nothing remains of her strange beginning except for two scars where the fluid drained out of her once swollen-to-bursting legs. Over the years, I have asked many horse people and vets what could have caused it and no one knows. I think, perhaps, it was from being in the same position for too long in her mother's womb, but that is only speculation.

Baby Fuzz

The bay mare's last foal had been one of those disasters that sometimes is impossible to prevent. I had allowed her to foal out on the pasture without close supervision, as she had never had trouble with the previous ones. The colt had been a breech presentation and died before I could pull it.

Now this year's foal, huddled beside his momma, was as healthy as could be as he stared up at me with enormous brown eyes. Sure, all newborns are cute as buttons, except I was having difficulty finding very much cute about him. There are homely horses but I had to describe him as the ugliest colt I have ever owned. All four legs seemed to point in the wrong direction. I swear those big brown eyes were set in a skull built for a camel. His colour was nondescript brown, the baby fuzz on his chin was long, coarse and stuck out in all directions. Even his ears flopped to the side like a cold rabbit in a snowstorm.

I spent the first five months of his life trying to keep him hid in the back pasture, embarrassed for being the one responsible for producing such an oddball. When it came time to register the colts that fall, he remained unregistered, placed far in the back of my mind as he had been placed far in the back pasture. In those few short months since his birth, as impossible as it may seem, he had grown even uglier. For the life of me I didn't know what to do with him.

The two little red-haired granddaughters of the lady I rented the land from came to his rescue. Somewhere along the line he had been given the name Little Ben. In their young hearts they couldn't understand why I couldn't see just how beautiful Little Ben was. They went to great lengths to make me understand the story of The Ugly Duckling, the story of how the ugliest of ducklings grew into the most gracious and beautiful of swans. Knowing that all my foals were for sale and not knowing what was to become of Little Ben, they were adamant in their quest to be his new owners. Well, at least somebody wanted him. So far, everybody else who had caught a glimpse of him had only laughed. So, after school and every weekend until the snow filled the ditches, the two girls picked bottles. With these traded in for a wee bit of money, topped off with being paid for any chores people would pay them for, they were ready. They came to me, their expectant little faces shining with hope. In their hands they held one hundred and some odd dollars. How could I say no, for Little Ben was their ugly duckling. I even threw in a brand new halter and lead rope. I didn't mention that normally one of my foals would sell for many, many times that amount.

Wouldn't you know it, Little Ben became Big Ben, in his own way not bad to look at. He carried those girls to many a first place ribbon in the local 4–H Club and youth riding competitions. That nondescript brown coat became a rich bay in colour. Those four legs now travelled straight and true. He even had a half–decent shaped head with two perked ears. Isn't it great that the Little Bens in life can become Big Bens?

WIPE OUT

Excitement abounds when hot on the heels of a wild old cow or hard–to–catch horse. Besides the thrill of the chase itself, there is the added fun of trying to stay on top of the horse you are riding.

I was lending a hand rounding up cattle one fall on a huge grazing lease. The timber was tall and the scrub underbrush thick. I was born and raised on the prairies, and still fairly new to popping bush. Not one to be left behind though, I kept up with the pack the best I could. I was mounted on a good stout gelding who had been after cows down through the timber enough times to know what he was doing. Maybe he knew what he was doing but I was starting to have my doubts about myself. No matter how I twisted and turned in the saddle, I already had some good scratches from slap–happy tree branches. The crew boss right about then let a holler out, "Get that nag of yours in high gear, them bloody yearlings are splitting up and heading back into the rough bush!" My gelding didn't need to be told what to do, he was off like a shot after the running cattle. I simply hung on for the ride. Ducking my head low over his neck, I closed my eyes and prayed we didn't hit a tree. He was flying around trees and over fallen logs, and I didn't even know if there were cows still ahead of us. So I raised my head for an instant to find out how things were going. Wham, I took a tree branch right across my forehead. That branch lifted me up and over the back end of the running horse as slick as a whistle.

I picked myself up and watched his rump disappear through the trees. From the crashing going on up ahead, he was still after the cows. Now, whether he was chasing them in the right direction or not, I had no clue. You know, I didn't really care either. For once in my life I felt good being on the ground. I wasn't much of a walker in my riding boots, so I just sort of hung around for a spell until the crew boss sent someone to find me. When he showed up, leading my gelding, I was happily intent on the birds in the trees and the pretty autumn colours. The boss man was disgusted with me for not being better help, but right in love with my horse. Seems the horse rounded up a dozen cows all by himself, without me. Chased them back through the timber, to the open meadow where the main herd was being held, with reins dragging. Actually, the day finished off pretty darn good. I sold the boss man my gelding for three times what I had paid for him. I would gladly get wiped backward out of my saddle once in a while for that kind of money.

Ups & Downs

Not meaning to brag or anything, but I'm a lot better cow chaser out in open country. I just might be able to run circles around a few other cow chasers down on the prairies. Sometimes!

I was trying to move a high-headed Charolais cow and her calf out of an overgrazed calving pasture through the gate into a fresh pasture where the bulls were waiting to meet her. My intentions were good, hers were not. Splitting that pasture right down the middle was a deep, rough coulee. She was more white-tailed deer than cow, the way she could go up and down those steep banks. Up and down she went, barrelling over the banks going down, bounding up the other side. If it had been deer-hunting season, I think I would have shot her and claimed poor eyesight as the reason for her being a cow instead of a deer.

Every time she went up and down, me and my horse had to go up and down after her. I was riding a nice three-year-old filly off the race track. Fire was doing her best to keep a level head about chasing this cow, but her hot running blood was also starting to show. Each time I had to go downwards, I would stop her at the top and ease her down in a sensible fashion. Going up, I angled her upwards without letting her lunge up and maybe lose her footing. We had the cow back on the right side of the coulee and even part ways across the pasture towards the gate, when Mrs. Cow decided to pull the deer act again. She threw her head up, bellowed at her calf to follow close, and whipped back in a dead run for the coulee. As the cow disappeared over the bank, Fire and I were close behind. Except Fire had had enough. There was no stopping her or even slowing her down at the top of the drop off. In a split second we were airborne. I bet we were twenty to thirty feet down before we made ground contact. All I could do now was make the ride of my life. We plunged to the bottom, almost on top of the cow. Before I could gain some sort of control over Fire, she reached out and took a chunk of hide out of that cow's rear end with her teeth. Maybe the bite was what the cow had needed all along, because she spun around and shot back up the bank we had just came down, Fire still trying to get on top of her with each upward leap. Again I just hung on, by a fistful of mane hair, to keep from going over backwards and maybe the mare too. We topped out onto level ground at a record-breaking speed. The sorrel mare and white cow were neck and neck in the race to the finish line. The cow beat us by two lengths through the gate, her calf still glued to her side. I was just glad the ride was over.

Follow the Leader

A rancher and I were trying to quietly move some herd bulls off pasture into a holding corral, where they could be loaded to be hauled out to pastures full of waiting cows. One big, mean Charolais bull was always a pain to work with horses. He hated horses–not people, just horses. Besides, it was springtime and all the bulls were spoiling for a fight, so we were taking it slow and easy to keep them from getting anymore riled up. Down the centre of this pasture was a deep, but dry, irrigation canal that had to be crossed. The bulls piled up on the bank of the ditch, shoving each other around and being ornery, rather than taking one of the cattle trails down and up the other side. The rancher was mounted on a tough quarter horse gelding. Swinging his lariat, he moved amongst the bulls, trying to break up the shoving matches and keep them moving. I was riding a colt with only a week or two of riding, and was busy at that second with the colt acting silly from all the tension in the air.

With a nasty bellow, that horse–hating Charolais bull lowered his head and slammed into the rear end of the rancher's gelding. He lifted the gelding right off the ground. The gelding's feet no sooner hit the ground when he lit into bucking. He was a rough horse to ride when he bucked, and the rancher had his hands full staying on. Staying on was even harder when the bull nailed the horse again, knocking him over the rim, into the canal. The horse and rider landed upright and the horse bucked up the other side and towards the corral. The mean Charolais bull was still trying to get close enough to the horse to hit him again. I knew that the rancher was a top bronc rider, and he was staying on top easily now that the horse was bucking in a straight line. One bull was already following them, so I didn't interfere when the other bulls started trotting after them too. We made quite a procession, heading for the corrals. First, a bucking horse and rider, then a mad Charolais bull, then twelve more bulls of every size and colour in a line with me on a colt who was buck jumping his own little show, bringing up the drag end. Within minutes the bulls were corralled, and sorted into pens according to where they were going. All and all, the job got done, maybe not quite like it was supposed to, but done.

Slap Happy

Chasing horses can be hazardous to a person's health. Take the time MK was helping round up wild horses for Vern Franklin in the Moose Mountain area. Like me, the time I tried to help round up cattle on the grazing lease, he was mounted on a well–broke gelding that knew what he was doing. Like my gelding, once the chase was on, he could really fly after them critters. Also like me, MK was getting pestered by slap–happy tree branches. So, like me, he ducked his head down to protect his face and eyes. It wasn't a tree branch that helped him dismount in a hurry though. No, it was two trees only a couple of feet apart or so. Seems he had his head down, letting the horse do the steering, when the sorrel gelding tried to fit between two trees close together. The horse made it, he did not. Both trees caught both his knees and off the back end he came. The gelding kept going wide open after the wild horses ahead of him. MK's knees took quite a beating but he was tough and walked three to four miles back to camp. By the time he limped into camp, the sorrel gelding was back too, resting in the shade. He says the horse gave him one of those "Where the hell have you been all this time" looks with big innocent eyes. MK was not impressed.

Going Up, Coming Down

I purchased nine head of snorty broncs off a fellow one time for next to nothing in the dollar department. The only catch was, I had to catch them. They were running free on a section of heavy bushed land. The local hotel owner's son was always looking for a horse to ride and someplace to go, so I hired him on to help me spook those nags out of the bush into a corral. I tied a couple of mares up in the corral and left the gate open. Then Bruce and I went to the far side of the land on two of my best saddle geldings. My idea was to work back and forth, pushing the broncs ahead of us, and when they broke out into the open and saw other horses already in the corral, they might co-operate and go in too. Everything went as planned. They stayed ahead of us in the bush, came out in the open and spotted those two tied mares. Meek as lambs, they trotted into the corral.

Once we hit the open ground, we broke into a gallop to get to the gate and keep them inside. My horse slid to a stop in the open gateway. Bruce, right behind me, turned his horse to the side, passing the back end of mine by inches. My gelding kicked the passing gelding right in the flank. He bogged his head and turned from saddle horse to saddle bronc in about one second. Bruce was nineteen years old and just getting good at riding, so was no bronc rider. The first jump, he lost his left stirrup. The second jump, he lost his right stirrup. The third jump put him away up in the air, looking down. What goes up must eventually come down. He came down all right, smack onto the saddle horn. I guess you know where the saddle horn got him, seeing how his legs were spread in an outward position on his way down. The horse only bucked those three jumps, then came to a complete halt. So I guess you could say Bruce was back in the saddle again. He sat there frozen for several long seconds, before ever so slowly falling over the side to the ground. I didn't know Bruce shall we say on a personal level, so I wasn't much help. I ran into Bruce at a rodeo a few years later, and he introduced me to his wife and kids. I guess if he had two kids, he must have healed up all right after all.

Air, Beautiful Air

Getting drowned while chasing horses isn't easy to do, but I came mighty close to having a watery grave. I was working on a horse ranch one summer when I almost met my maker. I had ridden a pinto gelding out to the pasture to bring in a mare and her foal who needed a cut leg doctored. She wasn't halter broke so I eased her out of the bunch of horses she was with and herded her towards home. She drifted ahead of me with no problem. We had a fairly deep stream to cross on the way, but if I held my legs up on my pony's neck, I could keep my feet dry enough. We had reached the bank of the stream when I heard the rest of the horses thundering up behind us. I shooed the mare and colt into the stream, and followed her in, my feet up high on the gelding's neck. We were halfway across when the pinto slipped and fell head long into the water. I floated free of the struggling horse, but never got a chance to surface for air when the twenty–some head of following horses galloped into the water. They couldn't see me under water and proceeded to trample over me. Hooves and legs were all over me, pushing me back down every time I tried to get my head above water. The ordeal was probably over within seconds but to me it was an eternity. How I wasn't knocked unconscious by those galloping hooves, I will never know. Finally my face broke the surface and my gasping lungs drank in the much–needed oxygen. Except for some mighty black and blue bruises, I was fine. Made me kind of wonder though, what I was doing working on a horse ranch for only a hundred dollars a month and room and board. Especially since I had good marks in school and could have gone on to be a teacher, or doctor or lawyer or something sensible. It still makes me wonder why I like getting half-killed every once in awhile by some hair-covered nag. It must be love.

A ROPER I'LL NEVER BE

Can you imagine going through life breaking horses and punching cows and not being able to rope them if need be? I think about the only time I ever caught a critter around the neck when I wanted to, it was just pure luck on my part. I could catch them just about anywhere except around the neck. Get that blamed cow in throwing distance, let fly with my loop, catch only one horn, watch the rope fall off the horn, watch the cow jump the fence and leave the country.

Get that sick-looking steer that needs to be doctored in throwing distance, let fly with my loop and catch the bull ten feet on the other side of him. Throw my loop at the hind legs of the calf needing to be branded and catch his mother by the horns. Then discover it is the meanest, chargy black Angus cross cow on the place and try to get the rope off her horns without being killed.

Gallop my gentlest old ranch gelding after the colt needing to be caught and doctored and catch my gelding's tail with the rope. Find out he may be pushing twenty years old and still knows how to buck. I never met a horse yet who likes the idea of a rope coming out of nowhere and getting sucked up under his tail. It's amazing how tight they clamp their tails down on your rope. They don't like it but seems to me they don't want it to fall down off their rear end either.

I recall one good–looking, sweet–talking cowboy I was itching to rope for myself, if you know what I mean. I think he must have thought I was interested in a different kind of roping than what I had in mind for him because he set out to teach me how to rope. Big mistake. I had already had one too many teachers in the let's learn to rope department. Each and every one of them had given up. He was a determined cuss, though. There we were, him showing me how to build a loop, me knowing how to build a loop but still acting all sort of shy and interested. Him showing me how to recoil the rope properly after a throw, me knowing how to recoil the rope properly but still acting plumb girlish about the whole affair. Him showing me how to get that loop up there above my head, swinging around in the perfect motion, me knowing how but acting breathless with wonder about it. He threw and caught the plastic steer head mounted on a hay bale, I threw and caught the dog's tail halfway between me and the steer head. He threw and caught the steer head, I threw and scared a chicken on the left side of the steer head out of laying eggs for a week of Sundays. After a couple of days of this, I could see that just being cute and cuddly like I was acting wasn't going to be good enough for him. The fact I had caught the rear end of the bale a half dozen times didn't impress him all that much. He even hinted rather strongly that if he was to ever marry a girl, she would have to be able to rope to help him out in the life of being a cowboy on his own ranch.

Boy, he was some catch. But I couldn't catch anything so we kind of drifted apart. I didn't feel too bad about it because I could out–ride him with both hands tied behind my back, and you know I was kind of looking for someone who would be able to help me out in the future when I settled down and became a horse girl on my own ranch.

To this day I can't rope a fence post, even if it is standing still. And to this day that good–looking, sweet–talking cowboy is still married to the woman he chose to be his bride. And to this day, she still won't even leave her fancy new ranch house to go down to the corrals and give him a hand. Why, her hair might get mussed up or she might get dirt under her fingernails. As for holding one of those yucky, smelly old ropes, no way.

Serves him right, don't you think?

Ducking & Dodging

There was one time, though, when not being able to rope cost me a small fortune. Even if I could rope, to catch this horse, you had to be able to actually get the rope around his ducking and dodging head. Applejack was a sixteen and two hands high leopard Appaloosa gelding that I bought down next to the Montana border. I purchased him for a lot less money than a good ranch gelding with his size and training should have gone for. Why? Because you couldn't catch him, that's why. He would pack you all day rounding up cattle, you could load him easy, he ground tied perfectly while you opened gates or worked on foot, and you could catch, rope, and hold a big bull with him (notice I said you, not me, because I can't rope, remember), but to catch him up to ride was next to impossible. Unless he was in a box stall or small pen you couldn't catch him. That is, you couldn't catch him unless you were a durn good roper. So you trapped him in a feedlot or a fair–sized cattle pen when he came in for water or extra feed by closing the gate on him. Then you better know how to rope because he had been roped for so many years, he never got excited. You threw your loop, he ducked. You got him loping around the pen, you threw your loop, he stopped dead and watched it fall neatly to the ground in front of him. You threw, he dodged. You had to be good to catch Applejack.

As it was, I moved a bunch of my horses, including him, to a small pasture. In the spring I got an offer I couldn't refuse for Applejack, a lot more than I paid for him. This rancher knew all about Applejack's being hard to catch but since he had been roping since he was knee high to a jackrabbit, it didn't bother him. The only stipulation was I had to deliver him to this rancher's place. I needed the money from the sale of this horse or I might have passed on the deal. My problem was I never even had a big corral on this land. Nothing but open pasture, no way to catch Applejack. What's a girl going to do? I had to have a corral, but it was rented land so I wasn't about to set posts in the ground and buy the planks to build one on someone else's property. So I bought panels and presto, instant corral. And presto, the money was spent on steel panels to catch the horse, to sell the horse, to pay other bills. He was a good horse, but you know, I never missed him all that much once he was gone.

PRETTY AS A PICTURE

For horses to be pretty in my books, they have to have more than the colour of their hide, more than winning conformation. They have to have the right kind of temperament too. I've known lots of shiny blacks, bays, sorrels and chestnuts, every colour under the sun. They were all nice to look at. I've raised lots of perfectly built horses, seen even more champion horses in the conformation department, but only a few really pretty horses come to mind, for they also had lovely temperaments.

Red Boy, a friend's Morgan stallion. Now there was a horse to remember. I was approached by his owner one spring with a proposition I couldn't refuse. He had to go away from home to work and was in a bind. He had mares booked to his Morgan stallion and no one to handle him during breeding season with him gone away to work. I had the knowledge, the corrals and a Morgan mare I too wanted to breed to this horse. The deal was I would keep Red Boy at my place, handle the breeding and get my mare bred at the same time for no stud fee. Of course I accepted. Now let's remember, I had only seen pictures of this stallion, and had recommendations from other horse people as to this horse's beauty.

Ken chose to ride Red Boy across country to my place, a distance of twelve miles or so. To Ken, I must have looked like a love struck teenager standing in my yard, with my mouth hanging open as he came up the driveway. That big chestnut, long mane and tail flowing, ears pricked, legs like oiled pistons covering the ground, was completing a twelve-mile journey with only a halter and lead rope on him for control. This was a five-year-old breeding stallion who would have had to pass by many other horses in that journey, and he was under total control with a halter on. All around him in my corrals were mares, geldings and even a couple of two-year-old colts in their pen raising a ruckus and showing off. When Ken stepped off him, he turned his head, gave one soft, non-aggressive whistle and then rested his head on his master's shoulder. I was hooked. In love at first sight.

He stayed at my place for three months. During that time I handled him daily, and a gentler stallion I have never known before or since. The rich chestnut coat, with his forelock reaching down past his nostrils and his tail dusting the ground, was a sight to see. His conformation was that of the splendid Morgan breed. Neither of these would have been enough for me without his gentle nature. He never tried my patience in all the usual little ways a mature stallion will try. The only time I ever raised my voice to him was when he accidentally stepped on my toes. When I let a yell of pain out, poor Red Boy was shocked. He was beside himself with apologies. Nuzzling my shoulder and blowing soft snorts of unhappiness. What a guy!

The Best

Rusty. From a wild, roaming sorrel to the prettiest gelding I ever rode. I fell for this colt when I was only sixteen years old. During summer holidays I had gone to work on a horse ranch. It was at this tender age that I found out the difference between broncs and barnyard pets. The lady who owned this ranch was widowed. Since her husband's death a few years before, the herds of horses had gone untouched. The horses I was to work with ranged in age from weanlings to five–year–olds.

The boss stallion in charge of the mares did what herd stallions have been doing from the beginning of time while running wild and free. He kept all the other stallions run plumb right out of his territory. The pasture was several sections in size and it was my job to round these little bunches of stock up and into corrals. Even with lots of help from the local cowboys, it was no easy task.

Rusty was a two–year–old colt, running with another two–year–old colt and a three–year–old colt. In the first week, we managed to corral seventeen head of young fillies, colts and five–year–old geldings. These geldings were the last to ever have felt a rope on them, and only once to be thrown, branded and castrated. My work was sure cut out for me this time. I had taken the job thinking I was real hot stuff with a rope and saddle, and when I left, I knew the difference between the half-dozen pets I had trained and horses who had never felt a human hand touch them before.

During the second week, before the heat of the day became unbearable, the elderly ranch foreman and I would go hunting for that little sorrel and the two bays he ran with. I had already given him the name Rusty and hadn't even got close to him yet. Harry told me as much as he knew about Rusty. He was out of an Arabian mare and that old thoroughbred herd sire. He said that Rusty was always a little bit on the spooky side and for the last year hadn't even come close to the corrals for salt or extra hay in the bad winter months. When I finally put them through the gate into the main pen, Rusty was on the inside only because those two bays were worn out from all the chasing. They herded like cows down the hill and through the gate, him following reluctantly.

After loosening the cinch on my saddle pony and telling him what a great little roundup horse he was, I stepped into the corral with Rusty. The two bays were off in the far corner looking like a pair of trapped rabbits, but not Rusty. Snorting, he came halfway across the corral to face me. Ears rigid, nostrils flared, he let me know that if it was a battle I wanted, a battle I would get. He was pretty all right, with his bright colouring, almost white matching mane and tail, and delicate Arabian head. He was also not in the mood for socializing. I wanted this colt for my own. I had to have him.

Now, on top of getting paid for working with these horses, part of the deal was the pick of any horse I wanted at the end of the summer. There was between fifty and sixty horses to choose from and I had made my pick without laying a hand on him. I eased the other two into a separate pen and left Rusty to think about things alone.

Since I was getting paid to halter break horses and get them started under saddle so they could be sold for something besides foxmeat, I decided to put off working with Rusty. Instead, I fed and watered him in a pen next to the round corrals where I would be doing most of my work. This way, I hoped he would gentle down some just by getting used to seeing and hearing me around.

Well these range-raised horses were finally getting to me. I was black and blue. I had been kicked, rolled on, bit and bucked off so many times I had lost count. My parents hadn't raised me to be a quitter and I loved working with these horses, but man oh man, I was starting to hurt all over. So I told the ranch fore-man that I wanted some changes made. As in no more putting off gelding these young stallions. I made him a deal. I hadn't had a day off since starting. I had been working from sun up to sun down. I would take two days off, and when I came back, there had better be some geldings standing around. He agreed to get the neighbour men over to do the job and Rusty would have a change of mind too at the same time.

On my return, I headed for the breaking pens to start work and on passing Rusty's corral, I nearly fainted. There he stood, head hanging, gelded and with one front foot held pitifully off the ground. Because I hadn't worked with him yet, they would have thrown him by letting him lope around the pen and then roping his front feet, jerking his feet out from under him. One man then kneels on the horse's neck, holding his nose up, while another hog ties him for the operation. I know it sounds cruel, but this is about the only way to castrate a horse quickly with minimum injury to horse or man, when the horse has never been handled. With Rusty, things didn't go as planned. They roped him, they hog tied him and they gelded him. When they let him up, he came off the ground with one giant leap. He shot straight for the top rail of that pen, a pen eight feet high, made of huge logs. A pen built many, many years before, to hold the toughest of broncs. He only managed to get one fore foot over the top. As he fell back down, that leg was caught tight on a jagged splinter. The flesh from the top of his cannon bone all the way down to his pastern was ripped open by the downward pull of his falling body.

As Harry stood beside me telling me what had happened, I was silent with shock, staring at my beautiful Rusty. When I heard him explaining that I was not to worry about it, I could just pick another horse as my bonus and that they would load Rusty up and take him to the meatpackers, my heart went out to this poor colt.

Every afternoon, because of the extreme heat, I did not work the horses for about three hours. I would saddle three or four up and leave them to get used to packing a saddle but not having to sweat it out with me riding them. Others who only needed lessons in halter breaking were left tied to posts, without me working around them until the worst of the day was past. This is the time I spent with Rusty. Quietly I would move the injured horse into the chute. Once safely confined I could doctor the horrible mess of his leg. Twice I was forced to cut away dead and dying flesh before applying medication. Kneeling beside the chute, my hands reaching through the bottom rails, I fought the flies trying to lay eggs in the torn flesh, I worked to keep the proud flesh from forming, and I talked to Rusty. I told him how everything was going to be okay and to trust me. And he listened to me. He did not fight me, but stood unmoving while I worked on him. And the day came when I placed a halter on him while he was in the chute. When I let him out of the chute, he did not fight the halter and lead. He simply listened to my voice and trusted me.

Because I was already late returning to school, I left Rusty there at the ranch to finish healing. In the fall, my father returned with me to get him. Although Rusty still remembered me and my gentle handling, he had enough fire in his eyes again to warrant us tranquillizing him just to get him loaded for the trip home. When I broke him to saddle as a three–year–old, Rusty never fought me. He accepted the bridle, the saddle and me on his back with little more than a toss of his head. What a great saddle horse he became. Swift and sure footed, with the heart of a lion, he never refused to do as I asked. He was by nature as brave as any warrior and as gentle as any lamb. I am proud to have owned him.

I Thank You

Dee Bar Bright. I only saw this great stallion once. Only once did I place my hand on his glistening ebony hide. Only once did I look up into his eyes as deep as liquid pools of darkness. That's all it took for me to know that as clearly as I had touched him, he had touched me in my heart. He stood over sixteen hands high. His pedigree was impeccable. He was a winner not only on the race track but in the breeding shed too. When his owner led him out of his box stall for me to see him, he stepped beside her, big, black and bold. He was like a baby in her hands. His ears cocked towards her, waiting for her next command. His manners were as proper as any English gentleman's. He was Dee Bar Bright, and the pick of Alberta's running quarter horse stallions to breed my best little race mare to. It was on that day when I met him that I knew from then on, I would breed only the best to the best. It was then that I knew that it's not how many horses you have, but the quality of the horses you have, that's important. Since meeting this grand stallion, I have always endeavoured to breed horses who will go on and become willing partners with whoever shall own them and ride them. They must be not only beautiful to look at, but also must have the temperament that really makes them shine in my eyes. Thank you, Dee Bar Bright.

Nice As Pie

Copper Cat. I don't know when I started referring to her as The Cat, instead of her real name. The Cat was and is the only sorrel-coloured horse I ever owned, the exact same shade as a brand spanking new copper penny. If I laid a new penny on her back before showing her to people, there was a good chance, no matter how well they looked her over, they would miss seeing it. I remember telling this to a cowboy one time at the local watering hole. He sort of sneered at me and let me know that he was a fine judge of horse flesh and would no more miss seeing a penny as miss an obvious defect on a horse. It wasn't more than two weeks later that I found out he was on the way to my place, to look at some colts I had for sale. Before he got there, I put a spot of glue paste on one side of a penny and went out to find The Cat. She was relaxing in the shade, so I pasted that penny on the inside of the fetlock on a front leg. Mr. Cowboy showed up and I was set to have a little fun. First, he took a look at the colts just about long enough to tell me I wanted too much money for them. Then I brought him over to see The Cat. I joked around a bit about maybe having a new copper penny some-where on that mare. Then I proceeded to make a bet for a couple of bucks that he couldn't see the penny. He went for it, hook, line and sinker. Boy, he was good too. He never missed a single hair out of place on her. That little rub mark on her rump was spotted right off. The chip out of the corner of a front hoof came next (he did tell me, though, that it wasn't anything serious). About the only thing he did miss was that penny.

The Cat was a well put–together little quarter horse mare. Stout for her size, but good legs and hooves to pack her around. She was out of one of my mares who had a good temperament. Her sire, Rocky Tom Cat, was a sweetheart of a stallion. She was as nice as pie. From day one, she was a people horse. Practically sitting in your back pocket all the time. The first time I rode her was the first day I threw a saddle on her and all this in front of about twenty people standing around. They were horse lovers who were willing to pay to watch me work with unbroke colts, to learn the hows and how nots of green breaking. Every last one of them was disappointed because The Cat never put on any kind of a show for them. Some were actually muttering that she must be already broke because she kept dozing off during the sacking out and did nothing but yawn when I stepped up on her. I was plumb happy about her gentle nature even if they weren't. Not wanting to let these budding bronc riders think all horses were so easy to handle, on the second day of the clinic I brought in a tough acting brown who, before the dust settled, had every last one of them on the outside of the arena. So much for standing around and getting in my way.

Copper Cat was trained and eventually sold to a nice young couple who were just learning about horses and riding. I know she went on to be a fine companion for them, and I imagine she took real good care of them too. As for the tough-acting brown, he took a lot more work before I could sell him, but he went to a ranch hand who had a disposition to match his own. I imagine that if they haven't killed each other yet they are still riding the lonesome trails.

HORSE ABUSE

Abuse of horses or any of God's creatures is a sin. What people do through ignorance and stupidity to their horses is unforgivable. When you don't feed them properly, when you don't take care of their hooves or teeth, when you don't take care of their health are all classed as abuse. The worst abuse of all is purposely beating on them, letting your anger and fear take over so you viciously hurt the animal. More times than not, it isn't just a matter of losing your temper, it is because people are afraid of horses. Because of this subconscious fear, people beat and abuse a horse to show not only the horse, but themselves, that they are in control.

I once was neighbours to some ranchers who continually abused their horses. They never fed them extra in the winter, but let them run on cattle pastures where the grass was grazed down to the ground. Every spring these horses were a rack of bones. Every spring, regardless of their condition, they were put to work, hard work, working cattle. Their feet were never looked after and were in terrible shape. The kids had no respect for horses and ran them from morning to night.

I admired their stallion, a splendid creature. What happened to him still makes me angry today. One summer, the rancher used this stallion to rope a bull with foot rot out in the pasture. By the time he had half chased, half drug the bull to the corrals, both the bull and the stallion were on the fight. Once in the corral, he snubbed the rope around the bull's horns tight and short to the saddle horn, then he dismounted and walked away. He thought it would teach both the bull and stallion a good lesson in manners if they were left to fight it out. An enraged bull doesn't have any manners. An enraged stallion, tired of being hit by a bull, doesn't learn any manners. This rancher didn't have much in the brains department either. The ensuing fight was deadly. Again and again the bull charged the stallion, hooking him savagely with his horns. Tied to his tormentor, the stallion bit, struck and kicked the bull. The rope was soon tangled around the two fighting animals, making it impossible for them to distance themselves. After dinner and a couple of drinks, that rancher went back down to the corral to see who had won the battle. There lay the bull with his head twisted at a gruesome angle. The stallion was sunk down on top of him, pinned there by the bull's horn, which pierced his side under one front leg and exited out the chest. The tip of the bull's horn showed through the horse's chest, and a great chunk of meat clung to it.

Did this rancher feel any pity for these suffering animals? Did he know what he had done and be sorry for it? The answer is no! His only emotion was anger at them. Both combatants survived the battle: the bull long enough to be shipped for slaughter, and the stallion to be crippled up for the rest of his life.

Too Much, Too Long

I bought a big sorrel rope horse one time to see if I could straighten him out with patient retraining. He had been pushed past his natural capacity to such an extreme that he was a nervous wreck. His owner thought of himself as a real good horseman. If the horse didn't stand in the roping box just perfect, he beat him over the head. If the horse didn't rate the calf just perfect, he beat him over the rump. If he missed the calf when he threw his loop, it had to be the horse's fault, so he beat him all over. If he did catch the calf, and didn't get back quick enough to hold the calf, he beat him on the chest and head. This poor gelding was so afraid of his master that the second the man swung up into the saddle, the horse broke out in a sweat, his muscles trembling. The gelding's mind was unable to comprehend what he was doing so wrong, so he pranced, reared and developed the habit of leaping sideways every few strides. The man simply punished him more. He attempted to control the horse by the most savage of bits, and a twisted wire nose band used as a tie down, tied so tight to the horse's cinch that the horse was in constant discomfort.

I worked gently with this gelding for several months, using all my knowledge to show him the abuse was over, that he didn't have to be afraid of his rider anymore. When I felt he was ready, I sold him to a cowboy who I knew was good to his horses. A year later, I ran into the cowboy again and asked him about the big gelding. The abuse the horse had suffered in his past had surfaced the second the cowboy had tried to rope a calf off him at a local rodeo. He had been fine at home, but the second he saw that arena he came unglued. First he had crashed into the fence, going into the roper's box. Then he reared up and over backwards. Although no one was hurt, all my training turned out to be in vain. The cowboy wanted a horse he could use at jackpots and rodeos for a few extra dollars in winnings. The gelding was sold to someone else and finally the end came for him at the slaughterhouse.

Unhappy Ending

I purchased a little blue-grey three-year-old mare with running bloodlines for a brood mare, from a For Sale ad in a horse publication. I don't often purchase an animal sight un-seen, but I wanted her type of breeding in my program. I was at work in town when the owners delivered her to my farm. As per my instructions, they had left her in a pen equipped with water and fresh hay. It was late in the day before I came home to see her for the first time. My, she was pretty. I stood outside the pen, taking in her shiny coat and dainty build. She stood quietly munching her hay and watching me with ears pricked forward. I entered the pen and began walking towards her. She whirled to face me, head up, muscles starting to tremble with tightly controlled tension. The closer I got to her, the more frightened she became. She was absolutely rigid with fear as I reached out to touch her shoulder. My fingers barely brushed her skin when she fell to her knees in uncontrollable panic. She quickly straightened up and stood frozen. I was shocked. This mare was badly abused by someone, somewhere. Yet in my phone con-versations with her owners, they had given me no hint as to her condition. They had talked about how much they loved her, how much she meant to them, how sorry they were to have to sell her.

Within seconds that blue-grey mare was sweating all over, her breathing rapid, her heart pounding. I left her and headed for the telephone. For three solid weeks I phoned them, morn-ing, noon and night. For three weeks the adults in that house-hold never answered the phone. Little kids would answer and inform me that mommy and daddy couldn't come to the phone, or that they are outside right now. I left my name and number every time with the kids, no one called me back. Finally, in frustration, I phoned after midnight when surely the kids would be in bed. It worked. The husband answered. I barely had time to tell him my name, when he informed me they would not take the horse back, that she was my problem now, and basically I could go straight to hell if I didn't like it. I asked him what made him think I wanted to give the horse back to him, maybe I was only phoning to find out what had caused her to be so deathly afraid of people. He proceeded to swear at me. All this from a man who loved his horse and was sorry to have to sell her. I hung up, never to know what had happened to the mare while in their hands.

Sometimes, when a horse has been abused too badly or too long, he or she cannot be brought back to being a usable animal. Such was the case with the grey mare. Although I kept her for several months, and worked gently and patiently with her, she would not or could not get over her fear of humans touching her. I started her under saddle and then enlisted the help of another lady trainer. This kind lady also tried her best, without good results. The mare was too nervous to think straight, thus being a danger to people and herself. I would not breed her in case part of her problem was in her genetic makeup. I was forced to sell her to a local horse dealer for slaughter, as I could not see her not being a danger to someone else too.

Don't Hurt Me

Princess came from a well-known cutting horse breeder from the Medicine Hat area. Although he was himself a good, kind horseman, one of the trainers he had hired to work for him was not. He fired the man within weeks for cruelty to his horses, but the damage had already been done to Princess.

She was a small mare who never grew much in height, so she was not started under saddle until she was four years old. Her disposition was of the nervous, flighty type, and along with being four before being worked with, she was quite a handful. This hired trainer's idea of handling such a horse was to beat her for every tiny mistake. It only took a couple of lickings for her to become neurotic. As the lickings continued, she went to pieces.

She came into the horse sale ring, stepping as if walking on eggshells and being afraid she might break them. Her responses to the reins to stop, turn and back, were lightning quick. Too quick. I could tell she was fired up too much, trying too hard to please. When the rider reached up suddenly to adjust his hat, she froze, her tail clamped down, her eyes wild. I knew instantly she had been handled roughly, abused. Because of her smaller size, plain brown colour and even being a mare, not a gelding, she was going cheap. I knew the bloodlines from her papers, and I knew her conformation was good, so I bought her.

Princess wanted to please me in every way, but fear of me kept her on edge. I rode and worked with that mare for two springs and summers. She allowed me to handle her, but trembled and broke into a sweat every time the farrier or veterinarian had to work on her. So I trimmed her feet myself, and all but once took care of any cuts, scratches or bruises. I never owned or rode a horse before or since with her natural ability to get down, look cows in the eye and put them where they were supposed to go. I also never rode a horse before or since where I had to be aware of any sudden movements of myself, as I did with Princess. If I forgot who I was riding and reached up to scratch my head, she shot straight sideways. If I didn't think, and shifted positions in the saddle suddenly, she jumped out of her skin. She had learned to trust me, but only so far. It was not safe for anyone riding beside us to make any sudden or unusual movements either. She was always watching for punishment to come out of nowhere, and remained a pain to ride and control.

Thankfully, once her training was as complete as possible, I found a cutting horseman from North Dakota who could live with her unusual, manmade habits; he bought her from me for the profit I needed to make.

Horse From Hell

Dusty came into my life much like Princess had. It was at an auction sale I found him. Once more I liked the bloodlines of this young stallion. Once more I didn't really like the way he moved out in the sale ring. Unlike Princess though, he wasn't quick as a cat, instead he was shuffling around the ring with his head sort of hanging, not really paying attention to the rider at all. I put him down as spoiled and lazy. So I bought him. Spoiled, lazy horses are fairly easy to retrain compared to abused horses. He was only two years old, so he should be easy to work with. I loaded him, shortly after buying him, and headed home. It was a long trip from that sale ring to my place. Several hours later, I backed the horse trailer up to the lighted area in front of my barn to unload him.

I was tired from the trip, it was dark and I was confused about the horse I had bought. Hadn't I loaded a quiet, half-asleep colt in my trailer, back there at the auction sale? When I opened that tailgate of the trailer to unload him, I was looking at the HORSE FROM HELL. He was dusty yellow-coloured like a cougar, and acting like a caged cougar too. I got back in the truck and worked that trailer backwards until it rested tight against the barn door. I then opened the sliding cattle door on the back end and Dusty slammed out of it, into the barn. He charged straight down to the box stall on the end and I was right behind him to slam that door on him. There I stood, plumb ashamed of myself. I now recognized that shuffling walk and half-asleep attitude of the colt in the sale ring. He had been tranquillized. Now I was thinking about it, he had let himself partly descend out of his sheath in the sale ring. A sure sign of a doped–up gelding or stallion. I had ignored it, like some green–horn horse buyer. Boy was I mad at myself.

Dusty turned out to be the kind of horse who, once abused too long and too bad, decides to go on the warpath. Few horses are natural–born killers, most are manmade through mistreat–ment. Dusty was one of them. I didn't know the people I had bought him from, but one phone call to them confirmed what type of people they were. The man told me the horse was as gentle as a kitten, and in the few short hours I had owned him, it was me not them who had made Dusty what he was. He also informed me I was a stupid, worthless female and he hoped the young stallion killed me for all he cared.

Using a provincial landowners' map, I looked up these people's ranch land. Luck was with me, because the neighbours to these people listed on the map were people whom I had sold ranch horses to in the past. I called them up to get some insight into Dusty's past history.

After chatting with them and finding out they still had the two geldings I had sold them and were proud to own them, I mentioned I had purchased a yellow dun, two–year–old stallion from their neighbours. The telephone line went dead silent then they told me to shoot him or ship him for meat. Here is their version of Dusty's life.

Apparently the husband had the bad habit of beating the hell not out of horses, but his wife. Apparently humans also go a bit weird in the head after years of abuse. So she beat the hell out of her husband's prize colt, who just happened to be Dusty. Seems the husband would beat her up for any silly excuse, and in her anguished state she would go down to the barns, tie Dusty up and beat him with whips, ropes, fence posts, even a chain. She had even been reported to the police for her cruelty against the horse. Before the police got too nosy around the ranch, maybe before they could come after the man himself, he had sold Dusty.

I figured Dusty was too good of a piece of horseflesh to sell him straight to the meatpackers without first at least trying to work with him. I warned everyone and anyone who might enter my premises about the horse, telling them to stay away from his corral.

It only took me a couple of days to make the discovery that I could enter his pen, providing I wasn't carrying a rope or halter in my hands. He would not attack me if my hands were empty. He seemed to grow quite fond of my daily visits, learning to like being scratched and talked to. I could discipline his boyish behaviour by simply raising my voice with him, but if I made any other threatening moves around him, I better be on my way up and over his high fences.

I made the mistake one day while in his corral of spotting a piece of bale twine lying on the ground, without thinking I bent down and picked it up to throw it in the garbage. In an instant he was on top of me, teeth bared, front feet striking. His initial charge knocked me to the ground and before he could get me with his teeth or hooves, I managed to roll under the bottom rail of his corral. I stood there in shock, the thin piece of string still in my hand. He paced back and forth on the other side of the fence, ears back, shaking his head in anger. I knew then that it had to be one of three things with this horse. Either I shot him, I took him straight to the slaughterhouse or I fought it out with him, not to hurt him but to show him once and for all that he could be handled with ropes without being abused.

The next day was Sunday, and my husband, Gary, could be home to help me work on him. The shed in his pen had been enclosed to make a large box stall. One side of it was two by eight planks, up to eight feet high. I closed him in this shed and told Gary I would try to throw a rope over his head, while his attention was on Gary in the other corner. I told Gary to be ready to go over the planks if he attacked. While Dusty was watching Gary, I tossed a noose around his neck. The second he felt the rope, he lunged, teeth bared for Gary. Gary went over the rails instantly. Enraged, the horse, slammed into the fence, again and again, his eyes fixed on Gary, thinking he was the one who had touched him with a rope. The planks splintered and gave way from his deadly assault. As he lunged out into the corral, I went with him. Quickly I managed to get a couple of wraps around the snubbing post in the centre, then I got out of there. He fought the rope until he choked himself down. Once he was down, I raced over to him, released the tie, and knelt on his neck, keeping his nose pointed up with my arms. In this way, a person can hold a big horse down, while someone else ties his legs together so he can't get up.

Gary quickly hog tied him, and then I went to work on him. Again and again I trailed a soft rope over and over his body. I rubbed his neck and face with it repeatedly. And I sacked him out by slapping him every where on his body with a light piece of tarp. After an hour, we rolled him over and worked on his other side. It seemed like forever before Dusty stopped fighting what was happening to him. I was exhausted by the time he finally came to realize that he wasn't being hurt. Slowly his muscles relaxed, he was finished fighting. When we let him up, he stood quietly as we once again touched him all over with the tarp and different ropes. Maybe he didn't have to be destroyed after all.

I only had one more savage go around with Dusty after that. It was the first time I saddled him up. While he was standing tied to the snubbing post, saddled and bridled over the halter and lead, I saw that the big gate into the pen had come off the top hinge bracket. I carried a square hay bale into the pen to stand on to give me the height to replace it. Without thinking I left the bale there. Making sure the cinches were tight, I tied the bridle reins moderately loose to the saddle horn, and released the halter from the post. I walked away, leaving Dusty to pack the saddle around loose in the round pen. He started ambling around the pen, not overly concerned with the weight on his back. As he moved on, he brushed up against the fence, the stirrup pulled back away and then with a small whumping sound fell back in place. He blew up. Dead ahead of him lay the square bale I had left on the ground. I'm glad it was a bale of hay and not me that he proceeded to vent his anger on. He attacked the bale, grabbing it in his teeth and throwing it in the air. The second it hit the ground, he was at it again, striking it viciously, mauling it with rage. When he quit, there was nothing left of that bale but a scattered pile of hay all over his corral.

Maybe with years of work, Dusty could be converted back into a normal horse but I was in the business of buying and selling horses. I did what I could with him, then gelded him and put him up for sale. I was totally honest with potential buyers. I sold him for way less than what I had paid for him, and the buyer knew exactly what he was getting. I turned down offers from anybody who was not an above-average horse person, finally letting Dusty go to a rancher who knew how to bring out the best in any animal. I hope that yellow cuss went on to become a good saddle horse, but probably not.

Winter Kill

Anybody who has ever been in the horse business at some time or another has heard this expression: winter killed. "Yup, old Blaze winter killed." "He was fat and happy when I turned him out in the fall, but he winter killed, because I found him dead in the spring." "I sure did love that old horse, I sure will miss him." "Heck, I was telling my neighbours up the road about it, and they say that over the years they have had several horses winter killed."

The winter didn't kill your horse, mister, you did! You have the nerve to sit here and tell me how much you cared for old Blaze? You killed him as sure as if you had pulled the trigger on a gun aimed right between his eyes. Except the way you killed him wasn't quick and painless. Instead, it took weeks for him to die, a slow tortured death. The death of starvation.

Why is it that people seem to think a horse should fend for himself all winter long? When the grass is green, up to the horse's belly, they probably give him extra oats every time they ride him or go near him. Winter comes and because it's too cold to ride, they kick him out until spring. No extra feed now, buddy. See you when I'm ready to start riding you again. "Why, horses have survived for generations out pawing snow." "My daddy never fed his horses, nobody feeds wild horses in the winter." I have listened to so many of these stories. Well, maybe it's true, your daddy never fed his horses, maybe we don't know how many of your daddy's horses winter killed either.

I have wintered many a horse out on pasture too. There are a few things to take into consideration though. I have never had a single horse winter killed. Why? Because I only turn healthy mature horses out for the winter. I check the pasture land they will be running on. I make sure there is an abundance of grass. There must be some sort of windbreak from the freezing, blow-ing snow, whether it is manmade or hills, coulees or thick willows or timber. I know that the horses are worm-free, so the feed they eat goes to maintaining their weight and body warmth, not for fighting a losing battle with internal parasites. And I check those horses all winter long. I don't kick them out and forget about them until spring. I check them and if they are losing too much weight, I either feed them extra hay or bring them home to be fed the rest of the winter. The two biggest reasons for a horse starving in the winter are poor pasture with not enough grass left from being over-grazed in the summer, and the snow getting too deep. If it's a bad winter with pro-longed excessive cold weather and more snow than usual, my horses come home to feed and shelter.

As I said before, I don't expect weanlings, yearlings, bred mares or horses past their prime age to winter out on pasture.

The horror stories I can tell about horses starving to death are many. The worst part of a lot of these stories is their owners actually do love and care about horses. It is ignorance that lets them go on year after year believing horses don't need to be fed in the winter. It is ignorant of people to say, "Nobody feeds wild horses in the winter." No, nobody feeds wild horses in the winter, and it is Mother Nature's unwritten law that the winter is meant to weed out the sick, the weak and the old. It is nature's way for these horses to winter kill.

One of the most majestic birds of prey in the world is the bald eagle, with his tremendous wingspan, his grace in the air and his savage ability to catch, kill and devour his prey. Eagles will also eat carrion when they find it. I remember sitting quietly in my truck with a pair of field glasses, watching five eagles perched on and around a carcass out in a field. They were enjoying an early springtime meal, their beaks ripping and tearing at dead flesh. That carcass was a dead pinto mare.

She had winter killed. The other horses had come through a long, cold winter in fairly good condition. She didn't have to starve to death in that field, growing weaker every day until she laid down and no longer had the strength to rise and go on. She didn't have to because all the summer and fall before, I had been after her owner, a good horseman in his own right, to get her teeth floated. Even in knee-high grass she was thin. When she got a bucket of grain, she slobbered more out of her mouth than she was able to chew and swallow. I had examined her teeth, finding one badly abscessed and the sharp edges on her grinders jagged and irritating her cheeks and gums. I had told him the one had to be pulled and the sharp edges filed off. He professed to loving that pinto mare but just never got around to doing anything about her teeth. He forgot to mention to people the problems with her teeth when he went looking for sympa-thy in the spring because she had winter killed.

I don't advocate violence against other human beings, but one time it was nip and tuck whether I was going to kick a man to death or just injure him for life. Better still I would have liked to lock him in a room, put plates of food all around the outside of that room where he could see them, but not get to them, and let him starve to death. The punishment would have fit the crime.

My heart had gone out to five starving colts from a PMU barn (a PMU barn is where pregnant mares' urine is collected for use in estrogen replacement supplements for women). Although most owners of these barns are very good to their horses, there are always a few duds. Eventually this particular owner was investigated by the SPCA for starving his horses, the horses were confiscated and he received a large fine. When I bought the colts, though, he was still in operation. He had hauled his yearly bunch of colts to an auction market for sale. All the colts came and went through the sale ring, except for these five being held in the back pen. I think the auctioneer was too embarrassed to even attempt to try to sell them to the public. The other colts were in poor shape but those five were nothing but skin and bones. Too young to have left their mommas, too long without decent food of any kind. They stood or lay huddled in that back pen, with no one to take pity on them except a meat man who agreed to give the owner twenty dollars a colt, and take them away to put an end to their misery. After the sale, I was out back, loading a couple of two–year–olds I had purchased to train and resell for a profit. This horsemeat buyer and I were friends of a sort and he approached me about taking these colts off his hands for the same he had paid for them since he figured they would get trampled to death in the liner full of horses on the way to the slaughterhouse. I had no use for these colts, but I could not say no. I had to try to save them, perhaps put some flesh on their bones and sell them next spring as yearlings, to good owners who would always care for them.

For six weeks, I fed them the choicest of hay, gradually adding rolled oats to their diet and fresh water at all times. I wormed them, treated their cuts and bruises and fell in love with all of them. From frightened little weaklings they became trusting, devoted pets. As their strength returned to them, they learned to jump, buck and play.

In order to care for horses, any livestock or any pet you need money. I had not made as good a profit that year, buying, selling and training horses as I had hoped. I was going to have to leave my farm for the winter, and find employment to tide me over until the horse industry picked up the following spring. I moved my whole herd to a friend's hay field nearby. The hay had not been cut and baled and was more than adequate feed for the winter. There was a heavy stand of timber on the north side for shelter and the people would keep a close eye on them for any injuries or sickness.

The five colts I left at home where they would have access to a shed and water. I bought a large supply of grain and hay for them.

Then I make the biggest mistake of my lifetime. I trusted someone to live there and feed them every day. I hired an older horseman who was out of work, being too stove up to get much good paying labour anymore. I gave him the keys to my house and one half the total sum of what I offered him to feed them for the first two months. I explained that I would stay in touch with him by telephone and gave him the number up north where I would be working in a camp. I hugged each one of those colts and told them that I would be back in a couple of months to scratch their itchy spots for them.

That January was one of the coldest I recall, with blizzard after blizzard. Every week I phoned my friends and asked about the welfare of my horses out in the hay field. They were all mature, healthy horses in their prime and doing fine. Every week I phoned home and inquired about how my five babies were doing. That man told me every week that they were getting fatter by the day, cleaning up their hay and grain just fine. And I believed him. I trusted him. One horse person trusting the judgement of another horse person.

Without telling anyone I decided to return home a week early, glad to be getting a break from working seven days a week, twelve hours a day. With the weather and road, what was an eight-hour trip going to work became a twelve-hour trip coming home.

Even though I was exhausted from driving so long, even though it was away past dark when I came up my driveway I pulled in towards the barn first to check on my pen full of five fuzzballs. With my truck headlights shining in the corral, I searched for those colts. I could faintly see into the shed, but no colts. Grabbing a flashlight from behind the seat, I ploughed through the snow and into the pen. The pen was level with deeply drifted snow. I reasoned that maybe the fence was down and they had got out. Climbing over the fence for a better look, I immediately stumbled and fell over a log hidden in the snow. As I started slogging around the inside fence looking for a break, I stumbled into another log under its snowy blanket. I was so tired it took awhile for something to sink in. There were no logs in that pen. Slowly I reached down and brushed the snow off the lump. It was the brown colt I had named Nicker for the way he always called to me when he saw me coming with his oats. I kept going until I had found all five of their lifeless bodies. After all my work to save them, they had been starved to death after all. With the stack of hay and a bin of oats in front of them, just out of reach on the other side of their jail, they died. With the flashlight I counted those bales. Not one had been fed to them. I checked the sacks of oats. Not one had been fed to them.

If that son-of-a-bitch had been in my house then, I might have gone to jail for murder. The local townspeople filled me in the next day on what had happened. He had taken the money I advanced him for feeding my colts, and moved in with another old wino from town. He stayed drunk on cheap booze all week, only returning to my farm on Sunday afternoons to wait for my weekly prearranged phone call and to help himself to the food in the deep freeze. While he was getting fat on my food, those little babies were dying one by one. The townspeople did not know he was supposed to feed any horses. They thought he was only supposed to stay at my place and look after the house while I was gone.

Before I could have charges laid against this man for the crime he had committed, he left the area. Even a year later, neither I nor the police were able to locate him. All I know is he should have been made to suffer as those five colts must have, their eyes fastened on the feed just out of reach. Damn him to hell.

MEAN TEMPERED

Some horses are born mean and nasty tempered. It has little or nothing to do with being spoiled or abused by mankind. They are born looking for a fight or somebody or something to kick and stomp on. Sometimes they reach maturity before their true dispositions come out into the open, but sooner or later they are going to wreak havoc.

I raised a blood bay gelding one time, who had inherited a bad disposition from his grand sire. His grand sire spent his entire life trying to take a chunk out of any fool who messed with him.

He should never have been used for breeding, because a wicked temper can be passed on to the offspring. Although both the sire and dam had good dispositions, the bay was born with a chip on his shoulder.

At only a couple of weeks old, he would bite and kick his own mother, and he ruled the roost, not the mare. By the time he was two months old, he would go out of his way to terrorize the other foals. I halter broke him at weaning time and he was sulky but seemed to know I would not put up with any of his temper tantrums. Except for gelding him as a late yearling, I didn't handle him all that much. At two years old I trained him to ride, and once again he was fairly well behaved although a problem with the others because he was prone to dominating them even at that age. He turned out to be a quick learner with an exceptionally nice build, so should have been easy to sell. It was not the case though. Every prospective buyer who came to see him would spot that he had an attitude problem. If another horse or even a dog walked by, he would pin his ears back, and if given the chance, take a bite out of the poor animal. If a buyer rode him around in a different way than I rode, he would hump up and kick in anger. If tied to a post for longer than he liked, he would paw the ground and act silly. So, his training continued all that summer and fall, with more than the usual hours spent on him.

By the summer of his third year, I was no longer interested in selling him. He was a big, strong gelding and my favourite mount for any heavy riding I had to do or for snubbing other colts to. I had learned that him and I were never going to be best friends in life but he never really tried my patience too much.

By the time he had been around for six years, he had fully matured in size and mind alike. His mind and the way it worked was what bothered me. I was beginning to think he might someday harm someone. He was sullen and nasty around other people, and seemed barely to tolerate me. The actual only times he was half decent was when he was tired right out from a hard day's work. It seemed hard work took the starch out of him.

He was seven years old when I knew he had to go. I had hired a girlfriend of mine to help with all the horses during training time. She had a three–year–old boy who came with her to the farm. To keep the boy out of harm's way while his mother and I worked, I had put sand in the box of my half–ton truck, which I then parked in the main corral. The little fellow would spend hours with his toys, playing in the truck box. This way we could see him at all times, and he knew he had to stay up there and not get out under the feet of some bronc who might be around.

His mom was in one corral saddling horses for me while I took a first ride on another colt in another corral. Stopping the colt for a rest I looked towards my truck to see how the boy was doing. That blood bay gelding had him firmly locked in his teeth. Ears flat back he yanked the boy clear out of the truck and stood holding him. At the same time he dropped the child, I was off my horse and running as hard as I could go. I screamed for his mother but she was even further away from them than I was. The bay stood over the boy, teeth bared, his front hooves savagely pawing the ground, missing the petrified child only by inches. As I ran, I grabbed up a stick lying on the ground and hurled it ahead of me at him. The second the stick struck him in the side, he leapt away from the child and stood glaring at me. Panting and out of breath, I stood facing him. He laid his ears back, struck out at me and squealed in rage. I continue to stay between him and the child as the boy's mother scooped him up and carried him out of further harm's way. The enraged gelding made one jump towards me, before turning and trotting away. Seconds later he attacked a yearling on the other side of the corral in his savage fury.

Although the boy was badly frightened, he was physically unharmed. His jacket was torn from shoulder to shoulder where the bay had first grabbed him. The bay signed his own death warrant that day. I shipped him for meat soon after, knowing he had finally reached the dangerous stage where he was going to kill someone, someday.

No Pollyanna

What makes an unruly tempered horse finally turn on people, even after being controlled for years, has no definite answer. I once asked a fellow how he got so many scars on his shoulder and the broken bones in his face. His story was enough to make my hair stand on end. He had purchased a broke saddle mare, Pollyanna, a five–year–old brown/bay quarter horse. She was pretty good looking, and he did not have real problems with her, even though she had a naturally inher-ited bad disposition. The next spring he needed a saddle horse in a hurry and she was the only broke horse handy to be caught and ridden. Even though she had a two–month–old colt on her, he saddled up and headed out, leaving the colt at home in the corral. He made it about one hundred yards when she lit into bucking and piled him. A good rider, he got back on and headed out again, this time making it about two hundred yards farther. She again bogged her head and went to bucking. He was good but she was better, off he came. Determined he swung back up in the saddle and forced her onward. He made it a whole half mile before she lost control. Bawling and screaming, she reared, plunged and bucked until he hit the ground. She did not turn and run for home; she attacked. Teeth ripping and tearing, front feet smashing into him, she vented her rage. Only after he was unconscious did she quit attacking him and leave. The brutal assault left his entire body torn and bruised. His cheek bone was demolished, his jaw broken and his shoulder bone pulverized, with the muscle torn right off it. After a long, complex shoulder operation, he remained hospitalized for over a month.

When he was finally released from the hospital, he made his way slowly down to the mare's corral. On seeing him she faced him with ears pinned flat back, on the fight instantly. He sold Pollyanna to Vern Franklin's Rodeo Company, where she went on to become one of Vern's top bucking horses for the next five or six years until dying one winter out on the open range. The colt, who had been only two months old at the time of the attack, inherited his dam's bad-tempered disposition and ended up also sold to Vern. Bar Ko, as he was named, sired many wicked bucking horses in his own lifetime. The vicious streak carried on down through each generation.

SKUNKS, PORCUPINES & OTHERS

Regardless that I was born loving all animals, some just don't fit nicely into the farm scenario. I was very young when this was made all too clear to me. Take porcupines for instance.

A big old porcupine took to coming into the combination grain and supplement feed bin next to the main corrals. I had no fear of him and neither he of me. While he laid in the doorway, content after licking salt stored there, I got up the nerve to reach out slowly and stroke his blunt nose. He actually closed his eyes and seemed to enjoy the attention. Because I had petted his nose, I fell in love with him and promptly declared to the whole world that this porcupine belonged to me. My father was not impressed. Dad knew that the porcupine had to be disposed of to protect the livestock from his quills. He also knew that his only daughter would have a fit over it. So being the good father that he was, he tried to compensate by attempting to just herd the critter out of the yard and across the field, in hopes he would not return. Well Porky didn't want to be chased anywhere and kept waddling back, past Dad to the grain bin. Even though I, in my youthful wisdom, assured him that I would live twenty-four hours a day in the bin so Porky would not go near the cattle or horses, Dad was determined to escort him off the premises. He ended up scooping him up on a grain shovel and carrying him out across the field to some willows surrounding a slough. Porky was back by night time. I had to got to school the next day and according to Dad, he persuaded the porcupine to take up residence someplace else during my absence.

Horses and porcupines usually don't tangle with each other like dogs and porcupines do. If they do, though, it's the horse who always ends up the loser. Dad's chestnut mare, Judy, kicked a porky one summer. Judy was not being rode and was running out on pasture away from the yard. It was probably six weeks or longer before I got close enough to her to see the damage the quills had done. Although she was not lame in that hind leg, it was grotesquely swollen with infection. The one thing about Judy was you could not catch her out on pasture. As she was alone with only the cows for companionship, it would mean bringing the whole herd across country to the corrals to catch her. If even one cow was not rounded up and herded home, she would buddy up with that cow and stay out in the pasture. There were not enough hours in a day or days in a week for Dad to find the time to round up cattle before the fall gather. He was too busy and I couldn't do it by myself, so it was decided that as long as she did not exhibit signs of lameness, then nature would have to take its course and heal her. She healed up finally after the quills were naturally disposed of. That hind pastern and fetlock joint remained enlarged and unsightly for the rest of her life.

A gelding of mine pawed a porky with the result that at least fifty quills were stuck in his front pastern and fetlock. I caught him and spent the afternoon, sorting through the hair and pulling them one at a time. The horse was not too pleased with the procedure and seemed to blame me for the pain in the first place. For a year after he was difficult when it came time to hold that one leg up to trim his hoof.

Oh, Momma

Now, animal lover or not, I don't like skunks. Sure they are cute, charming, even attractive to look at but that's all. They harbour many diseases including rabies. Worse even than the horrid smell when they spray is seeing your family dog frantically rubbing his eyes, in obvious distress when he takes a shot right in the face. So us children learned early in life to dispose of a skunk anywhere on the property. My older brothers would use their .22 rifles for the job, I would use large rocks thrown from a safe distance. It was a necessary evil, destroying them, but it had to be done.

I was training a buckskin stallion one time when I crossed paths with a skunk. Both dogs on the premises had recently taken a skunk's spray and stunk to high heaven. I was about two miles from the ranch when I found the culprit. Now this was the three-year-old's second ride and he was still prone to blowing up. I was leery about getting off him so far from the buildings in case he raised a ruckus when I went to get back on, but I also wanted to dispose of the skunk which on closer inspection was also thin and unhealthy looking. Stepping off my bronc, I held the reins tight while I found a large, heavy rock. By then, Mr. Skunk had wandered into a thick stand of buck brush.

Here I was, leading this stallion, whom I had only halter broke a week before, stepping gingerly through the buck brush, looking to get close to a skunk I couldn't even see to dispose of him with one neat throw. Ahead and off to the right of me, the brush moved, showing the passage of an animal. Intent on the wiggling bush, I pulled a blooper I wouldn't soon forget. I stepped right on Mr. Skunk. He raised his tail and let me have it. This was no long-distance shot: he soaked my leg. Gagging and choking, I dropped the rock and back-peddled out of there. Tears streaming out of my eyes, I felt violently sick to my stomach. Through all of this I kept a death grip on that horse's reins. It took twenty minutes before I adjusted to the smell so I could at least see where I was going. One half of me said to peel my pants off right then and there and the other half said no way was I riding back to a ranch, part naked. It soon became clear that I wasn't going to be riding anywhere. The buckskin had no intention of letting me anywhere near him, smelling like I did. He just kept rolling his eyes at me and snorting like mad. Every time I tried to work my way closer to him, he would shoot straight in the air to get away. You guessed it! I walked those two miles back, leading him at the end of the reins. Even the dogs would not get close to me, having learned their lessons about skunks already.

Those blue jeans of mine were brand new but they hit the garbage barrel the second I got them off. The stink was embedded in my skin, and even washing repeatedly out behind the house with tomato juice wasn't much help. I took a lot of ribbing from everyone else at the ranch for many days until I managed to scrub the stink off me.

Giving Chase

Coyotes have a place in the world of nature but not around ranches during calving and foaling season. Given half a chance they gladly make meals out of a newborn, a cruel death for the young and a costly one for the person depending on making a profit from raising them.

When I was twelve years old, I discovered a way to have fun with coyotes one summer. One of Dad's Hereford cows had bloated and died on the side of a small steep hill. There was an extra large population of coyotes back then and many came to feed off the rotting carcass. Mounted on my faithful mare, Lady, I would slowly and quietly come up the far side of the hill and work my way around its base towards the dead cow. It never failed that there was at least one coyote there. As I came around the last bend, I would let a war whoop out of me and Lady would break into a mad run. Startled, the coyote or coyotes would head across the field with Lady and I hot on their tails. Lady loved this game and put her heart and soul into chasing a coyote. Ears back, she really ran, but the coyotes were always faster and stayed ahead of us with ease. The chase would last until we came to a barbed wire fence, the coyote dashing under it and Lady and I coming to a sliding halt. I decide it was such a fun game, that after the cow was no more than a few scattered white bones and the coyotes long gone, Lady and I made do with the family dog. The dog loved the game as much as we did, and would run back and forth in front of us, barking, until we took up the chase. When he tired of it, he too would escape under a fence, there he would lay puffing and panting until he got his wind back. Then back for more he would come.

One thing about Lady was that she was a very protective mother when she foaled her first colt. I was boarding with Granddad at the time on his retirement acreage next to town. Lady didn't like anybody messing with her colt when he was very young. Being pastured next to town was hard on her nerves, with people always coming over to see her baby. Worse, the town dogs ran free.

One German shepherd dog insisted upon playing with her colt. The colt had no fear of the dog and was glad for the chance to run, kick up his heals and play. First the dog would chase the colt, then somehow in their mad racing in circles the colt would end up chasing the dog. Lady was not pleased at all, but the dog had sense enough to stay clear of her. A housewife from town got in the habit of strolling down to the fence line to say hello to the horses and was witness to the dog's demise. Seems the German shepherd got a bit carried away with the chase. Excited he lunged for the colt and bit him hard on the flank. The fright-ened colt screamed in fear and pain. This time Lady was close enough to the pair of them to catch the dog. A twelve-hundred-pound demon in the form of a very protective mother smashed the dog to the ground with her slashing front feet. As the horrified woman watched, the mare kept after the crippled dog until the life was beaten out of him. Later, when I heard about it, I went out to the spot to drag the dead dog away to be buried. Every bone in his body was pulverized. I felt sorry for the dog but had asked his owners three times to keep him tied up and away from my horses. Three times they had said, "Town bylaw, what town bylaw says its illegal to let your dog run free?" In breaking the law and letting the dog run free, would they have cared if he had run the colt through a fence or seriously injured him? I doubt it very much!

The Hunters

One day I walked out to check my mares and foals, and my approach went unobserved by a pair of coyotes intent on a newborn victim. As I topped a hill, below me I was startled to see my half-dozen mares in a rough semi-circle, their foals huddled behind each mare, and two hunting coyotes lazily circling them. The varmints were staying just out of reach of the angry mothers, wearing the mares down by keeping them on their guard at all times. While one coyote rested the other one kept up his continual circling, occasionally making a quick feint toward the horses to keep them on their toes. I probably watched this deadly play for an hour unobserved, watching first one, then the other coyote rest while the other kept up the pestering. One of my foals had been born weak, with crooked legs. That was the one that interested the hunters, no doubt. Seeing that the mares had had enough and were getting sloppy in defending their young, I let out a holler. Two furry, grey heads whipped around in my direction, four eyes catching sight of me at the same time. They were off like a shot, well aware of the power of a two–legged human. I moved the mares home until their colts were a month older and the weak–legged one had gained strength and his legs had grown straight with time as I had hoped they would.

Bird-Brained

I like crows. I find them to be very intelligent birds and make good and amusing pets if captured young enough. They always fly south in the late fall, and revert back to their wild state very quickly.

My two crows, Dirty Bird and just plain Crow, were a pair of devoted troopers to me, their adopted momma. Long after they were fully feathered and quite capable of flying, they chose to follow me on foot. After all, momma didn't fly, so why should they? Off I would go to the corrals, walking along with the crows following at my heels, single file. Two little black soldiers, marching in perfect rhythm.

They always kept a watchful eye out for the dogs and cats, but fully expected me to rescue them from either. Should a dog or cat dare to make me, their momma, mad by going anywhere near them, they would stand tight against my legs and mock the animal, with outrageous calls and great shaking of feathers. If I wasn't close enough to protect them, they were quite capable of swiftly flying to safety.

Horses, though, were not animals of prey, thus nothing to worry about as far as Dirty Bird and Crow were concerned. They loved to peck at the stitches and toes of my cowboy boots. I could not feel their hammering beaks through the leather and never minded this. If I stood still long enough, they would bring me all sorts of treasures, piling them up on top of my toes. Anything from bits of sun–touched glass to shiny pebbles were neatly piled on each boot. If a piece fell off, it was placed gently back where it belonged. If they could get away with pecking at my toes, then surely they could also peck at horse toes. The horses might not have minded if the crows had just stuck to the hard hooves. But no, the horses had to be pecked on their tender coronet band where the hair met the hoof. It normally only took a couple of sharp jabs before the horse stomped his foot. The crows thought this was great fun, but I was always petrified they were going to get squashed flat. So I would scoop up the pesky birds and throw them up onto the shed roof, out of harm's way.

Maybe this was what they wanted all along, for the fun could really begin now. Horses were meant to be dive bombed, right? Marching back and forth on the roof, they would get a horse's rump lined up, with great care. With squawks of joy, they hurdled off the roof, every time hitting their destination right on the target, the target area being the startled horse's tail heads. Their strong claws grasped the hair in a death grip. Even the quietest old plug would jump out of his skin. After a jump or two from their prey, they would fly back up on the shed roof, laughing like idiots. Dirty Bird and Crow may have thought this was a great sport but it made a nervous wreck out of me when trying to saddle up some bronc.

HORSES & CHILDREN

When I was a kid, my first horse wasn't exactly a saint. I suppose you could say he never actually set out to do me harm. But Patches didn't really like children, or adults for that matter either. Number one, by the time he let me catch him to go riding it was often too late in the evening to have much of a ride. He never really ran away with me, unless you count the couple of dozen times he decided to gallop home, even though I didn't want to go home yet. He never was much of a bucker unless you count the times he dumped me in the dirt, once knocking me unconscious for over an hour. He never really kicked me much or was it that I learned pretty quick to get out of the way of his heels? I wonder why it is that I don't have any great memories of Patches.

Take Pokey for instance. She was halter broke only. She was used as a brood mare only, for the simple reason that her neck was severely damaged, if not broken, when she was young. Her owner before me was a proud Granddad who when approached by his two little grandsons with the request to halter break a colt all by themselves, had said sure, go for it. They had gone down to the corrals and closed the gate on the several mares and colts standing in the shade of the barn. All those colts were pretty skittish and didn't let the two aspiring young cowboys anywhere near them. Except for a four–month–old bay filly. She stood right there and let them put a halter and lead rope on her. She even let them shoo her over next to the snubbing post. She stood watching them with big eyes as they knelt down and tied the end of the rope to the very bottom of the post, instead of whither height where it should have been tied. She was just too quiet for the youngsters, because when Granddad halter broke a horse it always fought like the dickens. So they took their midget–size cowboy hats off and spooked that filly. Terrified at the waving hats, she made one frantic lunge towards her momma over in the corner. The downward pull from the too–low tied rope was her undoing. When she hit the end of the rope, her vertebrae, up high in her neck, snapped. She toppled to the ground and lay there, unmoving, eyes begging for help. The boys knew something wasn't right when she wouldn't get up and ran to get their Granddad. He came, surveyed the dam-age, took the halter off her and left her there while he took the boys home to their momma's place, for he did not want to shoot an animal in front of the crying children. When he came back later with the rifle, she had got up and was hiding behind her dam. Seeing how she had got up by herself he thought just maybe she would be all right.

I bought her two months later because I felt sorry for her. She was able to graze by spreading her front legs or partially kneeling. She was unable to turn her head and neck to the right side, and the spinal column was jutted out on the right side beneath the skin. I don't have a clue as to why I bought her. I surely could not make her better, so why was I paying hard–earned money for this cripple?

She was not in pain and thrived on the extra feed and attention I gave her. She went on to raise many fine colts over the years. And if any horse loved children ever, it was Pokey. She knew not what such small humans had done to her, and she loved them.

A child to her, the smaller the better, was to be treated as one of her own children. Looking over the fence and seeing a child approaching she never failed to nicker at them, calling out to them, the same way she called to her own colts. When they were within reach, she would gently nuzzle them with her soft nose. Pokey would get upset if dogs came near any small child in her area. She would lay her ears back at a dog who bounded up to one of her human babies. I remember one time when Angie's four-year-old boy, Danny, was crying out in the corral because I said he couldn't ride Pokey anymore and had to come to the house for supper. His pitiful wails broke poor Pokey's heart. I think she was positive that her human baby was starving to death, for she kept turning her flank to him, offering her own brand of supper. Her fine muzzle caressed his hair and she talked to him with soft whinnies of love, just like she did with her own young.

Even though with her neck I had never broke her to ride, any child was more than welcome on her broad back. She would lead quietly beside me, careful to not disturb her precious cargo. Older children could sit on her all day without me anywhere near and she never attempted to get rid of them. Instead she would move extra slow and gentle as she grazed my lawn. Only God knows what a special bond he created the day he put Pokey and children together.

Horse Tails

There are many tales of horses and children. Surely these sometimes large, sometimes small, animals hold a special place in many people's youths, such as Old Mary and her master, young David. Old Mary was a bit spoiled and could be a fairly obstinate at times with adults, but the boy David could do no wrong. If she decided not to be caught, then she wasn't going to be caught. Then along comes David and she would sigh and stand still for him to catch her. That is a special bond.

I had an old pinto gelding named Old Booze because he acted like he had been on the sauce for one too many years. Old Booze didn't like me much and had nipped me more than once. He was only a small Shetland and if he took a kick at me, I didn't worry too much. After all, in his strangely sort of permanently drunken state, he couldn't really hurt me very much. Old Booze didn't just tolerate small children, he loved them. He would take a bite out of me and then turn around and softly whisper sweet nothings in a child's ear. If I walked behind him, he would raise a hoof and look back over his shoulder to get me lined up in his sights for a swift kick in the pants. Children could crawl over his rear end, play tug a war with his scruffy tail and he kept both hind feet on the ground. He was a stumble bum, always falling all over his own four feet, tripping over anything bigger than a fly perched on the ground. He never stepped on as much as a child's toe. He would happily pack one or more kids around all afternoon, never once laying his ears back in annoyance, but let me come up to him and he pinned his ears at me like I was the biggest pain in the world.

Hee Haw

Somehow I ended up with a donkey, named Jack, short I suppose for Jackass, which he was in more than one respect. Donkeys are generally sweet-dispositioned creatures. Jack was only if he felt like it. Most days, he thought he was put on the earth to chase the cats and dogs, pull tail feathers out of the chickens and just make a complete nuisance of himself with the horses. I kept Jack because he was a child's dream come true. A rascal of a child could do anything to Jack, and he never got mad. They could jump on him, crawl under him, slide off his rump and crawl over his ears, and he stood still for it. They could pull his tail, wrinkle his ears and pile three deep on his back, and he would just close his eyes and give a big sigh. Not with adults though. Even though he was quite capable of packing an adult around on his sturdy frame, he would start to hee-haw the second you climbed on him. If the tortured sound coming from his lips didn't make you feel sorry for him and get off, he would collapse in a furry grey heap on the ground. If that didn't make you leave him alone, he would bare his yellow teeth and try to make a meal out of some part of your anatomy. God forbid if you pulled his tail or wrinkled his ears. He could kick faster than greased lightning with both his front feet and his hind feet. On top of being so trustworthy with people's little ones, I sort of kept him around because he was a great alarm clock. The second the light of day broke he would face the house and begin to holler his lonesome call. Nobody, unless totally deaf, could sleep any longer with that awful noise carry- ing on. Thus my chores were done bright and early every morning, Jack only quitting when all the animals including himself were fed and watered.

Four-legged Teacher

I purchased Chico when he was already very old. The dun- coloured gelding had seen a lot of winters come and go. He was still sound in body, though, and just what I wanted for my stepdaughter's first horse. I knew how much she wanted a horse of her own, one she could ride all by herself with no adults to help her, for she was very independent minded at a young age. She didn't want a pony either, it had to be a horse. Chico had already taught an entire family how to ride, from the oldest to the youngest. He proceeded to show my stepdaughter how to ride properly: he would ignore all but the correct commands from reins and his rider's heels. If you wanted to go left or right, you better learn how to correctly neck rein him or he continued in a straight line. He was as gentle as a kitten with her, never shying, never galloping any faster than she wanted him to. He stood patiently for her grooming and repeated attempts to boost the saddle away up on his back. He dropped his head down, so the girl could easily put the bit in his mouth and bridle over his ears. He was a grand old man, looking after his precious mistress like a real trooper. Horses like Chico are few and far between; he gave his whole life to youngsters, taking splendid care of each and every one of them, and asking little more than a pat on the neck in return.

RUNAWAYS

Most of us have had a runaway at sometime in our lives. I suppose that you could say that when I was in my twenties, I had my fair share of runaways. Saturday nights seemed to be the usual time for them. The evening would start out okay, just a couple of us girls getting out for a beer or two, then before you know it, a runaway happens. You know the kind, bright lights, loud dance music, and even maybe a good-looking cowboy would happen along. Not that I had much more luck roping these fellows than I did roping a hard-to-catch horse, but it was fun trying.

The other kind of runaway is the one you really don't want to happen. That's the one where you and your horse can't agree on when to stop, halt and desist. Not a fun time.

I was riding a pinto three-year-old one summer, who after ninety days of riding was, I thought, ready for sale. Two Spot had a sweet mind and I enjoyed training him. After the colts were well saddle broke, I would usually ride them bareback a time or two before selling them, so their new owners could handle them without a saddle too.

We had lazily trotted up a steep, rutted road, barely more than a set of vehicle tracks, to a government dam that was stocked with trout and jackfish. In the summer time, the camp grounds were swarming with families of city folk, expensive rods and reels flashing in the sun, as they fished to their hearts' content. I rode quietly amongst them, chatting with the ones who oohed and aahed over the pretty horse. I was sitting relaxed on Two Spot, talking, and he was half asleep in the hot afternoon sun. A pair of children must have had the devil sitting on their shoulders, because they decided to spook my sleepy horse. Working quickly, they tipped over a forty–five gallon drum, used for a garbage barrel, and with a shove sent it rolling down the slight incline towards us. To Two Spot it was a demon from hell, coming to eat him alive. He spun around so fast, had I not grabbed a handful of mane hair, I would have been left sitting in midair. He hit that rutted road heading for the safety of home, going full out. I was on a runaway.

The bit was clutched solid in his mouth, pulling on the reins had no effect what so ever. Ahead of us, bumping its way slowly down the trail, was a polished new car. In seconds we were on top of its bumper. A runaway horse has no sense nor reason. As far as Two Spot figured, if he had to gallop over that car to get to the safety of home, he would. In the back window, the fright-ened faces of children were staring at us. To try to turn him to the side, would surely end up in us falling on the rough ruts, his feet tripped out from under him. Twice we almost went down, when his front hooves clipped the car's bumper. The driver did not know I had no control over the horse yet, and was angrily waving his fist at me. Mad as a hornet, he yanked the car over onto a level patch of prairie grass. We shot by him now, Two Spot still not listening to the reins. As we rounded the last bend for home, I knew my time was running out. At the bottom of the hill, a pasture gate was closed, four strands of lethal barbed wire waiting for us, strung across the road. Riding two–handed, I see–sawed the reins back and forth. It seemed to take forever for his brain to connect with the reins and he started to listen to me. We slid to a halt, his chest against the wire.

Now that my wild ride was over with, I started to shake violently from my head to my toes. The car owner pulled up behind us, and leaning out the window began to berate me for endangering his car with a stupid horse. I never said a word. I just swung off Two Spot and stumbled away, leading the now calm, happy pinto, glad to still be in one whole piece.

Low Flyer

Smokey showed me that even in a large flat field, a runaway could be next to impossible to stop. He, like Two Spot, was coming along fine in his training, and was of good mind and disposition. When you're training nice colts like these, you tend to relax your guard on them, not expecting the shenanigans from ranker type horses. We were trotting a few circles, working on his lead changes, and he was relaxed and responding nicely. I didn't pay any attention to the droning noise of an approaching light aircraft. How was I to know that it was a crop spray plane, about to drop out of the heavens and skim over our heads close enough to ruffle our hair on its first approach to the neighbour's field. Smokey bolted. In a split second I was on another runaway. The field was large and level, so I began forcing him in a circle to the left, planning on gaining control over him with ease. My plans changed for the worse, when we ran into a grounded flock of prairie chickens. They burst from cover on our left side and Smokey completely lost it. Blinded by fear, he ran straight ahead, his eyes rolled back in his head. There was no fence line to worry about hitting, but the gravel road, dead ahead came complete with two steep ditches. A runaway horse going full out does not go down and up a steep ditch like a sensible horse at a sensible speed. We made the near ditch in one tremendous leap, we left only one track in the middle of that road, and we went ass over tea kettle in the opposite ditch. Thank heavens I was thrown clear, coming to rest in a twisted heap in the ditch. As I rolled to my feet, I closed my eyes, not wanting to look at the horse lying still on the ground. Surely his neck must be broken, the way he went down, with his head bent under his falling weight. With tears in my eyes, I approached him. Suddenly with a groan, he came alive, scrambling to his feet. We were both bruised up some, but otherwise fine. Smokey went on to become a much-loved member of a family who doted on him like he was another child. He never once attempted to run away on his rider again, but then maybe a low-flying plane never ruffled his hair again either.

Bad Habit

Pepper is another story entirely. He was a confirmed runaway, having already gone through two other trainers when I agreed to work with him. He was a beautiful bay colour, with a blaze face and four white socks. He was exceptionally well bred, so his owners wanted to break him of this dangerous habit and save him from a dogfood can.

The last trainer to work with him had tried everything possible to break him, even having used a running W rig on him, and throwing him to his knees whenever he refused to stop. Pepper was a smart horse and soon learned that when the rig was on him, he had to behave, but you can't ride with this tripping rig on him all the time. My hope was to completely retrain him, starting at square one. He resisted the bit in his mouth, by bulling his head down to his chest if you pulled on the reins, and kept going. He had a short heavy neck, which when bent allowed him to actually touch his own chest with his nose. A rider had absolutely no control over him like this. As he had a hard mouth from being pulled on so much, I switched him to a bosal. I didn't use a gentle colt hackamore either, I used one that was hard core, rawhide braided over a steel nose band, meant for controlling rank older broncs. If anything, a bosal like this one, if used wrong, will make a horse carry his head too high, even rear if handled roughly. Surely with this head gear, he would learn to quit bulling into it, with his neck bent. Pepper sored up some under his jaw, and started listening to me. It looked like maybe he didn't have to go for doggy dinners after all. Or so I thought. I had been riding him for about thirty days when he decided to ignore the hackamore and fly home with me, out of control. We were back to square one. His owners had been out to see him, a time or two, and had been looking forward to having a decent saddle horse after all. It was not to be. You could ride him at a walk, even at a trot, and stop him nicely with the bosal. But you could not lope or gallop him out in the open. He simply ran away with me. I was the third person to try him, and the owners decided he should be shipped, because a runaway is too dangerous to himself and people to keep him around.

That week, while I was waiting for the truck to come and pick him up, I told his story to a friend of mine, who was ten times a better horseman than me. This man was not afraid of the devil himself. No bronc ever got the best of him, there wasn't a horse born, I don't think, who could put this man down. He said he had a mind to try something on Pepper, which had worked once before on a rank, older, spoiled runaway. I told him to go ahead, Pepper's days were numbered anyway. He saddled him up, and headed out into the heavy timber in the far pasture. I rode beside him, asking what he planned to do. He said, "I'm going to run his blinking head into a big tree, every time he runs away with me." Once well into the forest, he booted him into a gallop. As always, when he tried to stop him, Pepper just increased his speed. Sure enough, as the horse tried to gallop between two big trees, he swung the horse into one. Bang, he was knocked onto his haunches. I know it sounds cruel, but going to the slaughterhouse is a lot more final. Again, he loped away; again Pepper would not stop. Wham, into another tree, head first. The third time he would not stop, he was also leery about running smack into a tree. When the horseman pulled him over at the last second to hit another tree,

Pepper thought not. He twisted at the sight of the approaching tree, and fell heavily, sideways into it. His weight pinned the rider against the huge trunk, hard enough to break the man's trapped elbow and two ribs. The horseman was laid up for a month or more, after which he bought a pair of greyhounds. He claimed he bought the dogs so he could watch them eat their supper, in hopes Pepper was part of their meal. Just maybe he was. He was a real good-looking gelding, but useless to society. I hated where he ended up, but there are too many nice horses out there needing good homes to mess with a confirmed runaway.

HEAVEN & EARTH

Once I tasted the majestic splendour of the mountainous region north and west of Rocky Mountain House, my heart was captured forever. No human can put down in words the natural beauty of this wilderness. The written word can only give a tiny glimpse into its true existence; you must go there and live it, to fully understand the power of its creator and the glory of its being.

The air alone is worth going for. So crisp and clean, untarnished, it fills your lungs with the feelings of being alive. Flowing water so pure that you relish every mouthful. The scented forest of green brings peace to the most troubled soul. High above the ending treeline, the peaks rise up to meet the clouds, their tops forever covered with an artist's touch of swirled snow caps. The clouds drift their whiteness, to mingle heaven and earth together. It is the beginning and end all rolled into one.

Camp–robbing jays flit from tree to tree, ever on the alert for a morsel of food. Woodpeckers fill the morning air with the hammering of their beaks, a steady drumming of sound. An eagle's piercing cry floats above, as he glides with the gentle breeze, hunting, always hunting. Bush rabbits, squirrels, rock marmots and packrats scurry through the underbrush and among the granite stones. High up, blending in with the barren cliffs of rocky terrain, the noble mountain goats look down from their personal domain. Bighorn sheep are little more than moving shadows as they cross from mountain to valley and back again. The soft tread of wolves, as they pad silently by, is unheard by all but the forest creatures they hunt day after day. This area is but a small part of nature's wilderness, this beauty, as yet undestroyed by man.

The most common entrance to this great land is through the Blackstone River Gap, vehicles left behind. Man and horse are a team, traversing the rock–strewn trail, criss–crossing the river, careful of the water-washed boulders hidden in the rushing river. Horses and riders, with pack horses in tow, claw their way up and over the seemingly impossible walls of jagged granite to what awaits them on the other side. Once through the gap, many miles still lay ahead for those who wish to see untouched splendour at its best.

I was born and raised on Alberta's prairie, and was spell–bound with this new land of forests and mountain peaks. The two summers I worked for an outfitter up there were perhaps the best two summers of my life. Each trip in held new and splendid sights for me.

On my first trip in, through the Blackstone River Gap, I was mounted on Whiskey, my trusted and best saddle mare. The river must be crossed several times when going through the gap, and I gained new respect for Whiskey. She had never crossed a river even once in her life, let alone a fast-flowing rush of water, with slippery, hidden boulders on the bottom. She was, from the first, petrified of these crossings, yet she never gave a single hint of refusal. Trembling and snorting, she entered the river each time with true determination. If we rested the horses, next to a riverbank, she would not relax, standing rigid, eyes wide, until we moved on.

One of my jobs was to bring up the rear, keeping the pack string moving along because each day's ride was several miles long, until base camp could be set up. There the customers could enjoy, relax, fish the streams and lakes, and be one with nature. Whiskey was to prove to be too high-powered for bringing up the drag because she would not walk easily, always prancing and asking to be allowed to move out at a faster pace. Her constant jigging was hard on me and her too. So it was decided that she and I would lead the head of the column instead. Again she was not the right horse for this. The lead horse must move out briskly, yet maintain an even walking pace, so the gentle dude horses and pack horses are kept at an even ground-covering walk behind. Whiskey's go, go, go attitude meant the other horses were always breaking into a trot to keep up, resulting in the inexperienced riders bouncing all over their saddles, soring themselves and their horses' backs up. The pack horses then had trouble with their packs shifting around on their backs from trotting on steep terrain.

So while the outfitter took a more dignified lead, I allowed Whiskey to move out as she seemed determined to do. I was often a mile ahead of the others, before I would make her stand still and wait for them to catch up, once again. The higher we climbed, the more narrow the single-file trails became. We were now up on the side of a mountain, with the trail banking on the left side by a sheer wall of rock and the right side falling away sharply to the forest several hundred feet below. Whiskey was pushing ahead when we started to round a sharp bend in the trail, and she suddenly froze to a stop. She stood, muscles tight, consumed by fear. Something terrifying lay just out of sight around the bend. There wasn't even room enough to turn her around and go back. I had visions of us plunging to our deaths below if she panicked and leapt off into space. Finally the boss man appeared behind us, leading the string of horses. Seeing that Whiskey wasn't going anywhere and might get her and I killed if she went over the edge, he decided he had no choice but to inch his way past us.

He was mounted on a strong thoroughbred stallion who after years on such trails as this knew what to do. Head down, his every step placed with care, the stallion eased by us, his feet dislodging chunks of stone that sailed downward into the depths below. Once past us, he too paused, his nostrils quivering at something around the bend, but a touch from his master's heels sent him forward. Now that the stallion was leading, Whiskey followed at his heels. We rounded the curve of rock, and only then did I smell the lingering trace of what the horses had smelled. It was a musty, strong scent of something that lived on meat, often rank with age. The boss man pointed out where, only minutes before, a grizzly bear had been lying on the trail, probably sunning himself. Some rocks held strands of the great beast's hair, where he had scratched himself as he lay there. Thank heavens, Whiskey had not continued around the bend, straight into the bear's sight. Most of all, thank heavens the bear decided to leave, instead of making a stand against an approaching horse and rider.

The one thing I can say for Whiskey, though she was a pain on the trail, was that she was the only horse on the trip who did not have to be hobbled near camp. Each morning when I got up, I simply had to holler for her, and she came quickly to my side. She always stayed within calling distance, even when the hobbled herd ended up as much as a mile away in their grazing. I could then saddle her and go bring the rest of the horses to camp for the upcoming day of riding.

After that first trip, I rode horses I was just starting in training. Ten days to two weeks of mountain riding sure put a handle
on green horses in a hurry. True, on the steep trails and when
picking my way through muskeg, it would have been nice to be
mounted on a well-broke horse, used to the ways of the mountains, but you can't have everything on a silver platter. Green
horses can have quite a bit of difficulty crossing muskeg bogs.
The boss man knew his business well, and could usually cut a
trail around such spots of seemingly harmless ground, but
sometimes it was cross one or turn back.

On one trip I was riding a sorrel mare who picked her way
through a bog by carefully staying to firmer ground. One client
followed us through, coming to rest beside us, once our horses
reached the needle-carpeted floor in the timber. The boss man
and a guide working for him were pushing the pack horses
through at a different spot. As each horse passed, the water-
soaked ground was being churned into deeper and deeper mud.
Suddenly a pack horse, new at his job, decided to get off the
oozing trail and make it on his own. He made a couple of lunges
before suddenly sinking right up to his belly in a soft spot. The
more he struggled to free his trapped legs from the gripping
slime, the deeper he went. Finally exhausted, he gave up, with
only his head, neck and part of his chest showing. After getting
the rest of the riders and pack horses to safety, the boss said that
him and I would work our horses back to the trapped horse.
Then we would have to get off and dig with our hands until we
could work a chest rope under and around him, so we could
hitch our saddle horses on to pull him out. We made it back to
him, and turning our horses around so they would be in position to pull straight ahead, we dismounted and got to work. It
was slow, frustrating digging, but finally our hands met under
the horse's belly, and I passed the rope from my hand to the
boss's. He then added another rope to the secured belly band
around the horse. Then we both mounted and tied the ropes,
one to each of our saddle horns.

I had completely forgotten that I was riding a mare who had only a half dozen rides on her and wasn't actually broke yet. Together we both slapped our horses on their rumps and hollered at them to get up and pull. When the rope tightened up, my sorrel was caught by surprise and almost came right over backwards on top of me. It was too late now to stop, and I slapped her rump again to get her to keep pulling. She was a big mare, half thoroughbred and half draft horse breeding, and once she got down to pulling, the sucking mud didn't stand a chance of keeping a hold on its victim. Between the two horses, the trapped horse was wrenched from the clinging slime. But now things took a turn for the worse. The other horse and rider were trying to keep going straight ahead to safe ground, and the sorrel had her mind set on going to the side, to the path she had originally crossed over on. My two cinches were tight, but her sideways direction turned the saddle as neat as a pin from the pull on the rope. My rope was tied hard and fast to the horn. I kicked free of the stirrups, my head already dragging on the ground. Scrambling out of the way, I lost my hold on the reins, and the mare put her size and strength into not only getting herself and the still-downed pack horse to safety, but the other horse and rider too. She surged ahead, dragging the pack horse, who in turn was dragging the other horse, still connected by the second rope. Everybody made it to high ground, but oh, what a mess. The panniers on the pack saddle had burst, strewing their cargo all over because of my sorrel's chosen pathway. My saddle was one giant ball of dripping mud, from ending up dragging on the ground like it did. I learned that day to hate the sight of muskegs for sure.

Silly, Silly Man

One of the most wondrous trips in is the one up over the seemingly impossible Job Pass to a little-known lake, simply called Blue Lake. It nestles at the base of some adjoining mountains, so deep and pure that it is a dense blue in colour, which never fails to take each person's breath away, when first he or she lays eyes on it.

Job Pass tests the endurance of each saddle horse and pack horse as they climb upwards and upwards until the crest of the pass meets the sky. The high altitude robs you of your breath, leaving everyone, animals and humans alike, gasping for air. Then, high above the treeline, you start down the other side to the waiting green canopy. Both saddles and packs must be straightened before it is over.

Once camped at the lake, the fishermen in the crowd can get down to serious business. The icy cold water teams with fish just waiting to grace your supper plates. Here, when not at work, I can ride to my heart's content, winding my way through the huge trees, hoping to catch sight of the local wildlife in its natural surrounding.

Riding a nice bay gelding one day, I counted several species of birds as I rode, including sighting two grown bald eagles. As I rode out of the timber, towards the lake, I was to see the only wolverine in its own habitat I have ever seen. The drama unfolding before me was unreal. A devoted fisherman was staking his catch of prize fish in a narrow rivulet of water pouring down the mountainside into Blue Lake. He was busy reeling in yet another one, when a large wolverine appeared from a rocky crevasse and grabbed one of the staked fish. The man turned and spotted the animal raiding his catch. He started shouting and running towards the savage wolverine, who calmly turned and began scrambling up a wall of rock, still firmly clutching his meal in his jaws. This silly man was intent on getting his fish back, without realizing just what it was he was messing with. Grizzly bears have been known to back off from a wolverine on the fight. I started yelling at the man to stay away from the wolverine, but he was clawing his way up the steep wall of stone, practically on his belly. He was only a few feet from the unafraid animal when it turned around, laid the fish down, and face to face with the man began to snarl with deadly intent. Only then did the city slicker finally realize what he was messing with, as he stared at the cruel bared fangs. Had the vicious animal attacked, the man would have been badly injured or worse. After a few seconds, the wolverine picked up the fish again, resumed his upward climb and disappeared finally into another crevasse. Some people are just plain lucky.

On a different early season trip the next year, I too had a run in with Mother Nature. I was riding alone one afternoon, on a three–year–old mare, enjoying the solitude. She was coming good in her training but could still be sulky sometimes. Spotting a lone elk across a small stream, I rode towards it. The elk refused to turn and run, so I wanted to get closer, wondering why it did not take flight. The mare put up a fight about crossing the shallow stream, and I really had to get after her. Finally she splashed through and I approached the elk. I was almost right up to her before I spotted her calf hidden in the tall grass at her feet. I guess I was too close for comfort, because with a woofing snort, that cow elk attacked us with slashing front hooves. The mare spun around and we lit out, the cow elk right on our tails. This time it didn't take any urging from me to cross the stream: the mare cleared it with a single bound. At the edge of the water, the mad elk stopped, shook her head and trotted back to her calf. I learned yet another lesson about wildlife that day.

Mr. Bigshot

One of our best pack horses was an ex-saddle horse who got tired of being ridden one day and turned into a real bucking bronc from then on. He was fine carrying a pack saddle, but had not been ridden for four or five years by a rider. He was also just about the prettiest horse of the whole bunch, with a rich chestnut coat and proud bearing. It was the last trip up for the year and we had several dudes to contend with. Most were fairly easy to please and good people. One man, though, was fast getting on everyone else's nerves. According to him, he was the best at everything, at his city job, at fishing, at hunting, at cooking over a camp fire, at driving vehicles, at everything that ever came up in a conversation. Especially at riding a horse. The truth was that he couldn't even hold a candle to even half the other guests, let alone those of us who rode daily for a living. And Mr. Bigshot had decided he didn't like the gentle horse he was given for the trip, no, he wanted to ride the chestnut pack horse. For days, he harped about getting to ride the chestnut. We dutifully explained to him, over and over, that the horse was an outlaw. He guffawed at us; after all he was the best rider around. On the morning of the last day of the trip, he started again on the subject of riding the chestnut. The outfitter finally got mad enough to say go for it you impossible idiot, because all the rest of us here are witnesses to the fact that you have been warned about the horse, so if you get seriously hurt when he bucks you off, don't bother suing me.

I was instructed to saddle the chestnut and pack the gentle horse. Leading the chestnut to a clearing, free of sharp tree stumps and other dangers to a falling rider, I held onto his head, while Mr. Bigshot swung clumsily into the saddle. I kept a death grip on the horse, until the man was settled in the saddle. Then I stepped back and let him go. Nothing. The chestnut turned and took his place in the line of horses, eager to head out and get home. He never so much as humped his back under the weight of the rider. The last day's ride is always a long one, and the chestnut gelding performed like the well–broke horse he used to be. And man oh man, did Mr. Bigshot let us all know that of course the horse behaved himself, after all the horse was smart enough to know a top rider when one got on him. I don't think their was a single person on that ride who did not wish they could light a firecracker under that horse's tail.

The outfitter got thinking a few days later, that after all, it had been years since the horse was rode and maybe he had forgot all about bucking and could be used as a saddle horse again. It was not to be. The first time he stepped up on the gelding, the horse bucked right through a fence with him, like a crazy bronc. Then I took a stab at riding him a week or two later. He piled me easily. Perhaps he had just been tired out from packing heavy panniers for several long trips through the mountains over the summer and fall. Or god forbid, maybe he had let Mr. Bigshot ride him just to make the rest of us suffer listening to the man on the long ride home.

A HORSEBACK WEDDING

Getting married is always stressful for the bride. Between getting invitations printed, sending them, ordering her attire, getting it altered, arranging for flowers and a photographer, finding a caterer, deciding on the meal, renting the reception hall and hiring a band, most brides are lucky indeed to not end up with ulcers. Migraine headaches seem quite frequent around this time.

Now on top of figuring out what to do about Uncle Henry's drinking and wrecking everyone's fun at the wedding, try getting married on horseback. You still have all the usual things to take care of, plus a whole bunch more. After doing it once, not for a million dollars would I do it again, even though Uncle Henry has quit drinking and joined the church.

The last few days and hours of preparation were so hectic, I never had time to get a migraine headache, let alone ulcers.

First the matching horses for Gary (the groom) and me. I had a pair of beautiful black geldings. Apollo was the perfect horse for Gary. I had done an excellent job on this young gelding. His training had resulted in a gentle, well-mannered horse, nothing bothered him, a perfect mount for standing steadfast amongst a crowd of well wishers and ladies' dresses blowing in the wind. Sun was a black gelding of a different colour, if you know what I mean. He was an ex-bareback rodeo bronc. I didn't start his training as a saddle horse until a few weeks earlier when I decided on black mounts as the way to go for this wedding. More than one bet was placed by the people who knew this horse that I would end up in the dirt before the ceremony was over. Now, knowing people were betting against me made me even more determined to be married on top of him.

I had my work cut out for me. I knew that Sun was an above–average horse in the brains department. I knew, regardless of his career as a rodeo bronc, that he could be retrained with patience and kindness. I also knew I was slightly crazy in the head to think that what should take a year to accomplish was going to be done in only a few short weeks. I set my goal for Sun being ready a week prior to the wedding. My plan was to ride him in the yearly rodeo parade in Rocky Mountain House. If he handled the parade all right I knew he could handle the wedding. If not, I would have to find another black horse.

I train horses with snaffle bits and/or bosals. I chose the hackamore for Sun because in my experience you get a lot more done with a horse in a lot less time with one, especially one you know is going to be hard to control. Besides, Apollo could also be ridden with a bosal instead of a bit and I figured matching black horses had to also have matching gear, and you just can't be too fussy at your own wedding.

Sun was indeed a quick learner and things progressed smoothly once he figured out he wasn't supposed to buck his rider off anymore. The day of the parade came, and Sun never turned a hair with the crowd of happy watchers lining the streets. The drums and various musical instruments in the band following his tail end never bothered him. Sun was as ready as he could be for my wedding the following week.

I sure wasn't ready yet though. At midnight the night before my wedding, I was still trimming horses' manes and tails, clipping their fetlocks so they looked clean–cut, and wishing this wedding had been someone else's idea, instead of mine, so I could holler at him for doing this to me.

I managed to squeeze in about two hours of sleep before sunrise and then things really picked up. It looked like rain was coming and I had to decide if we could pack two hundred guests on top of each other in Lenore and Roger's living room. The lovely couple who owned the acreage where the wedding was to take place had their huge lawn trimmed, decorated and ready to go. Was all their hard work to be in vain?

Rain wasn't the biggest worry by far. Plans had to continue, either way. The gentleman supplying the French carriage and team of horses that Gary's mother, my mother and their attendants were to ride in phoned to say he might be late. "How late," I ask. Well, he knows the wedding is scheduled for two o'clock and he hopes to make it, but maybe more like three or four o'clock. I shudder and head for the beauty salon to get my hair done, just why I don't know because I'll be wearing a cowboy hat anyway, but the bride always gets her hair done, that's what is done, so it must be done.

It's now noon. The phone rings; the girl bringing two of the saddles can't get her vehicle running. She promises to try to get there on time. The phone rings again and I start to really hate that annoying ringing sound it makes. Gary's best man for the wedding can't find the place. Come to think of it, where is Gary? It's pretty hard to have a wedding without a groom. I remind myself to give him a piece of my mind, as soon as we are pronounced man and wife, because then it's too late for him to do anything about it.

When the girl who was to bring the buckskin mare for the best man to ride phoned to say she was having trouble loading the mare, I lost it. I disconnected that phone without bending down to remove the plug from the wall. Then I jammed my hat down over my ears and went looking for Uncle Henry: maybe he could give me something to settle my nerves.

When I say it was the best wedding in the world I do so not because it was my wedding but because everything went without a hitch.

At two o'clock sharp, Helen Hunley, Lieutenant–Governor of Alberta, stood before us, ready to join Gary and me in holy matrimony. My father, riding my favourite mare, Whiskey, escorted me across the lawn to join Gary on Apollo, with his best man astride a fine buckskin mare. My maid of honour, also astride a pretty buckskin, completed the picture. Our mothers and their attendants were seated in a polished French carriage, a team of splendid horses harnessed to it. The sky was crystal clear, the sun shining down. No breeze was present to bother my mount, Sun. It was the best day of my life.

As for those buddies of mine who had placed their bets on Sun dumping me in the dust, I made sure they all paid up for thinking this cowgirl couldn't handle a bronc on her own wedding day.

POOR FENCES & JUNK PILES

Awhile ago I was booting it down the highway for the city, involved in one of my favourite pastimes: every horse I spot as I go past gets the once over. I only have a second or two to take in their colour, type of breed, whether they are young or old and if they would look good standing in my corral. As I passed an older type farmyard, my eyes rested on a sorrel next to a barn that was half fallen down. My vision had been impaired by the trees, and I never really got a good look at him. Something had been wrong with the picture though. I couldn't put my finger on what was troubling me. Perhaps it was the way he had been standing, head down, looking dejected.

I went to my appointment in the city, and being short of pocket money, headed right back down the highway for home. As I whizzed by the same barnyard, I took another look at the horse. Four hours had elapsed and the sorrel still hadn't moved an inch. I was a mile down the road before what was wrong, hit me. I turned around and went back, driving slow. I stopped and took a good look at the horse. My suspicion was correct. The horse was tangled up in a junk pile of broken boards and twisted wire. He hadn't moved and still looked terribly dejected, because he couldn't move and by the looks of him, hadn't been able to for a long time. I drove in and knocked on the door of the house, but no one answered. I approached the horse quietly and was shocked to see that he was dehydrated badly from lack of water. His trapped front legs were already swollen out of shape, showing he had been trapped a long, long time. He was gentle and not frightened of me, so I got my fencing pliers from behind my truck seat, and went to work, cutting wires, and pulling them from around his legs. One of the strands of rusty old barbed wire was embedded in the flesh, right to the bone. He must have been in continual pain, as he struggled to free himself. Once I had him cut free, I led him over to a tub of filthy water, which appeared to be his personal watering trough. I was in the process of hanging a note on the front door of the house to let the owners know about their horse's condition, when a young woman drove into the yard. I asked if she owned the sorrel in the corral, and she said yes. Before I could tell her he needed the services of a veterinarian, she told me how much she loved her horsey, and as soon as she got changed out of her work clothes she was going to go out and give him a big kiss on his nose for being such a sweetie.

Here was a horse owner who loved her animal but didn't have a clue about horses. When she finally quit chattering long enough for me to tell her to call a vet, she was devastated and

burst into tears, running down to her horsey, then really starting to bawl like a baby. I stayed to assist the local vet when he
arrived, and found him to be a pleasant fellow who after caring
for the injured horse was as determined as I to educate her
about the proper care of her pet. The both of us sat down with
her and explained about death traps, commonly known as just
an old junk pile. After I told her some horror stories about
horses cut to ribbons when they step into junk piles, the vet
told her about horses needing good quality food and fresh
water. The girl had no clue. She was from the city originally and
had always loved horses. So one day she rents this old farmyard
so she can live in the country and then she spends her last
dollar to buy a horse. She promised us she would clean up the
snarls of rusting wire and splintered boards right away. Too bad
she hadn't had the brains to do it before the sorrel suffered like
he did.

I rented some pasture land one time to run my young stock
on because I didn't have the feed to keep them around home. I
walked the fence line, doing any repairs necessary, and then
criss-crossed back and forth over the land, checking for junk,
old wire on the ground, anything that might harm the horses.
All I found was an old car frame, sitting on its axles. I certainly
could not remove it by hand plus it didn't appear to be dangerous to horses anyway. Big mistake!

The second week I pastured the land, my most expensive
race-bred, yearling filly managed to get a front leg hung up in
the frame. She stripped the flesh from the knee down to the
fetlock joint, right off the bone, in her struggles to free her
trapped leg. What a mess. The attending veterinarian seemed to
think I could save her with hard work and perseverance. She
was forced to live in a small box stall for weeks, to restrict her
movements. Once in the morning before going to work and
again before I retired in the evening, I had to change her bandages and doctor the mess that was once a leg. She learned to
hate needles as the weeks went on, but I felt responsible for

what I had allowed to happen to her, and would not give up.
After the first fourteen weeks, she was responding to treatment
and at least could exercise in a small pen. I saved the dainty
bay's leg and by the next summer, it was strong enough for me
to train her. The leg was horribly disfigured for life, and she
would never blast out of a starting gate to win any races. She
broke out nicely to become a fine saddle mare, and eventually I
was able to sell her to a family who wanted a top–of–the–line
brood mare, who could also be ridden lightly, once in awhile.
She found a home for a lot less money than I paid for her, and I
learned still another lesson about junk in pastures and corrals.

I realize barbed wire is a necessary evil on most farms and
ranches. Always in the past and always in the future, horses are
going to be cut to ribbons by it too. There are ways to try to stop
some of the injuries though. Keep the wire stretched tight, and
horses won't be as likely to catch a front foot in it and if they hit
it, running full out, a tight wire does less damage than a loose,
sagging one. They are still going to be cut up, but not as bad.

Barbed wire gates cause more horse–related injuries than
anything else. Horses hang around these gates, knowing they
get to go through them sometimes. If the gates are not high
enough or not in good repair, presto another veterinarian bill to
pay. Time and time again, I have seen people open a wire gate
and just leave it lying on the ground. Along comes Mr. Horse
and steps right in it. Sometimes he walks through it without a
scratch, but sometimes he gets caught in it and, guess what,
another vet bill to pay. A couple of years ago, it took my vet two
hours to put almost a hundred stitches in my favourite old
mare, because a man drove a tractor through a barbed wire gate
and, thinking my horses were nowhere around, left it lying,
open, on the ground. Had I not found this mare within minutes
of getting tangled in it, she would have bled to death from a
severed artery, never mind the ensuing vet bill and hours and
hours of doctoring to save her. When I confronted this man over
the damage to my horse, he shrugged his shoulders and said in

all his years of ranching he had always left the gates lying on the ground and hey, none of his horses ever got hurt. Bully for him, because my horse did get hurt, bad.

Some horses must have a guardian angel. Like my fine gymkhana gelding, Yes Sir. Yes Sir always thought he should be on the other side of his pasture fence. He had fresh water, grass up to his knees and other horses for companionship, but he was not satisfied. At least once a week I had to rescue him from an unusual predicament. I would come home from work to find him straddling the wire fence, his front legs on the outside of the pasture, his hind legs on the inside. I guess he was a lousy jumper and could only figure out how to get his front end to freedom. While hung up like this, he never panicked or struggled in anyway. He simply waited patiently to be rescued, with the barbs on the top wire digging into his fat belly. I cut that top wire so many times to remove it, so he could step over the middle strand, that the whole top wire was nothing but a series of chunks and short pieces. Except for missing a lot of hair on his under side and quite a few scratches, he never hurt himself. I loved riding Yes Sir but I sold him to somebody who had nothing but pipe fencing on his property, so I could stop having to worry about him all the time.

When Tammy, a tall grey thoroughbred mare of mine messed with a barbed wire fence, it was the worst injured horse I ever managed to save. She was a sweetheart of a mare and I often used her to pony two-year-olds to leg them up for the race track or to just condition them. I was leading a filly off her who had cysts on her ovaries and was wicked tempered from them. This brown two-, coming three-year-old needed many miles of poneying, coupled with hard riding to get her in shape for summer racing. Tammy and I had led her at a long trot for about four miles when one of Alberta's unpredictable foothills rainstorms caught us. We were soaked in seconds, the rain pelting down so hard and fast that the sun was almost blacked out. Quickly I turned in at a neighbour's place and put the hot, steaming brown filly in their small cow barn. I closed the sliding door on the barn and left Tammy in the only corral, leading into the barn. The neighbours gave me dry clothes and a towel for my dripping hair. We sat and visited until dark, before the rain let up. They said I could leave the horses there over night and I could come for them in the morning, rather than ride home in the darkness.

It was about three o'clock in the morning when the jangling phone pulled me from sleep. It was my neighbours. Seems all night they could hear the filly in the barn, kicking the walls and making a fuss something fierce. Then they had heard the sound of breaking boards and finally the sound of loose horses crashing through the bush.

I was dressed and at their place in minutes. It was pitch black out in the heavy bush, but I knew their few acres was fenced and the horses couldn't have gone far, so I headed out on foot, following a fence line. Up ahead I suddenly heard the brown hellion's savage squeal and the sounds of her heels connecting with the other mare's body. I broke into a run and soon found them in an open patch of land where the dim moon helped illuminate the scene before me. The grey mare had attempted to get away from the brown by jumping the too-low barbed wire fence. She was hung up by the hind legs in the wire, and the brown was backed up to her, kicking like a demon.

Frantic, I caught the brown and tied her to a tree. My heart sank when I realized Tammy was badly tangled in the wire, and worse, that she had tried to jump the wire right at the picket post. In the near darkness, this sharp post appeared to have speared her in the belly and she was hung up on it too. I could hear the neighbours coming, so I shouted for them to go back and get my fencing pliers out my truck and a flashlight. She was still struggling, hurting herself even more, so I quickly haltered her and pulled her head around tight to the side, managing to throw her over, off the post, to the ground. While

I sat on her neck, keeping her nose up to restrain her, the neighbour cut her bloody hind legs free from the deadly wire.

It was only after we had led her back to the brightly lighted yard that I could access the damages fully. Although the post hadn't broken the skin, already a fluid-filled sack the size of a football hung down from the injury. The right hind leg was bleeding profusely but could be doctored. I wasn't sure about the left hind leg. Not only was the skin hanging in shreds, but the leg was almost severed from the body, the ripped flesh dividing the flank from the leg itself. The wound was deeper than the length of my hand and laid open, six inches in width. We blanketed her heavily and kept her as calm as possible, while I tried to reach a vet at that ungodly hour of the morning. Finally I reached one in a town about thirty miles away. When I explained her injuries to him, he said that if she had walked back to the yard by herself, then possibly no tendons or vital nerves were destroyed. As for the damage done by the post, I could always hope it was just tissue damage and no internal organs were damaged. He gave me little hope of being able to come at all that day, as seconds before I reached him, another horse owner had phoned with a mare having a difficult birth and after that he was booked solid with regular customers. I was stuck, as I had just remembered that my own vet was away on holidays for a week. So I doctored her myself as best as I could in their yard and took her home in a stock trailer.

Tammy was a fighter though and no matter how bad her wounds were, I felt I had to try to save her. She greeted me every morning with a nicker of welcome, and stood for me to change her bandages and put evil-smelling salves and concoctions on her torn joint where it once met her flank and now gaped open. Where once the bone showed through amidst the gore, finally one day, nature took her first step in laying a healing hand to the wound. Slowly the savage wound healed, along with her other ones. Finally came the day, many weeks later, when the now-thin grey mare was actually able to trot away from me, in a show of determination to get better. Then one day I looked out the window to see her break into a slow gallop, running to visit with some other horses. Tammy was going to make it after all. It took a full year before she was sound again. Her scars were not pretty to see, but she was glad to be alive. Barbed wire had almost put an end to her life; only her strong will to survive against all odds had enabled me to save her.

Now, on my own property you will not find a single scrap of junk or a single strand of lethal barbed wire. I may still have to doctor the occasional bump, cut or bruise, but no more brutal wounds from these two things that can destroy a horse in a few seconds. I just shake my head, when I go someplace and see old wire lying useless on the ground, broken boards with nails and spikes sticking out of them and manmade junk piles out in the horses' corrals and pastures. No horse deserves to be submitted to these hazards, especially by people who call themselves horse persons and horse lovers.

AUCTION SALES & THREE-LEGGED HORSES

If you're in the market for a horse, buy privately and stay away from auction sales. Unless they are production sales or select sales, you just might get burned.

For over twenty years, I have been buying and selling horses. Sometimes I've even made money at it too. I've also ended up with my share of horses I was forced to sell for a loss. Three-legged ones can be hard to spot. They look sound in all four legs, then you get them home and find out they are lame in at least one leg. If you're an honest horse dealer, that means reselling them for probably less than you paid for them. If you have the time and money, maybe you can treat the horse and return him to usefulness. Most times the injury is past repair and the horse is good only for the slaughterhouse.

I pride myself on being able to spot defects or injuries on a horse in the sale ring, and after all these years I still get burned. They are only in the ring for two to four minutes and the bidding is fast and furious. That doesn't give you much time to really look the horse over for problems.

Chances are, first off, you look to see how old the horse really is. You watch his ears for excessive nervousness or a bad temperament. Are his eyes clear, his nostrils dry and his breathing normal? Are all four legs working properly, as he turns, stops, backs and moves forward? They don't have to have visible scars, lumps or swelling for the horse to be lame. Is he high headed or trembling, showing fear or aggression? If he's packing a rider, is he as well broke as they claim? You have to know the difference between just started under saddle, green broke, well started or fully trained. How many bad traits is he exhibiting from either poor training or improper handling? When you get him home, are you going to be able to retrain him the right way? What one person may consider well broke might be a whole lot different from what you consider as a well-trained animal. Does he back up good in the sale ring? If he doesn't, he's not going to back up when you get him home either. Did he hump up when the rider stepped on him? If he did he's only half broke or going to buck with you once he's home in the corral. Is he doing a good job of neck reining in the ring or is he being forced to turn by yanking and pulling on the reins? You have only those few minutes and seconds to make a good buy or end up sorry you even went to the horse sale in the first place.

Think about this: if he's such a good horse, why is he at this sale in the first place? If he's that good, how come the owner didn't sell him right at home for probably more money than he's going to get at this sale? Why is he really being sold? Yes, lots of people are honest with you when they sell a horse, but many of them don't give a hoot about you or the horse. They are there for the money.

Maybe you have heard the joke about the horse dealer who sold a farmer a horse. He admitted to the farmer that he knew the horse didn't look too good. The farmer gets the horse home and finds out it is blind. That horse dealer was honest, he told him the horse didn't look too good.

Some things you might get told about the horse for sale. "King has lots of get up and go" could mean that King never stands still once you're on him. He has one gear and that's fast forward.

"Once you get on Rocky, you won't ever want to get off." Maybe Rocky is the type that if you do get off him, five miles from home, he won't let you back on, so I guess you sure don't want to get off him then. "You will just learn to love Bertha's walk" maybe means that even with a whip and spurs, Bertha won't break out of a walk. "Prince can out-run anything" maybe means Prince is hard to catch and can out-run you on foot, out-run somebody trying to catch him with another horse, who knows.

The seller thinks the best thing about his horse is he is easy to catch and easy to load. Maybe that's all he is good for, maybe you had better stick to just catching him and loading him unless you're a professional bronc rider. You spot what looks like a bit of lameness in one front leg and the seller tells you in no uncertain terms that that leg is as sound as the other front leg. You get the horse home and yup, he's lame in both front legs. The seller never really actually lied, did he?

"Queenie isn't registered but her mother is and her father was one hell of a horse." Maybe he was THE HORSE FROM HELL too and Queenie has his temperament and bad traits. "That little wire cut on Red's hind leg has never really bothered him" maybe means Red hasn't been rode since it happened and once you do start riding him, presto, one lame horse. "Flash is even so good he is boss horse wherever he goes" might mean Flash is going to kick, bite and run your other horses right out of the corral when you get him home.

"This bay gelding is a ranch horse, a real good cow horse." Watch out for this one because if he's that good, why is he for sale? Ranches keep their best broke ranch horses. Lots of ranch horses sold every year never saw the wide open range or a herd of cows, or maybe they did help once, to chase the neighbour's milk cow back home. Lots of ranch horses have been handled and ridden all their lives by tough cowhands and plenty of them, so unless you can stick on a horse like glue, don't buy him. I have worked with and around ranch–broke horses most of my life and they are not barnyard pets. They are working horses, not kid's horses. Chances are they don't even like us humans very much; they are there to work, not be petted and kept in the backyard. If they have some age on them, chances are they are stove up and know plenty of mean little tricks to get even for years of hard work.

The age of a horse does make a big difference in how much money you spend on him. If he has a couple of good years left in him and is well broke, go ahead and buy him. Keep in mind, though, that it is cruel to buy a horse well past his prime age and expect him to pack you around all day, at a gallop beside your buddy riding his younger horse. If he's a good old sport, he will keep going and going regardless of his stiff old legs and the pain you're causing him. Older, gentle mounts make excellent horses for beginners and children. Put a stop to your child running him excessively and give him the care he deserves. Feed your older horse the extra hay and grain he will require to stay in shape, keep his feet trimmed and his teeth floated. Treat him the way you will want to be treated when you get that old.

Speaking of how old a horse is, sellers at auction sales are notorious for knocking a few years off Old Dobbin's age when they sell him. A horse that hasn't been worked to death is considered in his prime from four to twelve years old. When he comes into the ring and he's advertised as smooth mouthed, in real horse lingo they are saying he is past his prime years. If the seller says he doesn't know how old he is, but is still in his prime, check his teeth because the chances are the owner never figured he reached his prime until his late twenties, and horses should be the same. My favorite is the seller who doesn't know how old his horse is but he learned to ride on him, his son learned to ride on him and now his grandson rides on him. That little speech makes the horse old enough to forget about buying because he probably doesn't even have one year left in him.

One of the main things to realize at a horse auction is the way a horse acts in that small ring is possibly not what he will act like once at your home in a bigger area without the noise and crowds to intimidate him into behaving. I have jumped up on unbroke broncs and rode them around in that same small ring and made buyers think that the horse was halfway broke. There isn't room for him to line out and really get bucking, he can't run away and he is confused and possibly frightened into a false sense of submission. More than once I have misjudged horses' training and temperament and bought them only to have spoiled, half-broke and potentially dangerous animals on my hands. I have always had better luck buying good quality two- or three-year-olds out of a ring, who have had a minimal, if any, human handling, and doing all the training myself. This way you often pay less money for them and you're not faced with bad habits and poor training from other riders.

All of my top horses I have sold over the years were sold straight off the farm, or at select breed sales where they are guaranteed sound. Some of my good stock have been sold at local auction markets, and when I brought them through the ring, I was honest with the crowd and buyers and spectators sitting there. If they weren't kids' horses, I said so. If they needed an experienced rider to handle them, I said so. I told their correct ages and didn't try to pass a nineteen-year-old horse for a ten-year-old. The horses who were good only for meat, because they were crippled, too old or dangerous to ride, went for meat. That's what being an honest horse dealer is all about. There's one final thing for you potential horse buyers to think about, when someone is selling you what appears to be the best horse in the world: why is he or she named SPIT FIRE, BUCKY, DING DONG, JUMPER, SLOW POKE, DEVIL, TORNADO or SILLY WILLY. Just maybe the name says it all.

HORSES BY THE PAIR

Almost everyone in the world believes to some extent in one or more superstitions, like a black cat crossing his or her path and bringing bad luck. Walking under a ladder also supposedly bringing bad luck. Breaking a mirror too. I have never had bad luck with any of these superstitions. Nothing bad ever hap–pened over a black cat crossing my path except maybe to the cat, if I'm doing sixty or seventy miles an hour on the highway, and the cat was only doing three miles an hour when he crossed the road. Except for a couple of drops of paint on my shirt collar when I walked under a ladder one time when the carpenter was changing the colour of the house, nothing serious ever happened. As for bringing bad luck onto myself from breaking a mirror, I've probably cracked a few in my lifetime, when I sneak up on one early in the morning before my teeth are brushed and my hair is combed, but all in all nothing bad happened.

What brings me bad luck is buying horses by the pair or taking a pair from the same owner to train. This is heap mucho bad luck for me. Something always goes wrong somehow. There is absolutely no truth in the saying take two and double your pleasure, double your fun.

Take Salt and Pepper, for instance. I agreed to train this pair of fine–looking horses from the same owner, at the same time. Salt was a smoke–coloured mare who had gotten away with murder with her last trainer, resulting in her behaving like a totally untouched bronc every time you tried to saddle her and ride her. Pepper was a pretty bay gelding who had become a runaway from having inexperienced, so-called horse trainers let him get away with it. When the owners unloaded the pair of them in my yard, Salt was hell on four legs, fighting being even led across to the corrals. I put her down as maybe being more than I could handle. Pepper behaved like a gentleman, nuzzling my shoulder and letting me know he already liked me and we had just met. The next day, their retraining began. Salt blew, snorted and stamped angrily when I caught her in the round pen. By the time I got the hobbles on her and a hind leg tied up, to begin sacking her out, I was thinking about how nice it would be if I got out of the horse business and started raising rabbits or hamsters for extra money. By the time she quit fighting me, and was saddled for her ride, I had decided on raising chickens instead, because they are even less trouble than rabbits or hamsters. With my mind on chicken dumplings, I pulled her nose around tight, and stepped up. She wasn't much of a bucker, figuring just by squealing and bouncing off the fences, I would be like her last trainer and jump off, letting her have her own way once again. But with visions of a barn full of silly, smelly chickens I had decided to stick with the horse business for awhile longer. Salt gave up rather quickly, when she didn't get her own way.

Now for Pepper. He stood quietly for me to catch him and saddle up. What a nice gentle gelding, shucks, he was a good looker, maybe I would buy him for myself. We loped around the arena some, then took a spin outside in the pasture. Pepper promptly ran away with me, actually forcing me to jump off of him at a mad gallop, just before he plunged over a straight drop off into the Clearwater River. I jumped clear and hit the ground rolling, he sailed off into space and did a crash landing in the water below. Then like the good guy he was, he found a path leading back up, trotted over to me and nuzzled my shoulder, after all we were good friends, right?

Salt was a top little mare once I finished her training so I bought her, instead of Pepper. Because of my run of bad luck with pairs of horses, a city slicker, disguised as a deer hunter, shot her the following month during deer-hunting season. Although I know several people over the years who have lost cattle and horse to these great white deer hunters in bush country, Salt is the only horse I lost this way. Pepper the confirmed runaway eventually went to horse heaven in a dogfood can. Another pair bites the dust.

Big & Small

Pebbles and Bam Bam came to me to be halter broken and to learn to have their feet picked up for trimming. They were six-month-old weanlings at the time. Their age and their colour, both of them being bays, were the only things they had in common. Pebbles was a scruffy miniature Shetland filly. Bam Bam was a long-legged, trim thoroughbred filly. I had a barn full of different sized halters, not one was tiny enough to properly fit Pebbles. So off to town I go, to buy a newborn foal size halter for her. That scrap of rivets and thin leather cost me more than I was being paid to work with her. Pebbles did not want to learn to be led, so because of her size, I sort of just drug her along behind me where ever I went. I figured that even when she grew up, she would still be lightweight enough for the average person to drag her around. She wasn't mean, just stubborn. Teaching her to pick up her feet put a permanent kink in my back from having to bend all the way down to the ground to pick up her dainty feet. She was not impressed with learning to pick her feet up either, so I basically just used my strength to do it against her will. Once again, I figured an adult person should always be strong enough to pick her feet up, even when she grew up—we are talking small horse here.

Bam Bam was a young lady in every way. She was leading good in less than half an hour. In an hour, she would hold whatever leg up that you asked for. The second day I went to their corral to work with them, I find Bam Bam with a severe tummy ache from not being used to rich alfalfa hay, so off to town I go for medicine. I paid lots more for the medicine than I was being paid to work with her. Once again a pair of horses did me in. I was supposed to make money, not lose it.

Escape Artists

Early one spring day a man phones me up to see if I would like to buy two black Shetlands off him, as he had recently sold his farm and they needed new homes. He said they were not broke yet, but should be easy for someone like me to train. The price was cheap, so I told him to load them up and bring them over. It was three weeks before he showed up with them loaded on the back of his half–ton truck. I had almost forgotten about them, and if I had known what a pain they were going to be, I would have told him, after waiting three weeks, I no longer had any use for them. After he backed up to my chute, I asked him what had taken him so long bringing them over. He mumbled something about them being hard to catch, and opened the end gate. Two matching black cannon balls exploded off the truck and down the chute. While I stared at the pair of wild–eyed little demons, he asked for his money, wished me good luck and rattled off down my driveway.

What I had failed to ask him that first day on the telephone was the ponies' ages and sex. When he had said they weren't even halter broke, I had assumed they were still fairly young. The one was a mare about four to six years old. The other was a mature stallion about six to eight years old. Two fuzzy black tornadoes were busy searching for a way out of the alley they were in and one of them was a bloody stallion. He was small, but I had registered mares on the place and regardless of their greater size, I didn't want them getting anywhere near a Shetland stud. When it comes to stallions, where there is a will, there is a way.

My first job was going to get a rope on him, and get him into the escape-proof barn until my vet could come out and change his outlook on life, by gelding him. With lariat in hand, I eased my way into the alley, not wanting to rile the critters up any-more than they already were. Two steps into the pen, they both turned, dropped like Siamese twins and wormed their way under the bottom rail into a bigger, riding pen. Side by side, neck and neck, they raced around the pen. Muttering some sort of Greek language, I went for a hammer, nails and planks. I added another plank all around the bottom of the alley. Now I opened the gate and moseyed into the big pen, to chase them gently back into the alley, where they would not be able to scoot under the fence now. Two black hellions turned and shot under the heavy gate into the hay pen, without a backwards glance. They had perfected going under planks, like dogs. Well, now I had them, no planks here, instead page wire, high up and tight to the ground. They were as good as caught now, once I added yet another plank to bottom of the gate they had gone under. I was going to enjoy catching both of them, and teaching them a lesson in manners.

Grinning like an idiot, I started building a Shetland-size loop in my lariat. They wiped the grin off my face in an awful hurry. They hit the page wire fence full out, both their heads making matching holes in the square wire pattern, all four front feet fitting through the six-inch squares easily. They hit that fence in the one and only spot that wasn't one continuous fence line. It was a piece only about eight feet in length, stapled to two posts. The staples popped out with pinging noises and like a team of horses harnessed together, they tore off across the field, held together by a harness of wire around their necks and front legs. They headed for my other horses, who went from grazing peacefully to panicked flight at the sight of the Shetlands and wire bearing down on them. About the third lap around the field, the black team shed their harness without suffering as much as a scratch from their ordeal. Once the herd settled down, I poured grain out in the riding corral, and hollered at them to come and get their munchies. Once they were coming good, I hid around the corner of the barn, hoping the Shetlands would follow the bunch in. No such luck. They knew better and stayed on the outside, looking in. Two weeks later, one of my good mares came into season, and the stallion couldn't help himself. Bringing his black mare with him, he entered the reinforced alley where I had her tied up as if waiting for him. I snuck around and closed the gate on him, then got my big mare out of there before he could breed her.

I had had two long weeks to think about what I was going to do with those two escape artists. It took me three days of con-stant battle to get them halter broke good enough to phone what I hoped was going to be their new owner. This guy had been talking about buying a team of ponies for some time and getting into chariot racing. I wasn't exactly lying when I told him they had been hitched together once already. He loved the idea that one was a stallion and the other a mare, this way he could not only chariot race them but raise colts too. I kept my opinions to myself on that one, because if they hadn't produced a colt already at their age, they were not likely ever to. The fact that even for chariot ponies they were much too small, he never seemed to notice when he came to look at them. He sure did want those ponies so it looked like I was going to make my money back on them after all. Except he only had ex amount of cash on him, less than I had paid for them. I took that money anyway and just smiled as he loaded them up and headed home. I heard the next spring that he had told his neighbour hopefully some day he could catch his prizes and get started breaking them to harness. He had said they were a little wild but getting tamer by the day, as just last week he had got within fifty feet of them. I wished him good luck.

Double Trouble

I quit buying pairs of horses after I paid good money for a pair of stout grey geldings. They looked like a good buy when the owner unloaded them in my yard, but it was not to be. Zeller was a well-broke ranch gelding, nice to look at and with a gentle disposition. He looked a bit ouchy in the front feet, but when I saddled him up to try him out in the summer fallow field, he moved along with no problem. Bean Bag wasn't much to look at, as he was covered in long coarse hair. I figured a couple of doses of worm medicine would help him shed out. His feet were overgrown and cracked, but a rasp and hoof nippers would take care of that. He was only halter broke, but didn't raise much of a fuss over me running my hands all over him, so would be easy to break. I paid the man and took my greys to the barn. After spending the night in a tie stall with a wooden floor, Zeller seemed a bit more ouchy, so I examined his feet again. No external evidence of founder, but when I applied the hoof testers to his front feet, bingo, he jerked away from the pain. He was road foundered. In the soft, thick dirt of the field where I rode him the day before, his feet hadn't bothered him because the surface wasn't hard. I called a farrier who came out and shod his front feet. That was all he needed and he travelled fine then. He was a top broke horse and should have been easy to resell for profit. But try to find a buyer who believes you when you say, yes he is foundered some but as long as you always keep him shod, he will be fine. I finally found a horse-man who wanted him, but for the same I paid for him and not a dollar more. I was then out the forty dollars for shoeing him.

Oh well, Bean Bag was wormed now, so any day he should start shedding out his horrible shaggy coat, which made him look like an animal that belonged in a zoo or on a game farm. He was miserable to trim his feet, but I was sure he would get better in time. He didn't have any buck in him whatsoever, and in a month was as well started as most horses are in three months. He learned quickly and I knew by fall that I would be able to sell him as well broke. He wasn't getting any nicer about having his feet handled though, acting plumb mulish about it. Worse, even after a second worming he hadn't lost a single miserable hair. Every horse in the country was slick with their summer coats and he looked worse than ever. Summer became autumn and Bean Bag could spin on a dime with the slightest of rein pressure. He could put any horse to shame with his magnificent slide stop. He was ready for sale except for his hide. If anything, he was even funnier to look at, next to the smooth-coated other horses. The hair on his legs and belly would have done a muskox proud. So armed with my electric clippers and a friend to help, I decided to shed him out the modern way. It was the day before the sale, and it was now or never. Bean Bag thought even less of the clippers than just getting his hooves trimmed. I must have fought with him for hours, trying to give him a shave and a haircut, when I discovered that some horses can stand on two legs only, not three or four, just two. Because that's how he ended up standing while I whizzed the hair off his legs. My buddy had one hind leg tied back to a post with a slip knot and I had the opposite front foot strapped up on the front end of Bean Bag. He stood on only two legs with a fixed expression of "How dare you do this to me" on his face. When I finished with all four legs right up to his belly, we let him stand on all four feet. Now to finish his body. His hair was so thick and dense that my poor clippers started to overheat. I only got to make about two passes down one side when with a buzzing noise and a smell like burning metal, my clippers gave up the ghost, shorting out in my hand. So be it, I wasn't skunked yet. I would still haul him to the horse sale, early enough to purchase a new pair of clippers, and finish clipping him before too many people showed up to view the horses.

As soon as I got Bean Bag into a pen at the auction mart, I went looking for clippers at the western store in town. Sorry lady, we sold the last pair a week ago. No problem, the feed mill in town sells them too. Sorry lady, we sold the only pair we had last week. That was fine, I wasn't about to give up yet. I placed a phone call to the next town, and a sweet young girl told me over the phone that yes they had a pair for sale there. I drove thirty-five miles to find out they had sold their last pair in the spring and that the sweet young girl was three bricks short of a load. By the time I got back to the sale, a group of horse buyers were gathered around Bean Bag laughing their heads off. To me they sounded like just so many cackling chickens, with a couple of crows thrown in. Maybe he did look a bit funny, with his shaggy, matted body, and all four legs trimmed right up to it, neat as pins. Maybe the shaved swipe or two on one side did look a bit ridiculous. Not one to admit the trim job didn't finish out like it was supposed to, I sold him anyway. Except for the auctioneer almost falling off his perch, he was cackling so hard, everything went fairly well. I actually made a profit of a few dollars on him, though later the buyer claimed to be just point-ing at him, not really bidding. It irks me to no end, when even years later, some idiot has to bring up the story about my shaggy horse and the trim job on him. What do they know anyway?

HAULING HORSES

The rose–coloured dawn was just beginning as I saddled and bridled the two horses. After tying their reins up loosely to the saddle horns, they followed me to the open stock trailer. First, the bay mare walked past me, stepping up into the trailer, where she stood quietly as I closed the centre gate behind her. The sorrel gelding waited until I stepped back down out the trailer, then he too loaded himself without any word from me. Having closed the end gate behind him, I was ready for the road. Once on the highway, I had lots of time to think about how nice it is when horses are this good at loading and being hauled. Lots of time to remember a lifetime of other horses.

Long before I ever owned a horse trailer or a stock trailer, I made do with stock racks on the back of my truck. My first set of stock racks were home–built ones, perched on the back of a 1957 Fargo. The truck was almost as old as I was, with a few more scars than me though. I hadn't started to rust yet, like that old truck, but we had some traits in common. We were both known to be stubborn to get started in the early morning, and both known to be hard to stop once we did get going. I was built sturdy and low to the ground, giving me lots of power but not too much speed over long distances. Like me the old blue cuss was built to last but was missing out on the speed end of it. Once loaded with a pair of horses on the back, fifty miles an hour going downhill was the best we could do. Put either one of us in deep mud up to our tail gates, and both of us would manage to chug through it, me on my two legs, the Fargo on its four beat–up old tires. I made many miles with that old truck with horses' heads showing over top of the racks on the back.

As time went on, I upgraded to a newer truck with impres–sive, fully enclosed stock racks, factory built for hauling horses. In these racks, I often hauled some of my favourite horses. Like the bay mare with four white socks and a blaze face. I didn't have to back up to any form of loading ramp to get her to jump on, she would do so, with ease, jumping off of level ground. I never understood how she continued to load so easily because when hauled any kind of distance at all, she always got kind of sick, almost like getting colic, breaking out in a sweat, and turning her head to poke her muzzle at her belly and flank. If the distance was too great, she would collapse in the back of the truck, in total misery. Time and time again, I would panic, sure that this time she was really going to die on me, just me and my truck, barrelling down the road with a dead horse in the back of it. Each time when we arrived at our destination, she would lie there for a half hour or so, then miracle of miracles, she would get to her feet, as good as new, jump out of the truck and be ready to do whatever had to be done. I always had to be on guard with her if I had the truck in the corrals or pasture, to load or unload barn manure, because if she happened along and saw the tailgate lowered, she would try to get past me and jump in. It looked pretty silly, this big clown of a horse standing in the back of my half–ton without any stock racks on it.

Then there was the bay saddle gelding of mine who had the most annoying habit of all. Get him loaded, head down the road and he would immediately go into some sort of trance–like state, almost like he was sleeping. As he swayed back and forth, he would get the truck swaying so bad it was hell, trying to hold it on the road in a straight line. Rather than lose complete control of the swaying truck, I would have to hit my brakes hard enough to jolt him awake. In no time at all, he would be back in his sleeping trance, and his swaying motion would be putting me all over the road again. Hauling him was like this: pick up speed, clutch the steering wheel, swerve all over, stand on the brakes again, repeat, repeat.

The time I used my racks to haul one of my mares to an Appaloosa stallion to be bred was short and to the point. The stallion owner pointed to a mound of dirt out in the pasture, where he said I could back up and unload the mare. I backed up to the dirt ramp and opened the end gate. Before I could even think about unloading the mare, that leopard–coloured stallion appeared out of nowhere, shot by me with a squeal, bred that mare still standing on the back of my truck, then disappeared again in a cloud of dust. I guess that is what's called "Breeding Made Easy," or "Short, Sweet And To The Point. "

When I finally bought a two–horse trailer, I thought I was in heaven. No more putting stock racks on, taking stock racks off afterwards and finding loading chutes or natural ramps of banks of dirt to load from. I also quickly came to realize that horses load a whole lot easier in open stock racks than in narrow, enclosed horse trailers. Take my sweet old bay mare who loved to jump in my truck. Sure, she would happily load in the horse trailer too, but backing her out was a different story. She would not, even on the threat of death, willingly back out of the trailer. She couldn't even be pulled out, with two or three strong people staining on a rope run up and around her chest. No, I had to remove the partition, get it out of her way and then with great dignity she would turn around and walk out on her own. The same as in the back of my truck, she would get her sick spell and want to lie down. The time or two she did lay down, she would find herself trapped when she sprawled her legs under the centre of the partition, so it had to come off again, just to let her stand back up without injury. The bay saddle gelding came mighty close to causing some terrible wrecks as he managed to get the trailer swaying from side to side, all over the road, much worse than him being on the back of the truck.

Another one of my geldings who always loaded in the stock racks without a fuss fought being loaded in the trailer so bad that he spent his time going nowhere at all that first summer. Finally I parked the trailer, with wheels blocked in a corral, and leaving the end gate open wide, I placed both his feed and his water inside. The black fool went hungry and thirsty for quite a spell, until he figured out get in, eat and drink, or starve. After a couple of weeks, he loaded without a care in the world. But when I removed the trailer from his corral to use it, you would have sworn he was a baby colt losing his momma at weaning time. I'm convinced that if the fence had not been as high and strong as it was, he would have crashed through it and followed the trailer out of the yard and up the road. For as long as I owned him, he was not happy when the trailer left the yard without him, whinnying and leaping around in joy on its return.

Another one of my mares knew exactly how not to get loaded. The sorrel would just take one look inside the trailer and throw herself to the ground. She would lie there sulking with her eyes rolled back in her head. No amount of persuasion could get her up. One time in total disgust I took the halter off her and walked away. Later while cooking supper, I looked out the window and there she was still lying on the ground behind the trailer. I figured after we had eaten, I would go down and light a fire under her if I had to, to get her up. Lucky for her, I was out of matches when supper was over and besides, some-time during the course of the meal she had got up and was munching grass on the lawn. Catching her, I led her back to the pasture. To get to the pasture gate, we had to pass behind the trailer. She never made it by the end gate of it, like a horse who had suddenly been shot, she dropped to the ground with a moan. The silly nag had learned her method of never being loaded. I'll never understand some horses as long as I live. The day I sold her, I was completely honest with the buyer about her being kind of impossible to load. In fact, I gave him an extra good deal on the mare since I knew not how he would ever get her loaded to take her home. That old cowboy just snorted at the pea-brained woman who couldn't load a little sweetheart of a mare like her. He opened the end gate of his own horse trailer, took hold of that mare's halter and walked into the trailer, with her following on his heels like a puppy. Beats me how he did it. To this day the only answers I've ever come up with were either she just didn't like me or she just didn't like my trailer.

Jackass

The day I got sucked into hauling a donkey home in a rented horse trailer was one of my biggest embarrassments ever. First, he wouldn't load for me, so four macho cowboys simply picked him up and put him in the trailer for me. Of course all four of them thought it was funny. Then we headed out of the city limits, me driving my Chevy car with this beat-up trailer in tow. Wouldn't you know it, the rusty old hitch jumped off the bumper ball right smack dab in rush-hour traffic on a down-town bridge. The safety chain prevented an accident but that's all. There I sat, without a clue what to do, with the trailer block-ing two lanes of traffic and a donkey hee-hawing like an insane maniac inside it. Of course the pedestrians on the sidewalk thought it was funny. Even the police, who showed up to straighten things out, thought it was funny. The police insisted I unload the grey creature so the wreck of a trailer would be light enough for the other drivers and the police to push and pull back into line with the bumper. Then after it was hitched up again, properly this time, everyone laughed and thought it was just so funny, when the loudly braying donkey chose to sit down like a dog rather than reload. In my state of acute embar-rassment I really did think they all sounded like so many braying jackasses as they stood around roaring in laughter at my plight. They were making more noise than the donkey ever thought of as I drug him, still protesting back into the trailer. All this because a friend asked me to do him this favour and I hadn't had the nerve to say no.

No Refund

The time I had eleven horses to haul long distance, I decided to do it all in one trip by renting both van and driver from a company that specializes in hauling race horses. Each and every one of those horses was easy to load without any problems. That is until the van showed up. The driver and his helper asked me first thing if any of them were hard to load. Of course I said no. Of course they soon had me pegged as another one of those female creatures who have bad hormone days. Each horse in turn refused to go up the portable ramp into the side loading door of the van. Finally I managed to talk Whiskey into following one of the men up the ramp. Now once inside the horses must be turned around and backed up another slight incline into tie stalls. He got her turned around and backed up all right, but before he could snap the two tie chains onto her halter, she lunged right over top of him and with a giant leap exited that van without touching the ramp. Next I tried Pokey again with my tried-and-true secret weapon: a bucket of yummy oats. Always convinced that she was starving to death, she followed the bucket up the ramp. And there she stopped. Head and neck on the inside, the rest of her outside. The portable side railings on the ramp didn't look all that sturdy to me, and Pokey soon proved it by simply letting herself fall off the side of the ramp, making kindling out of the railing. I was starting to mutter under my breath about the whole affair, and those two men were keeping a close eye on me in case I lost control like women are sometimes known to do. About the time one of them latched onto my sorrel brood mare, got halfway up the ramp and then let her jump off the other side of the ramp, taking that flimsy railing with her, I was ready to call it quits.

The only problem was that I had paid in advance at their Calgary office and now they were telling me there would be no refund paid back for not getting the job done. Well, then we were going to haul us some horses weren't we? I instructed them to get rid of their silly ramp and pull up as tight as possible to the loading chute. Then to fill in the dangerous foot of gap between the end of the chute and the van, I got short planks and nails and tacked them to the floor of the chute and the floor of the van, which didn't impress them very much. Then I put all eleven head of horses in the narrow laneway leading to the chute and told them to get ready to catch and tie horses as they came up. Two men stood waiting with looks of horror on their faces, as I let out a holler and swatted rumps from the safety of the top rail of the laneway. Eleven horses stampeded up that chute, with both men working feverishly to catch and tie them as they thundered into the van. The whole operation took only seconds. Except for me getting a sliver in my thumb from the corral fence, nobody was hurt. I've always wondered if they ever changed their policy about giving refunds to customers whose horses don't want to load the conventional way.

TYING THEM UP

Unless a horse is a wild, unclaimed mustang, there is a good chance he is going to find himself tied to a post at some time in his life. If he is handled or rode much at all, he will spend even more time tied up.

The majority of horses soon learn not to fight a secured rope. They may dance around, paw the ground in annoyance and make a nuisance of themselves when tied, all this without ever pulling back hard enough to take the slack out of the rope from their halters to the post. Being tied up is the first lesson a horse receives in life, when he comes into contact with a man. Once he is halter broke, he knows that man is his lord and master, when the rope slips around his neck, he is no longer the boss.

It's a good thing most horses are so quick to learn this most important lesson in life. The few that don't ever learn it and wreak havoc with broken ropes, busted halters and injuries to themselves are a real pain to have around.

I bought a running quarter horse filly a few years back that was a confirmed halter puller, the worst one I have ever known. When she was led out of the barn, I looked her over for a long time, trying to figure out why she was for sale so cheap. Her conformation was excellent, she had no apparent lameness or injuries. Her manners were good, allowing me to pick up her feet, run my hands all over her, while standing quietly. She led beside her owner with ease and a calm attitude. Glad to have found such a nice piece of horse flesh for so little money, I dug out my checkbook. After the bill of sale was signed, and the filly loaded loose in my stock trailer, I remarked to the man that perhaps he could have sold her for even more money. He just shook his head and said getting rid of her was more important than money. Not having a clue yet what he meant, I bid him adieu and headed home.

She was on the place two or three weeks before I tied her solid to a post, while I went into the barn to get the nippers and rasp to trim her feet. I stepped back outside to find her wandering around with a broken lead rope dangling down. Muttering to myself I caught her and using a heavier cotton rope, I tied her up again. Slowly she faced the post, slowly she went into a crouch, a look of intense concentration on her face. Then in one explosive backwards leap, she broke the heavy metal snap on the end of the rope. Off she trotted. Yup, I had bought myself a confirmed halter puller, one of those horses who has learned they can break free by violently pulling back.

In the first place, I won't have such a horse on my place. In the second place, I will not sell a horse to someone else because I consider it a dangerous habit, to both horse and anyone near him when he throws such a fit. So this filly would have to be cured of her habit, once and forever. It can be a hard thing to cure, sometimes next to impossible.

Getting my heaviest halter and an unbreakable lariat, I set out to teach little miss race horse a lesson in staying tied up. I put the halter on her, attached the lariat in a loop around her neck with a quick release, safety knot, and ran it through the ring of the halter to the post. I had barely got out of her way, when she blew up. Her favourite backwards lunge didn't work, leaping straight in the air didn't work. But a combination of them did. What had seemed a solid enough post wasn't: with a crack like a pistol shot, it broke off at ground level. I simply moved her down the fence line to the next post, this one she managed to pull right out of the ground. I conceded, she had won round one of the fight. Before the week was out, I had found an immense used bridge support. I dug that new snub-bing post in by hand, as deep as I could go. I tamped the dirt tight around it and went to get miss halter puller. The battle was on. Never have I seen such a determined to escape horse. She lunged backwards and sideways, she reared and struck out with her forefeet, on and on she fought. When all else failed, she threw herself and hung there, choking, too mad to get up. They say a horse will never purposely choke themselves to death, but I had my jackknife out and ready to cut the rope if she was to the point of drawing her last breath. Still she hung there, the seconds ticking by. My knife blade was already against the rope, when with a squeal of rage, she leapt to her feet. She renewed the battle with out and out anger now. When she could not break free, she threw herself again, hanging there, lungs gasping for air.

For a week I left her tied to that post, packing feed and water to her twice a day. For the entire time, she blew up at least half a dozen times a day, first the fighting and then the hanging herself. She was a mess to look at, skinned up something terrible, but she did it all to herself. On the eighth day, she had learned her lesson. I could sack her out with a tarp thrown all over and around her and she would not tighten up on that rope. She could have been tied with a stream of bathroom tissue, and she would not have torn it.

I sold her to a nice young couple who had always wanted a race horse of their very own, but could not afford one. I let her go for little more than I paid for her. I was pleased to hear they won several races on the Alberta circuit with her, making a tidy profit. As for me, I was glad she was gone. I hate broken lead ropes.

Gilly was the exact opposite to little miss halter puller. The first time I discovered Gilly was invisibly tied up to a post, I felt sorry for her but had to laugh at the same time. I had purchased her for a brood mare, and although I also broke her to ride, I really didn't handle her that much. On this particular morning, I caught her and tied her to a post in the corral, so another hard-to-catch two-year-old horse would come into the corral. My scheme worked: seeing Gilly already in the corral, he came in and I closed the gate on him. I saddled him up and loaded him in my trailer to go riding all day at a friend's place. Just as I was leaving I saw that I had opened the gate to the corral but had forgot to untie Gilly. Quickly I reached through the fence and unsnapped the lead rope from the halter. I could take the halter off her when I came back. I also left the rope still tied around the post.

When I returned late in the day, there stood poor Gilly. She neighed unhappily to me as I unloaded the gelding. She was hungry and thirsty. She had pawed a fair–sized hole in the ground, troubled by being separated from her pasture mates all day. The silly goose thought she was still tied up. Well halter broke, she never pulled back or even attempted to tighten up the invisible rope. She stood there watching me with big brown eyes until I came over and took the halter off. She tore over to the water, gulped some down and galloped out to pasture and her buddies, happy to be free at last. In the years I had her, I often would put a halter on her, lead her over to a post and go through the motions of pretending to tie her up. She was always convinced an invisible rope held her tight, and would remain tied until I came back to her and untied her.

All Tied Up

First I rode Lady with a saddle and bridle. Then bareback with nothing but the bridle, and finally with nothing at all. I rode her many summers and many miles this way, the two of us, a true team of partners, as close as horse and master can be. All I ever carried with me to tie her up was a piece of bale twine in my pocket. Whenever I dismounted from her back, and needed to tie her up, I would lead her by her mane over to a fence post or tree, kneel down and fashion a loop of twine around her left front pastern and then secure it to the post or tree. She was tied as solid as any horse with a halter and rope. I could leave her like this for hours and she never pulled free. She was so good at it that I learned if no posts or trees were close by, placing a large rock on top of the end of the twine did the trick just as well. Wouldn't it be nice if all horses were so easy to restrain.

I love to listen to my mother tell stories about her horse, Flip, who faithfully took Mom to school year after year by buggy or sleigh. Mom loved Flip and I'm sure Flip felt the same about her. Flip's life had not always been so easy though. She had at one time been so badly beaten over the head that she could not be tied by the head, without it causing such fear and panic in the mare as to result in injury to herself and those around her. So once at school, in the horse barn out back, Mom would tie her in her stall by the front foot as I tied Lady. It seems the new teacher one year did not know Flip was tied by a foot and not her head. He addressed the classroom of students in a firm voice, saying whoever owned that particular mare in the barn should get right out there and tie her up because she was loose. Thinking Flip had broke free, Mom went out to do as he asked, and found her still tied. Seems the teacher checked again and saw the mare still loose. Mom said they had quite a go–around, her and this teacher, before he got it through his head that Flip was indeed tied up.

HORSES & HARNESSES

When autumn turns into winter, many of us horse people hang up our spurs, not quite into freezing everything from noses to toes just to take old Flame for a spin around the pasture. Years ago, the cold grip of western Canada's wintertime hardly slowed my riding time up at all. Bundled up in long johns, blue jeans and heavy coat, I pulled on my toque and mitts, saddled up a long-haired horse and climbed on. I'm not quite sure when I actually quit taking those frosty rides and settled for just thinking about one instead.

I knew that this is the time of year when cutters and sleighs are brought out of hibernation to take their places behind horses and harness. Seeing the laughing, happy faces of the people on board, as the horses feet kicked snow back at them, almost convinced me that it sure must be fun indeed. My only problem was the idea of sitting behind a moving horse instead of on top of him. What I needed was a lesson or two in driving horses instead of riding them.

A horseman I knew, who could drive them or ride them, it didn't make much matter to him which it was, decided to give me the lessons I was searching for. I was told to meet him one crystal clear winter day that was cold, but tolerable, down at his ranch to take a spin around the pasture behind a team of horses. First off, he said, we would have a go at driving a team hooked up to his cumbersome sleigh, used for Sunday rides for dudes from town. Had I been paying better attention than I was, I might have caught on that his big work team was nowhere in sight. I might have caught on that the two horses we were hooking up seemed a bit nervous about all that harness draped over and around them. You'd think that some little doubt would have crept into my brain when it took the two of us to get them actually hitched to the sleigh itself. While I clung to their tossing, wild-eyed heads, he took his place on the sleigh, long leather reins held tight. Then he said, "Okay, turn them horses loose and jump up here with me." I did what I was told and took my place beside him, both of us standing against the front boards just behind those pair of swishing tails.

Grinning like an evil hound, he slapped the reins against their rumps. The team didn't need any more urging and bolted. I lost my footing and landed on my backside with a thump. The sleigh was rocking and swaying making it a hard job to regain my feet, but somehow I managed. Grabbing a hold of the front boards, I held on for dear life. Just like I had seen before, I was being showered by flying snow. Unlike I had ever seen before, this team was not just moseying along, enjoying their work— they were doing their best to out-run each other, with the odd attempted dash to the side like they maybe didn't want to be harnessed side by side like they were. The man was using all his many years of driving skill to keep them running in a large circle within the boundaries of the pasture. Stealing a peak at him, I could see an insane grin plastered on his face. I sure hope it was just frozen there from the cold and not there because he was having fun. About the time I had decided to bail off the back end of the sleigh and let the man have fun all by himself, he started to gain some control over the horses. Before long, he had them slowed down to a trot and was getting them to make circles to the left and then to the right. Pretty soon they were coming to a halt on command, even though they refused to stand still for long. By the time they had rediscovered how to walk like normal horses, he was passing the reins to me, insisting I take them and start my driving lessons.

With all that leather in my hands, I was some nervous but I had hopes that with me driving, I might be able to head in the general direction of the barn and then have a reason for getting off the sleigh while I was still in one whole piece. We walked them around some, then took it slow and easy back so that the steaming wet horses could cool down. I wasn't entirely surprised after unhooking the team, when he told me that they were a pair of pack horses that had never been hooked up in their lives before. He claimed he didn't harness them today of all days just to scare me out of my long johns but because he really did need another team around the place. I wanted to believe him but just couldn't quite get over that silly grin on his face.

After warming up in the house for a spell, he took me to a shed and showed me his new pride and joy. There it sat, painted black with red trim, a one-horse cutter. He ran his hands lovingly over the sides, then reached down inside on the floor boards and pulled out a shiny new harness. When he started to get that irritating smile back on his face, I turned and tried to make a mad dash for the safety of my truck. He collared me and with great patience explained that he would never do the same thing to me twice in the same day. He looked and sounded so honest that I wanted to really believe him. I knew him to be the country's biggest dare devil when it came to horses. I knew he was lacking completely in that well-known emotion called fear. So why did I let him talk me into agreeing to hook another horse up to his new toy for a quick spin around the pasture? He swore up and down that this gelding was well broke. The horse did stand still while the harness was adjusted on him, and he did snort and blow only a little when he was backed between the shafts and hooked up solid. Then with much misgiving, I took a seat beside the man who after all was only trying to give me driving lessons. What a nice man to help me learn this way.

He clucked to the sorrel gelding who was watching us behind him. At the sound to move out, he took a step forward. We went with him. He took a few more quick steps to get away from us, but once again we followed him. Concerned now, he tried to turn around and face us, but somehow that didn't work either. His nostrils started to flare, his eyes started to roll and in desperation to get away from us he lit out across the snow-covered pasture. The faster he went, the faster we appeared to purposely follow him. Through the flying mist of snow, I was twice in the same day being subjected to the back side of a runaway. Clinging to my side of the cutter, I prayed for survival as we rocketed onward. I hurled the words at him, "You promised me you would not do this to me twice in the same day! You said this horse was well broke!" With that damnable grin back on his face, he shouted back at me, "I meant I wouldn't hook two horses back up again today, not just one iddy biddy horse and he is well broke, well broke to ride, I meant." For just a wee moment I truly wished I was married to this infuriating man, just so I could have the pleasure of divorcing him. Like the team, the gelding soon tired, and once he slowed up some, he began to respond to the reins, stopping and turning on command. Like the team also, eventually the reins were passed to me for my second driving lesson of the day. Even though the horses did all the work, I was totally exhausted by the end of the afternoon, too tired to even stay mad at my teacher.

The next winter I went along on one of his Sunday sleigh rides for people from town. He had hitched one of the original pack horses and a bronc together for this ride. The pack horse was by now well broke to the job of pulling a sleigh full of happy people down the winding trail cut through the forest to the edge of the frozen river. The bronc wasn't too pleased about his lot in life, but behaved as much as could be expected. Until we were almost to our destination that is. Then trotting around the last bend in the trail, he threw a fit, ending up with him on one side of an immense fir tree and the other horse on the opposite side. Nobody was hurt, no damage was done except for the tongue on the sleigh was broke in half.

The people had paid to have fun and fun they were going to have. With the team tied to a tree, we all headed down to the river where the snow had been shovelled off a good-sized patch of ice. There bales of hay became benches for everyone to put their skates on. While the crowd skated to their hearts' content, a large fire was built. They came to warm themselves and eat hamburgers and hot dogs until bursting. Thermoses of coffee and brandy were passed from hand to hand. Before anyone realized it, it was pitch dark and the chill of night arrived. Only then did someone raise the subject of how they were all getting back to the ranch. It was too far for people to walk and with the sleigh out of commission, what was going to be done? I was getting cold and tired so I asked the man if the pack horse was broke to ride also. He assured me he was, so I decided I would take his harness off and ride him bareback to the ranch. Then I would come back with the four-wheel crew cab, pile everyone in it and take them back.

Very little firelight reached as far back as the tree. I unharnessed the horse, stepped up on a log, and scrambled on his back. I don't know if it's just that particular ranch or what, but I was instantly on a runaway, in the black of night, this time on top of instead of behind some horse out to get me killed. Long reins were streaming out behind me, the horse and I thundered for home, closely followed by the other horse who must have broke free to follow us. We turned into the lighted yard going what felt like ninety miles an hour. The horse skidded to a stop in front of the barn, with me managing to hold on by the skin of my teeth only. I sort of fell off his side, still pretty much froze up with fear, and took my first good look at which horse had brought me home with so much speed. Yup, I had done it again. I had just dismounted off the bronc, not the pack horse. After I had rescued the rest of the people, I told the man that I thought I should maybe get paid for starting the bronc's training. He wasn't smiling for once. Seems this horse had a promising career as a saddle bronc and it looked like I might have wrecked him by running him all the way back through the timber, across the pasture lands to the corrals. Seems he felt it was all right to hook him up to a sleigh but not to ride him. I just shook my head.

Stubborn in the Snow

My grandparents made their living off the land with teams of horses. My father drove horses before he ever rode one. Before he even married though, tractors, trucks and cars had replaced horses both in the fields and on the roads. So what was he doing, in the middle 1950s, hooking his saddle mare Judy up to a small sled, which was normally used behind a small case tractor for cleaning the cow barn? It was close to seven miles to the nearest store and the winter roads were impassable with drifted snow. Mother needed groceries to feed her growing family, so Dad and his young mare were going to town.

Judy didn't appreciate being asked to pull the sleigh, but she co-operated all the way to the store. But once the sleigh was loaded and they had headed back, she decided just when she would pull and when she wouldn't. When the going was easy on top of the smooth layer of snow, she pulled, but when she hit a wind-swept spot of prairie where the land was blown clear, she stopped. No amount of cajoling from Dad would get her to move an inch. He was forced to get off the sleigh, unload it, drag it himself to the next layer of snow, load it again and tell her to get up. It took him forever to get back home to the farm, both frustrated and tired. Some horses were meant to be ridden and not harnessed, as Judy proved to my father in her own stubborn way.

TOUGH HORSES

When I talk about tough horses, I mean the ones who were born with long-lasting batteries inside them, because they just keep going and going and going. A tough horse does not know the meaning of the word "quit." A truly tough horse will keep going until he drops. They are few and far between, these horses who never seem to get tired, who always have that one more burst of speed, energy or power. They all have one more thing in common. They are not deadheads, often they are difficult to handle or ride, often they need a top horseman to bring out the best in them.

Whiskey was the toughest horse I ever owned. She only stood fifteen and one hands high, and in her prime wouldn't have made a thousand pounds in weight. She was thorough-bred/standardbred cross and homely as sin. If she hadn't been born as tough as she was, she would not have survived past four months old. She was more dead than alive the day I bought her. When I attend horse sales, I go through every pen of horses out back, long before the sale starts. It gives me the added advantage of having the time to look each one over carefully.

In one pen out back at an Innisfail auction sale, a four-month-old brown filly lay quietly, her hair brittle and scruffy, her ribs showing plainly. I passed her by without a second glance, for I was there to buy two-year-olds and up, not starving colts who have no potential for resale. I had forgotten all about her when there she was in the ring. Almost too weak to stand, she stumbled around the sale ring. My heart went out to her but she wasn't worth a plugged nicked so I did nothing. As usual the ring itself was crowded with Wanna Be cowboys and other ones who think it makes them important to stand down in a sale ring so everyone there can see them. I have a great dislike for these types unless they are really there to actually buy a horse. Many times the ring becomes so crowded with them that it diminishes the working space for people like me who need the room to show their mounts to buyers in the stands. One of these smart asses laughed and kicked dirt in the brown filly's face. In an effort to get away from him, she tried to speed up and her poor legs fell out from under her. Unable to find the strength to rise, she remained sprawled on the ground. Another of these jerks grinned like an idiot and grabbing her tail and one ear lifted her to her feet, to show his manly strength, I suppose. I was mad clear through at these uncaring nerds and my hand shot up in the air. Sold to the lady in the brown hat, one brown filly, for fifty bucks. I had out-bid the meat buyer by ten dollars. I was also mad at myself: no wonder I spent more money than I earned with horses, buying a scrub like her.

When the big truck arrived at my place, late in the night, with the load of horses I had purchased, she was lying scrunched in the corner. I unloaded the rest down the chute and then I had the driver back up next to the haystack. Three of us pushed her to the tailgate of the truck and then lowered her onto a soft bed of hay.

In the next morning's early light, I checked her. She had made no attempt to rise. I knew it was going to be a waste of my time and money but I phoned a vet anyway. The vet looked her over, gave her a shot of penicillin and wormed her by stomach tube. He said she wasn't going to make it and he had done all he could. Within a few hours she was in great pain, having colic on top of her already weakened state. The next vet I called out took one look at her, stood up and said I should put her to sleep. He was a good vet I respected, but by now I had two vet visits to pay for on top of the original fifty dollars. He agreed to do all he could for a day or two, but still thought she was past saving. He hooked her up to intravenous to replenish lost body fluids and drenched her orally to help pass the blockage in her intestines which was the cause of her colic.

By night time she had passed the blockage. Balls of dead worms. She was a living worm factory, every scrap of food she ate going to support masses of internal parasites. No wonder she was so near death.

I'm sure any other horse would have already been dead, but she was a tough one, finding the strength somewhere to keep trying to eat the hay and grain in front of her, taking shaking sips of water from the bucket I offered her. The food passed straight through her damaged system, being excreted much as it had looked before she swallowed it. I found myself determined to save her.

A horse cannot stay lying down for extended periods of time without the legs becoming paralyzed and swollen from poor circulation. Even their digestive system is impaired by this constant position. So I needed a way to get her on her feet and keep her there. I had seen slings used to suspend downer cows, so with the help of another horseman, I made one. By the end of the second day she was in a shed of her own, held up in a sling attached to the overhead beams. I had her suspended so her feet touched the floor, but she could not collapse down. In front of her was a net full of hay and a bucket of water, both at head height. I administered shots of crucial vitamins her body needed and antibiotics. Now it was up to her.

She was a fighter all right, and determined to make it. Once she quit struggling in the sling she took advantage of it, some-times standing on her own and sometimes relaxing and letting the sling support her weight. She nibbled at the hay, and tried to eat all of the crushed oats and bran I offered her. She laid her fuzzy ears back at me, as day after day I gave her intramuscular injections of vitamins and other necessary drugs. Slowly she gained strength.

Just when I thought her and I had won the battle of her survival, I found her lying on the floor of the shed. She had reared up and over backwards out of the sling. Still too weak to rise from the position of lying flat on her side, she had lain there prone, kicking and struggling to get up. She had repeatedly banged her head on the wall. Worse, she had struggled so hard she had forced her bowel and uterus part way out. With all my strength I managed to roll her up into a lying position with all four feet under her. Thankfully her internal organs were re-tracted back inside her. I let out a holler at the same time I pounded on the shed wall, which spooked her enough that she was able to lunge to her feet. I succeeded in getting her back in the harness before she collapsed again.

After that I made time to exercise her daily, taking her for slow walks to burn off her newly acquired energy, then return-ing her to the sling. She seemed to be doing so well that I thought she would be fine for a few minutes out in a pen, when I was called suddenly to the house to answer the phone. It was a business call that took over an hour to handle. I returned to find her flat on her side again and violently fighting to get up. This time her exertions had forced both the bowel and entire uterus out of her weakened body. Both organs were filthy dirty and already starting to dry out in the hot afternoon sun. One vet couldn't be reached and the other one refused to come, saying she should have been disposed of a long time ago. I couldn't give up now, she deserved to live.

Using buckets of warm, soapy water, I cleaned the bowel and uterus and using my years of knowledge with cows in similar situations, I worked them back into the body. Then more shots of penicillin were given. By then, help in the form of another horse-loving girl arrived and between the two of us, we got her up and back into the sling.

Well, I did save the scrawny brown filly. I could not have done it had she not had a powerful will to survive all odds against her. I named her Whiskey and she found a special place in my heart. She grew from a homely baby into a just as homely a mare. I prided myself on having good-looking horses on the place, and used to be ashamed of her when people saw her and made funny comments about her size and shape. I stopped being ashamed of her the day she won her first race, with me up on her, at the local rodeo. I never lost a race with her because her heart and spirit carried us over each finish line. As she learned to work cattle, cover mile after mile of rough mountain country and even endurance races, she became a beautiful horse in my eyes. Never an easy horse to ride, with her unlimited energy, inability to ever stand still for five minutes and desire to just keep going and going, she was one tough horse, the best.

A Top Team

Just like Whiskey, Roanie wasn't pretty enough to grace the covers of horse magazines, and just like her, he was tough until the day he died. His owner was a top cowhand and excellent horseman. He was a hard-working man who needed a good horse under him, one who could last from dawn to dusk, just like himself. The smoky blue roan gelding was the horse he needed. It didn't matter to Roanie how many miles there were in a day, he took them in stride. It didn't matter how many calves had to be roped by the heels and drug to the branding fires, afterwards his master and him would start in on roping cows that needed to be doctored. If it wasn't pitch dark out by now, maybe they would lope along a few miles of fence line to make sure all the wires were still up. The next day, Roanie was always as frisky as a young colt again, ready to start all over, his devotion to his owner obvious in the way he came to him, nickering a greeting. Seeing these two together always gave me the impression that any and all of us were somehow left on the back burner, compared to them. My hat is off to the memory I have of this pair of working partners.

No Quitter

Sometimes horse owners don't mean to be hard on their mounts, pushing them so long and hard while working that only the toughest of horses can stand up to the physical strain. Sometimes a person maybe doesn't realize he is being cruel to his horse by asking too much of him. This is the way it was with a rancher I knew and his personal saddle horse, named Drifter. Drifter was a big, rough–looking quarter horse gelding in his prime years when I often rode beside them, checking cattle, rounding up and herding cattle. It was on wide open range with a long way between fence lines. I was usually mounted on young horses, in various stages of training. I always took care of these horses, trying to never push them past their capabilities, making sure they did not sour on long, hard rides. A young horse, in training, can get over–hot or tired, resulting in them losing their ability to keep learning and even to become sulky and resentful. Nobody seemed to care about how Drifter felt. As time went on, he became more and more prone to buck, harder to catch and resentful of the bit in his mouth. Had Drifter not been such a tough horse, I think he would have either turned into a complete outlaw to get away from the punishing rides, or simply laid down and quit altogether. Instead, that big gelding lengthened his stride and covered the ground even faster and longer. It seemed that he was saying, "Okay buster, you want more miles done even quicker, fine, then hold onto your hat, so it's not left behind!" I would see him soaked with sweat, going hour after hour without as much as a drink of water, let alone a short rest. I believe this tough gelding just kept getting tougher as the years went by. I hope that if not yet, then someday he gets turned out into a lush pasture of waving grass, so that he might spend his last days free of a saddle on his back.

The Top Four

Sun was tough in a different way than most horses. He was tough because he saved himself. An ex–rodeo bronc I trained to ride, he had a bit of a disposition problem, meaning he didn't really like people, even me, no matter how many treats I fed him. His attitude was, "Show me what you want me to do and let's get it done as quick as possible, so I can get back home and snooze in the shade." I used him extensively for competitive trail and riding events. He was a master at twenty–five milers, covering the ground so quickly and effortlessly that I always had to stop at the two–miles–to–go marker and wait an hour or so before continuing. You see, first you must come in on time, Too early and you are disqualified, too late and the same. Second, you cannot stop your horse once you pass the marker saying only two miles to go or you are again disqualified.

I'm sure some of the other competitors thought I was crazy for pushing Sun so fast and hard, only to end up sitting there away ahead of schedule. I didn't push Sun at anything. Sun set his own pace, and pity me should I try to interfere with him. If I used excessive force in controlling him, he would fight me wearing himself out in the mean time. He knew exactly what he was doing at all times, I just sat up there on top of him looking at the pretty landscape rolling by. I don't mean that he was a rammy, go, go, go type either. When the ground was level for loping, he loped. He never lunged up a mountainside, thus taxing his muscles, he went up like an old cat out for a stroll. He didn't try to gallop down steep inclines, he sauntered down them. He did not hesitate at river crossings, then leap off the bank, charging across as if it contained live crocodiles. No, he moseyed down each bank, drank a swallow or two, then ambled across. He saved himself like an elderly man who knows it's time to hang up his football uniform and take up bowling. He then would break into a long trot, holding it for miles and passing loping horses with ease. Because he took care of himself, he never grew tired or needed a rest. When he grew bored and the terrain was good, he would break into a gallop, his long stride covering the ground and the wind whistling by.

Fifty-mile rides, when we advanced to them, were completed in the same style, Sun's way. I won the best-conditioned award on the majority of the rides, meaning the judges and attending vets found him to be unstressed and not sore after each ride. I never placed less than fourth out of an average figure of seventy-nine horses, when the ribbons and trophies were handed out. Why? Because Sun was a tough horse. On top of that, he was an intelligent horse.

OLD HERB

You may have all heard people talking about a certain horse as being an "ALL-AROUND HORSE." This means different things to different people. To one person it means that he can chase cows with his horse, then turn around and put the wife and kids on him. Or it means that a cowboy can chase cows all day on his horse, then turn around and haul him to a jackpot roping at the local arena after supper and win too. Or he can ride that horse all summer and when winter comes, turn around and hook him up to the cutter or sleigh and trot down country lanes with the snow just a flying off that old pony's feet.

This is the story of a real all-around horse. And I mean all around. In Old Herb's lifetime he did just about everything possible. Harry McKenzie, the owner, let me ride Old Herb just once and I was mighty proud having done so. Heck, I was mighty proud to have stayed on him because had he decided to buck, man oh man, he could buck. He was on his best behaviour, though, and didn't turn a single hair.

Old Herb wasn't much to look at. Sort of a dull sorrel colour topped off by a pair of little pin ears. Built halfway between a Sherman tank and a giraffe with frying pans for feet. What God never gave him in the looks department, he made up for in stamina and heart.

Harry was the best horseman I ever knew in my life. There are lots of top horsemen out there, but in his day, nobody could match him. Put Harry and Old Herb together and bingo, instant team of winners. I think these two were so good at everything because they both were as stubborn as mules and as wily as foxes.

Old Herb loved rounding up wild horses. No matter how gruelling the chase, how wicked the terrain, he was right on their tails. When Harry roped something off him, he didn't care how much weight was on the end of the rope or how hard it fought, he held his own. He could cover many a mile packing his master in the dark of night, always as sure-footed as a cat. When used in the mountains, he never hesitated to swim a rushing river or claw his way up a seemingly impossible mountainside. He never did take kindly to being used as a pack horse but if he had to do it, so be it. He could pack his rider or a pack saddle, loaded to the hilt, all day and all night too. Harry even hooked Old Herb up to his chuckwagon and raced him when he needed him. Old Herb was tough, all right. But all these things weren't what Old Herb really liked to do. Not really, you see, because what Old Herb liked to do was buck. He gloried in smashing someone into the ground. About the only person who could stick on him was Harry, because he was one of the few people just as tough and ornery as the horse.

Now you say how can this be? How can a horse be that good of a saddle horse and a bronc too? Not just a bronc but a rodeo saddle bronc. Harry used to loan him out to a stock contractor when he wasn't using him. When he came out of that chute, you sort of had to feel sorry for the rider because he was going to be meeting up with the ground pretty quick. To add insult to injury, Harry's son Allan, then just a young boy, would trot out into the arena, remove the flank strap, if not already done, swing up and gallop Old Herb out of the arena. Of course he would make sure to miss stepping on the cowboy who might still be nursing his aches and pains in the dust.

As Allan McKenzie grew into a teenager, riding saddle broncs earned him the titles of "National High School Saddle Bronc Champion of North America" and "National Youth Championship" at Fort Worth, Texas in 1983. The best two teachers he ever had were his dad and Old Herb. Herb was used as a practice horse often. I think everyone knew that when the day came when Allan could stay on him for the full ticking of the timer, he had it made. My hat is off to the memory of this great old warrior who was a real "ALL-AROUND HORSE" in every sense. Old Herb, he did it all.

SPEED DEMON

Speed demon, yup, that used to be me, all right. The faster the better. Take class C stock car racing and the ladies powder puff races. Long before each race would start, I would already be shaking, vibrating like the dickens. It was combination of intense fear of what might happen to me and of joyful anticipation to get at it. I would pace back and forth in the infield as the car owner and his personal pit mechanic went over the car one last time for anything wrong. Then on with the safety helmet, climb through the window and get strapped in. And they're off!!!

The oval track, with sharply slanted turns, took great driving skill to just maneuver around it, let alone win on it. My sweaty palms clutching the wheel, only letting go long enough to shift yet again, I gave each and every race my best shot. And I placed second, each and every race. I might have been good, but there was one lady who was better. Had she ever missed a race, I would have won hands down. I was only nineteen years old, and she was in her late twenties and had been racing these races in her husband's car for years. Her experience paid off, or was it because I was terrified of her? If I tried to pass her on the top side in a turn, she would bump me and I would concede that turn to her. If I was foolish enough to try to take her on the low side of a turn, she would bump me hard enough to put me off the track into the infield. So she won every race that year, and I settled for second spot. I loved the straight away on the track because I loved putting the pedal to the metal and getting everything I could from the car. But so did she, I'm afraid.

Now four-wheel drive racing takes more driving skill than speed. Besides that, man is it hard on your truck at these small-town races where monster trucks are unheard of. My poor little four-wheel drive half-tons look better in TV commercials, flying over immense rocky hills and valleys, than in real life. My inner conscious would not let me wreck my own truck, but look out when John let me drive his Ram Charger, bought and fixed up for these races only. Then I did win a few, speed demon that I was, combined with a certain amount of driving skill, put down as "My God, look what that crazy woman is trying to do to my truck, oh my poor truck."

Nothing, though, can beat a flat out horse race. The best horse races in the world have to be the ones run out in a farmer's field or on a small-town rodeo track, no holds barred.

Take Lady and I, for instance. At least a couple of times a summer, we would find someone to run against. The neighbour's children knew Lady by heart. Sensing a race in the coming, she would prance like a real race horse. Blowing and getting herself worked up over it. I would be perched on her broad back, bareback, getting myself worked into a pitch of excitement too. The other children, mounted on their splendid horses, would watch us closely, knowing Lady and I were set to run our hearts out.

Then, just to make things fair, to give the opponents a chance, Lady and I would take up our starting positions several hundred feet from the actual starting line. And they're off!!!

Lady would give me her all. Her great chest filled with power, we thundered ahead. Sad to say, though, the other horses always caught us and flew by us, like we were standing still. Yup, sometimes they gave us a good quarter mile head start in a half mile race, and they still passed us. So maybe Lady wasn't a speed demon, but it was worth a try anyway.

At Oyen's gymkhana events, sometimes there would be a quarter mile straight away race. If I entered one of these, I left Lady at home in my grandfather's pasture. Getting beat bad out in the country with no one watching was bad enough, getting beat in front of the local people would have been much more devastating to my young soul. So I would borrow the neighbour's horse, Spiker. The big grey was no hell to look at, compared to the other racers' sleek, well-bred horses, but they could not touch him in a quarter mile straight away.

The others would dance up to the starting line, carrying their fancy saddles and boastful owners, Spiker and I would walk serenely up to the starting line, me, as always, riding bareback. And they're off!!! The big grey simply exploded from a stand still into the running machine he was. Straight for the finish line, my knees drawn up high, bent over his racing neck, a fistful of mane keeping me in position, we showed the others what racing was meant to be. I think the others always found a reason in their minds why they lost to old Spiker, as they could not or would not admit to themselves or each other that the grey gelding was that much better than their own horses, fancy though they might be.

Chuckwagons & Barrels

I remember one race well, one I did not want to run but had no choice in the matter. A man had given me two chuckwagon ponies to train to ride. He had raced them as long yearlings, then again as two-year-olds. They were good ponies in harness, winning him some pony chuckwagon races, but by their third year they were fully grown and had matured to just over regulation height for racing. As they were too tall to race, he asked me to break them to ride. While he worked at training two replacements for his team of four, I broke them to ride. The bay was soon trained good enough for him to sell. The chestnut, Champ, was my favourite of the pair. I was a bit embarrassed being seen around town on such a small horse, but his willingness to please me more than made up for it. Champ still had the desire to run, so I started him on barrel racing. He was small in size maybe, but big in heart, and as we continued to practise, he was soon beating the recorded times of the Oyen gymkhana club members' racing times, according to his owner's stop watch. Finally the day came when his owner asked me to run him on the barrels at a Sunday's event day. A prospective buyer would be in the stands watching Champ's performance, and if he was really good, the buyer would pay top dollar for him, for his young daughter.

The barrel pattern was always set up in the infield of the round pony chariot and chuckwagon track. Now, let's remember that as a wagon pony, he was used to going around only two barrels, not three, and heading lickety split down that track, to the delight of the screaming crowd. There we were, Champ and I, bareback, about to run the barrel pattern for the first time in public. The crowd of people, the other horses around and the chuckwagon teams being warmed up for their races all had Champ's nerves on edge. For the first time since starting his training, he was fighting his head, wanting to go. And they're off!!! We left the starting position in one giant leap. We went around the first barrel, cutting it so close, my knee almost tipped it over. We drove on to the second barrel, I knew we were making the run in record-breaking time. We cut around the second barrel, dirt flying from his churning hooves. Then things started to go wrong. Champ did not leave that second barrel, striving for the third barrel, no, he came around that second one and lit out down and around the track, running the race of his lifetime. Hitched to chuckwagon or not, he knew what race needed to be won.

I did my best to pull him in, but the more I pulled, the harder he ran. The crowd was on their feet, cheering and clapping as we came around the final turn, and headed for the finish line. I crossed the finish line, my face flaming red with embarrassment. It didn't take me long to slink home, convinced that everyone would never stop laughing at me. Champ's owner still made the sale that day, with the assurance that the horse would learn which race he was running with a little more training. As for me, I didn't hang around the gymkhana days all that much any more. After all, I was just getting too old for such nonsense, at the ripe old age of fifteen.

Finish Line Express

Although I have raised and still raise some mighty fine running quarter horses, I do not believe I have ever owned or ridden a horse with more heart and try, when it comes to running, than Whiskey. She was that one special horse that comes along in a person's life who can do it all and do it right.

I raced her for two years at small-town rodeos, and we never lost a single race against the best in the country. Each time, the other riders and horsemen snickered and laughed at her big head and long mule-like ears. She paddled like crazy, her feet seeming to go every which direction instead of in a straight line. Strong willed and hard to control, she used her nervous energy to leap, prance and act silly when we entered the rodeo grounds. No matter what I did to try to keep her calm before a race, she was always soaked with sweat, making the competition think she would be worn out, tired, before the race even started. They were always wrong about my plain little mare. I placed many a side bet on her, each time the others betting happily against her, thinking the race was lost before it was ever run.

I taught Whiskey just one special thing to help us to win. She was too light in the hind quarters, making her too slow on the first jump away from the starting line. The other horses were mostly quarter-type build, with powerful haunches to propel them forward into high gear when the starting pistol was fired. I taught her that when I brought her into line with the others, she must stand still, and as I softly hissed at her, gather her hind legs under her. She would do so, seeming to be almost trying to sit down on her rump, as she waited for the signal to go. It was an awkward position, but it worked for her. And they're off!!!

I was often told that her first leap carried her as high in the air as it did forward, when she left the starting line, but that first leap usually put us already ahead of the pack. Even if it didn't, she simply out-ran everything on four legs. On a half mile, circle track, so common at rodeos, she left them all behind. I often would start pulling her up before the finish line, to save her, not even worried about the horses catching us from behind.

I would have liked to run her while riding bareback, to lessen the weight on her, but I needed the saddle to even come close to controlling her. I raced her only once as a five-year-old in a field only half a mile in length. It was a grudge match between me and a cowboy who claimed I had only beaten him by default on the track at Rimbey, two years before. He always claimed that I had bumped his mare, throwing her off course, resulting in him coming in second. He harped so often about this that I agreed to race him for a fifty dollar bet in my neigh-bour's level field, which was relatively free of gopher holes. I had not ridden Whiskey that year, and she was out of shape, where his mare was being ridden and raced all the time. I felt that I had beaten him the first time fair and square, but knew also that his sorrel was a worthy opponent against us. So for the first time ever, I decided to run her, riding bare back to get the extra weigh off her back. I knew I had little control over her, riding this way, once she started to run full out. On top of being bareback, and the fact she was awful snorty from not having been ridden for months, the field was fenced with lethal barbed wire. Whiskey was used to a half mile run, with all the time in the world for me to stop afterwards. Now I was going to ask her to win this race in only a quarter of a mile, giving me the final quarter of a mile to stop before hitting the fence line at the end of the land. The cowboy agreed, even shook hands on it, that the race was over, finished, halfway down the field, that no matter who was leading, he must pull his mare in, stop her, so Whiskey would quit running her heart out and allow me to also stop before hitting the wire.

The sorrel mare was nice, but we took the lead from the first jump. She was a length behind us when we hit the middle of the field. The finish line was marked by bright red five gallon buckets. Sitting upright, my legs clutching her sides, I fought to pull her in and stop her. The idiot just kept coming, full out, making no attempt to stop his horse as we had agreed on. There was the fence, coming up fast. Whiskey was still trying to beat the sorrel and had barely slowed her pace. I think I almost ripped her mouth apart, getting her slowed up enough that when she at last saw the wire, she was able to slam on the brakes, skidding right into it, with me flying over her head like a human cannon ball. Everything happened so fast, I was hitting the ground on the other side of the fence and hearing the snapping sound of breaking wire, at the same split second. I rolled over and gained my feet to see it was not Whiskey's chest that hit the wire with so much force. It was the sorrel's. Her rider was also on the ground, and she stood, blood streaming from her torn wound, flowing down from her chest, soaking her front legs and splashing onto the ground. Using my blue jean jacket, wadded up, I applied pressure to the wound, while he went to phone the vet. Once the vet arrived to stitch her up, I gathered up Whiskey's reins and went to leave. Hanging his head in shame, the no–longer bragging cowboy held out the fifty dollar prize money to me. I told him where he could put his blood money, and asked him just one question. "Do you always make agreements, shake hands on it, then become a fool and a liar breaking the agreement?"

I only raced Whiskey once more on a bet. She was by then fifteen years old and slowing up some with age. The race was indeed an unusual one, between us and a competitive dirt bike racer. The race was actually a combination of three short sprints, the distance being only the length between two power poles.

The winner with two out of three wins would take home the money. My mare hadn't run a race in years, but she instantly knew to gather her hind end under her when I hissed in her ear at the starting line. One of the onlookers would beep his truck horn for the sprint to begin. At the sound of the horn, she shot up and forward as she had done so many years before. The dirt bike also rearing in the air on its hind tire. We won easily. Round number two. She was slower this time on the take off, the bike and her, side by side to the end. The cheering spectators ruled this one to the dirt bike. The third round, she covered many feet with an unbelievable take off, putting us ahead for the entire short run. This time I pocketed the money, grinning like the Cheshire Cat. Whiskey blew and stomped, wondering what kind of race this was supposed to be. Forgetting her age, she danced and pranced the mile home, hoping for a real race like in the good old days.

Racing has long been known as the sport of kings. And who wouldn't feel like a king or queen, standing at track side and watching your own race horse crossing the finish line first? Whether one of my horses wins or not, I am captured forever by these born and bred running machines as they put their heart and soul into the race. If I have raised them from birth, watched them grow from fuzzy babies to sleek young adults and then had the chance to see them race, it makes all the money spent on them well worthwhile. It is these horses who have managed to help keep me broke, my bank account nil, for the last few years. But let me have just one win out of many races, and suddenly it is all worthwhile once again. More than once, I have given up on racing horses, saying to myself that I cannot afford it, but always comes the day when I have to buy just one brood mare or just one weanling and start dreaming all over again. Such is the life of a speed demon such as I.

STALLIONS

Stallions should not be all classed together as crazed sex maniacs. A stallion, handled with diplomacy, can be as gentle to work with as any gelding. As long as his handler keeps in mind that his hormones rule his head when around cycling mares and other male horses, he can be controlled using a little bit of sense on the person's part. I have worked with and ridden many stallions over the years. As long as they knew that I was the boss, they behaved themselves. Let one learn that he can walk all over top of you, and you suddenly are going to have a mighty big problem on your hands. Country people have loads of respect for bulls on the prod but seem sometimes to forget that a stallion can be twice as dangerous as a bull if he goes on the fight.

Take Diago for instance. I was only fifteen years old and he was the first young stallion I had owned. I was naive enough to believe Diago loved me, and would obey my every command as the other horses did. He was about a year and a half old when he taught me a lesson in stallion behaviour. I opened the pasture gate, and was leading him by a handful of his long mane to water as I did every day. Suddenly his head came up, his ears rigidly at attention, listening to something in the far distance. With a squeal, he broke away from me and loped away. Always before, if I hollered at him to whoa, he would, and stand patiently for me to catch him. This time he ignored me. Running to the garage, I grabbed a halter and lead rope and followed him on foot. He rapidly out distanced me, but by now I knew where he was headed. Three-quarters of a mile away was a small pasture full of ponies.

Out of breath, I caught up to him at the ponies' fence, but Diago was ignoring my verbal commands to whoa, so I could halter him. He was young maybe, but a male, as he traded bites and kicks through the fence with the pony stallion on the other side. Suddenly, he reared up, his front hooves coming down over top of the fence, catching the other stallion on top of the head. His hoof shaved the ear off the pony, as slick as a knife blade. Seeing the ear hanging there was sickening to me. As Diago pulled his trapped front legs free from the top of the fence, I managed to get his halter on and force him away from the fence. Never before had he bit me, but he promptly took a chunk out of my arm. This was no longer a gentle young horse, this was an angry stallion, on the fight. It was my first lesson in dealing with stallions, and not one I ever forgot.

A mare in heat attracts a stallion like bees to honey. Take Bingo for instance. He too was only a year and a half old. When one of my mares came in heat, I locked this pretty sorrel Arab colt in a box stall in the barn because he was at my place to be started in training, not to breed mares. I do not know how Bingo did it, but he managed to jump through a barn window, high up and half his size to get to that mare and breed her. He was skinned up some, but he had been determined to do what his hormones told him had to be done.

Poco was a satiny black quarter horse stallion, two years old, and coming good in his initial training. I planned on finishing his training and selling him as a broke horse and also a stallion prospect as he had good blood lines. He was easy to work with, until a mare would come into heat out in the pasture. Then teaching Poco anything at all was entirely out of the question. Even though the mares were separated by two fences, he could still see them and smell them. He would snort, whinny, prance, leap in the air, anything but listen to me. Only by gelding him was he to become the fine horse he was meant to be. As uncontrollable as he was around mares, at only two years old, he would have matured into an even harder to control breeding stallion.

My fine quarter horse stallion, Rocky Tom Cat, was a saint from day one. He had one of the sweetest dispositions of any stallion I owned or trained. His training was so easily accomplished, you would have sworn he was born trained already. The first day I saddled him, I rode him without him having a care in the world. By the forth or fifth ride, I rounded up a herd of old brood mares on him, and he never let on he was a stallion. After two weeks of riding, I chased and passed a running white-tailed buck on him, just for the heck of it, and he never turned a hair.

In the breeding shed, he was as proper as an English gentleman, going about his business without as much as a snort out of him. He was a beauty to handle at all times, proving once again to me, that not all stallions are accidents waiting to happen.

Squealer was sixteen hands high, a black thoroughbred stallion I owned. He was twelve years old when I purchased him. He had been pasture bred all his life, and a kitten around mares. I used him as a stallion in his first year with me, and then gelded him, so he could be used as a riding horse, with none of the worries about riding a stallion on trail rides with strange horses around. Had he been left a stallion, he would have ended up at the slaughterhouse, as nobody wanted him for breeding anymore and most buyers shy away from older stallions. All stallions as they mature develop a distinctly masculine voice, and this was what gave Squealer his name. I never heard or owned a stallion who could squeal as loudly and aggressively as he could. One bellow out of him, and your hair stood on end. You could hear him a mile from the house when he let loose. Even after being gelded for years, he never lost his squeal. He could be tied to a post, sleeping in the sun, and every so often, he would rouse himself, fill his throat with air and let a tremendous squeal out. It was the one thing he never quit doing, stallion or no stallion.

A stout dun quarter horse stallion I used for breeding was an idiot when it came to mares. He was afraid of mares, petrified they were going to hurt him. Hand breeding a stallion like this can be a real pain. As I led him up to a mare, he would act like a sex-starved jerk, until he was close to the mare. Then he would turn from being a macho man into a small boy who thought he should hide behind me. Well, convincing him it was okay with me and the mare if he wanted to have some fun could take hours. As dangerous as it sounds, that big horse and I developed a system, which enabled the job at hand to get done. He absolutely refused to look at the mare, let alone touch his muzzle to her, instead he would concentrate his attention on my lower right leg. He would nuzzle my leg from my boot up to my knee, running his teeth up and down without actually biting me until he was ready to breed the mare. Then quickly he would do so, then get himself away from her and turn to me for a treat and a pat on the neck. For safety sake, I kept my lower leg well padded with wrap-around bandages, but he never did take a chunk out of me. Different, but it worked for him and that's all that mattered to me.

Savage Attack

I only witnessed one all-out stallion fight in my life. The savage battle was horrible to see, two magnificent stallions, tearing chunks out of each other, their battling hooves smashing tissue and bone. I never want to see it again, ever.

I was working on a horse ranch one summer, where the herd stallion was a big chestnut, a splendid creature about nine years old. One morning at the breakfast table the owner of the ranch informed the ranch foreman and me that she had sold Big Red to another rancher. She was of the age where she no longer wanted to raise colts and the other rancher always liked the stallion, so she sold him. The plan was for me to catch Big Red and lead him from the back of the truck, across country to the other fellow's ranch. With the foreman driving, and me leading him, the stallion covered the seven or eight miles at a ground covering trot. The foreman kept his eyes open for one of the many free roaming herds on the sections of open land. At last we came upon a herd of about fifteen mares. The only trouble was, the mares belonged to a mature Appaloosa stallion, who on catching sight of us, started working himself into a rage immediately.

I told the foreman that we should keep going until we found a bunch of mares with no lead stallion, but he told me to release Big Red. Red was tired from the fast trip and choose to ignore the other stallion and mares. First he went to get a drink of water from a nearby dugout. While he was off guard, his nose buried in the water, the Appy shot down the bank and laid into him. Red scrambled up the bank and loped away, until the Appy turned back to his mares. Then poor Red tried to graze, minding his own business. The enraged Appy was having none of it, he wanted the chestnut right out of his territory. Squalling like a male lion, he lunged into Red, knocking him sideways with his chest and slashing front feet. Red had had enough. With a scream of his own, he met the Appy's attack head on. Their great gaping jaws and wicked yellow teeth tore chunks of hide from each other's necks and backs. They stood on their hind legs, front legs wrapped around each other like two wrestlers intent on throwing each other to the ground. The battle raged on, smashing kicks in each other's ribs from powerful hind legs. Both of them had blood streaking down their fine coats as they fought for supremacy. Red was tiring, taking the savage blows more now than he was able to deliver. Slowly, he lost ground, beaten back by the Appy. With another mighty lunge, the Appaloosa smashed him to the ground. Red was unable to rise, the other stallion actually kneeling on top of him, chewing on his neck, bloody foam covering his lips.

I begged the foreman to use the truck to break up the fight. Finally he put the truck in gear and roared ahead, blaring on his horn. The Appy, on seeing the truck barrelling towards him, turned and left the downed Red. The Appy quickly rounded up his mares and drove them over a hill and out of sight. Big Red struggled to his feet and limped away in the opposite direction from the other stallion and his mares. I wanted to catch Red and bring him home to the ranch to doctor his massive wounds, but the foreman said I was nothing but a bleeding heart and Red would have to fend for himself. Maybe that is the way it is done on these big cattle and horse ranches, but I was very upset. I am a lot older and wiser now than I was then, and a hundred times more outspoken. Now, I would never have allowed myself to be party to such cruelty, putting a strange stallion in another stallion's territory and watching them try to kill each other.

Experience has also taught me that a stallion is a massive hunk of deadly danger when he fights with not only another horse, but a puny human too. I personally know people who have been savaged by an angry, out-of-control stallion, some-times to the point of death.

One man had his ear bitten off by his gentle baby, who proved no stallion is a pet. Another man lost most of his cheek by letting his stallion kiss him on the face. Quite a kiss, all right. One woman used to wrap her arms around her stallion's head and cuddle him, until the day he bit her right breast off. A horse trainer beat on his stallion once too often, until the horse turned on him and put him in the hospital for six months and left him crippled for life. A neighbour who would not listen to me when I told him his pretty stallion was spoiled and had become a dangerous beast, barely survived being attacked and thrown around the corral like a rag doll.

CATCH THEM RIGHT

I was yanked from sleep one morning by the shrill whistle of my stallion. My mind was confused, my thinking groggy. Three Kits, nicknamed Skiddor, was not much for hollering to start with, but something else wasn't right about the whinny. Just about then, I heard a horse plunging through the snow past my bedroom window. That was it. What was wrong was that the noise had come from my front yard, not his pasture. Skiddor was on the loose. I have neighbours with horses who wouldn't be too happy to wake up with my stallion in their yards, messing with their own horses. My feet hit the floor at a dead run as I skidded around the house getting dressed as quickly as possible. Grabbing his halter hanging in the porch, I was out the door. Skiddor flashed past me, bucking and playing in the deep snow on the lawn. He had himself worked into a fit of excitement with all this newfound freedom. He was already soaked with sweat, steaming in the frigid cold.

One glance at his fence told me how he had gained freedom. He was sixteen hands tall, and the unusual amount of heavy snowfall that just never seemed to quit coming had allowed him to simply walk up and over a huge drift almost covering the north fence line.

Skiddor can be a big, and at that height and weight, I mean a big handful to handle when he's overly excited. But at the same time, he was one of my horses and well trained in my method of catching any horse that belongs to me. I walked straight towards him, halter curled over my arm, in plain sight. When I was close enough to the playing stallion, I simply said in a loud, no nonsense word, WHOA!! He froze into a statue, facing me, ears forward, eyes on nothing but me. I stepped up to his left shoulder, shook out the nose band of his halter and held it out. He dropped his nose through that nose band and stood perfectly still while I buckled the throat latch around his neck. He led beside my right shoulder, properly, back through a gate into a pen. The second I released him, he shot up into air with a joyful leap, then went bucking and kicking across the pen. What he did before I caught him and what he did after I released him, I don't care about. What I care about is that he is well halter broke. I do not consider a horse well halter broke unless you can catch them, anywhere, anytime, under any circumstances.

I dislike a hard-to-catch horse with a passion. I do not know anything more irritating than not being able to catch a horse. I think I would prefer to be bucked off and stepped on, rather than have to chase a horse, only to have it spin away from me at the last second. Or to have to hide the halter and rope somehow, while you sweet-talk your way up to the horse with a bucket of oats. It has to be a mighty good horse to last on my premises if he has the habit of being hard to catch, I dislike it that much.

I have never raised a single colt from birth, and trained him myself, that could not be walked up to in the pasture and caught. Any horse I've ever bought that was young enough to train, or in many cases retrain in the catching department, can be caught anywhere, anytime. Sure, older, mature horses who have gotten away with the habit for years can be difficult to train to be caught, but even a lot of them soon learn it's best to drop their nose down through the nose band on the halter, and stand still for it to be done up.

Consistency is the answer to teaching a horse to be caught. Horses learn through repetition. I also use my voice a great deal in training them. Every one of my horses knows when he or she has made me angry by the tone of my voice. They all know when I am pleased by the quiet, silly things I say to them.

Skiddor will practically turn himself into a kitten the second he knows he's pleased me by the sound of my voice. If he's being a jerk, throwing his weight around, he knows when he has pushed me too far. When I start to snarl at him, he listens up.

I never try to sneak up on a horse I want to catch. Right away the horse knows something is up, and is more apt to move away. I don't corner them to catch them, I walk up to them head on. They know. And I do everything the same, every time. Repetition, repetition.

I walk straight to their heads, and when I'm close, I say whoa, in a no-nonsense tone. My horses know what whoa means and stand still, because they know if they turn away, or turn their rumps, I'm going to get mad and really holler at them. They don't like that. I don't hide the rope and halter. It's right there so they can see it and know they are meant to be caught. And I do not try to flip the rope around their necks first, before the halter. Why? If you have halter broke them properly in the first place, why do you think you have to catch them now, improperly? I stand beside their left neck and shoulder, open the nose band of the halter up and they drop their nose through it, and stand still for it to be done up. Why? Because I have taught them that only after, and I mean only after, their nose is in the halter, do they get a treat from my pocket or a mouthful of oats. A couple of my horses now will barely give me time to hold the halter open for them to put their nose in it, because they want the treat or bite of oats so bad. They are poking their noses down into my hands, saying, "Hurry up, mom, get that halter on me, what's the slow up here." They are well halter broke.

Hard-to-catch horses are usually leery about being caught in a corral too. You know the type. The second you go to close the gate, they leap into action, beating you to it and out to freedom. I see people go to great lengths to sneak around the barns and trees to beat these hard-to-catch horses to the gates and get them closed, to trap the horse inside. These horses are not stupid. They know when the gate gets closed. Chances are something is about to happen to them, which they aren't going to like. They are going to get caught, maybe rode hard, maybe be given a needle or something.

With my horses, I can't keep them out of my corrals. I find myself making mad dashes for the gate to get it closed, to keep them out sometimes. They usually beat me to the gate and swarm inside. Now, I have to shoo them out, the gates wide open. I'm waving my arms, hollering and jumping up and down, and they suddenly are blind. They madly race around on the inside, after all mom's upset, but they can't see the open gate to make their great escape.

Why? Because they get caught in the pasture as much as the corrals so they are not afraid of being trapped in it. They get saddled wherever I feel like saddling them for that hard ride, not just in the corral. If the vet is coming or the farrier, they get treated anywhere on my property, not just the corral, so they have no fear of being trapped in it. Rather they like it, because if they hang around, they might get lucky and get some extra munchies while in it. Horses have brains too, you know.

My final secret to training horses to be easy to catch was taught to me many years ago, and I've found it to be effective most of the time. When I handle a horse, broke or not, I am continually touching them everywhere on their bodies, getting them used to the feel of my hands. I teach them to be caught by their chests. As soon as they are used to my hands on their chests, I use a hold, squeeze, release method on the loose skin in the centre of their chests to teach them they are caught and not to resist.

They learn this method quickly and never seem to forget it. Standing on their left side, I gather up a fold of skin in my hand. The second they go to move ahead, I apply a slight squeeze. This stops their forward motion. Next they will try to turn away from me, at which time I apply a mild form of twitch, by twisting the skin and holding it firmly. The horse feels caught and often his only recourse is to then attempt to escape by backing up, away from the pressure. I go with him as he backs, keeping the pressure on, until he stops. The second he stops, I release the squeeze technique and remain holding only the loose skin. Few horses will ever figure out that they are not in some way firmly caught. Once trained this way, it is a very handy way to catch a loose horse, perhaps while someone goes for a halter, or until I can do what needs to be done with him. I have retrained many seemingly impossible hard–to–catch horses with this method. They are wise in all ways of people sneaking ropes around their necks or halters over their noses, often standing still until the very last second to break away from you and trot away. They don't even really see your hand coming until it is already holding their chests. It is a good method that works quite well.

A LETTER HOME

This is the letter I wrote to my loving parents in September 1992. It is filled with the great beauty of nature at its best in the northern region of Saskatchewan's timberline. It also tells the story of a five–year–old mare who had a mind of her own.

Dear Mom and Dad;

I thought about writing this sort of diary–letter combination to you about my week's holiday, instead of just telling you over the phone. I hope it proves interesting. It will be my first true blue holiday I've taken in many years.

MONDAY–DAY ONE

I got everything loaded, including luggage, food, dog and horse at about three p.m. and headed out. My trailer pulled good at fifty–five m.p.h. but started to sway after that. I arrived at about six p.m. because I stopped twice to let Blaze do his puppy duties and to check on my mare, Fancy. She sweated up some but rode quite well actually. I arrived at the empty fishing and hunting lodge to find no heat, no water and a Ridgeling (when he was gelded, they left one testicle in him, which makes a horse twice as silly and unpredictable as a whole stallion) running loose in the yard. I managed to unload Fancy and get her into the only corral, about three hundred yards away, no fun thing to do with this snot–nosed Ridgeling and other horses charging around us. I felt like loading up and heading back home but decided to tough it out and head back the next morning.

Across the yard a young couple live, and the Mrs. promised her husband would come over later and fix the furnace and turn the water on. He came over later but the furnace was shot and he couldn't turn on the water because of a bad leak in one of the bathrooms. (No kidding a bad leak, the carpets went squish, squish where ever you walked.) Thank heavens for wood stoves in porches. Another friendly neighbour from across Fowler Lake showed me how to run the old wood stove, even helping me gather wood after dark (only after I repeatedly told him, no thank you, I don't wish to stay with you in your cozy little cabin built for two). This camp, Hunt Creek Lodge, sleeps up to fourteen people with some comfortable–looking beds and rooms, but I elected to stay in the not–so–nice and comfy room right off the porch where the heat was coming from the stove. Blaze and I got all tucked in and, except for getting up ten times during the night to refuel the stove and let Blaze do his puppy duties, got some sleep.

TUESDAY–DAY TWO

Blaze looks dog–gone happy, but my nose is stuffed up and

I'm lacking my usual eight hours of non-stop sleep, but hey, today is another day. The dog and I sit down to a hardy breakfast of fried prem and greasy eggs. Blaze really does have good table manners except for the constant drooling out of both sides of his mouth. Now tell me please, how do you saddle a five-year-old mare with a questionable disposition, in a yard full of strange horses, and let's not forget the Ridgeling shall we? Blaze helped a lot with his hackles up and four-month-old puppy bark, and it kept all the horses at bay except for (you guessed it) the Ridgeling. My friend Robert is an owner of this place, and only lives a couple of miles away, so I load the kicking, squealing, fourteen hundred pounds of mad mare on the trailer and headed for his place. Robert doesn't know it yet, but my horse is coming to live at his place. Robert runs a large cattle operation, so he has corrals galore. In fact, it looks like a smaller version of the old Calgary stockyards. Lots of empty corrals to keep Fancy in, as I've decided to stay one more night if possible.

Now it's time to go riding. Before deciding to bring Fancy on this little get away holiday, I was well aware that she needed lots of riding and lots of work done on her. Number one, she is not two, not three, but five years old and very set in her ways. Number two, she is spoiled rotten. Hold it, hold it, hold it!!! It's not all my fault. She has been spoiled like this since she was a filly, not by me, but by the people who boarded her dam and her from the time she was born, until I came home from working in the Great White North. I love horses but if I remember correctly, I had to get rough with her when I first got to handle her as a weanling. The girls who work as grooms and all around help on the horse farm had fallen in love with her, so they taught her cute little tricks, like rearing up and play fighting on command. When she bit them, they let her get away with it, when she walked all over them, they just gave her another treat. I guess they never looked to the future when she would be a full-grown horse, not a tiny filly, still trying to dominate us human beings with her manmade bad habits. I may spoil my animals with love to a certain extent, but I've never liked Fancy's attitude that everyone was put on God's green earth just for her pleasure (or to abuse, as she sees fit). I've never even figured out why I kept her, maybe because in all my years of raising top horses with the best blood lines, she was probably the best. She has picture–perfect looks and build, good enough to knock the socks off horse people who know what a top horse is really supposed to look like. Hey it's my story, okay.

Number three, not only is she five years old, spoiled, with an attitude problem, quick on her feet (cat–like), and built like a tank (giving her above–average strength), but worst of all, she's SMART, as in I truly believe some animals do really have the power to think, regardless of what all the books say. I've read entire articles on the matter, and they all say something like "...an animal such as a dog or horse cannot reason, does not in actual fact, have the power to think, but only reacts to basic stimuli and hereditary instinct." Horse punky! This mare has me worried because I think she can actually THINK. This ride goes fairly well, as I rode her enough back home to take the buck out of her, a good thing too, as she is such a strong powerhouse that she really snaps my neck and makes my back ache when she bucks. She still persists with her habit of tossing her head and angrily striking out with her front feet, something she does naturally running loose in the pasture too. The bit fits her properly and I've checked her teeth and know they are okay, but she seems to want to start rearing when she throws her head and strikes out at nothing with her front feet. She could easily resort to rearing, in order to evade the bit and anything she does not want to do. All in all, the ride went well but I feel she may have the upper hand still, some way? Back at the lodge, I find I can have water, yes, even hot water, but the leak isn't entirely fixed and the carpets still go squish, squish. Ah well, the scenery is beautiful, and all around me, inside, are stuffed deer, bear, fox, badger, great horned owl, wood grouse, beaver, wolf, etc. You did notice, I said inside the camp and stuffed didn't you? I never ran across any live wildlife today.

WEDNESDAY–DAY THREE

Blaze and I slept better last night. I finally figured out how to run the damper on the stove pipe and the funny wheel on the front of the stove to give the fire less oxygen so that I only had to cram it full of birch and let Blaze out to do his puppy duties twice during the night. I also figured out my breakfast of fried prem and greasy eggs went a lot smoother with the dog outside eating his own breakfast on the front steps. I'm fed and watered, Blaze is fed and watered, Fancy is fed and watered, so it's time to go riding. The scenery is once again majestic in all its glory. The trees are rich with their fall coats of golden tones. The air is crisp and clean. The lakes shine, misty blue. Mother Nature is at her best, glimpses of wildlife partially hidden in her foliage. HOW IN THE WORLD I HAD TIME TO SEE ANY OF THESE THINGS, I'LL NEVER KNOW! Fancy has gone completely nuts. I want to go north, she rears. I want to go south, she rears. I want to turn right, she rears. I want to turn left, she rears. I want to stop and gather my wits, and she rears. I get off and tie her head around to the back D ring on the saddle. She still won't turn to the pressure on the reins. She heads off by side–stepping with her head cranked around. I get back on and the fight is on again. The battle is all one–sided. I lose. I get off and find a club, a small club, as I'm not really into animal cruelty, and attempt to win the next round of this fight. She is not a normal horse, she is not trying to pull away, to escape punishment, to run for her life, she is fighting back, front feet flashing past my head, ears pinned back, teeth bared. The club wins round two.

Shaking like a leaf from my adrenaline rush, I lead the slightly more respectful mare back to Robert's ranch. At home, I have a large tack shed full of racks of training devices, which could help me teach this mare that rearing is an unacceptable behaviour. I go into the strange barn, there is nothing there except for an old dust–covered wire nose band tie–down. I tie her head down to the cinch between her front legs and walk away. I'm mad, she's mad, and the battle is far from over. Two hours later, I return. I'm calm and guess what, so is Fancy. She has fought the rigging until her nose was sore and she had figured out that maybe, just maybe, the boss of this outfit is me, not her. I get back on and go for a short, half–hour ride. Now remember, I don't believe in tie–downs, even though they have their place in barrel racing, calf roping, steer wrestling, etc., to keep a horse's head down and keep control of a horse forced to run full out for a short distance, then have to abruptly stop, without losing it mentally, so to speak. A properly adjusted tie–down can be a training tool that goes a long way. A tie–down as short as I have it right now is both cruel and dangerous. On level ground, maybe not too bad. The horse, generally speaking, with a tie–down on, cannot rear high enough to fall backwards, and at the right adjustment the tie–down still allows the horse to use his head and neck for balance. But I'm not riding on level ground and Fancy is used to being able to throw her head and neck all over the place. Somehow we survive the ride with the mare getting more used to having her head tossing restricted and with the combination of keeping her moving forward and the tie–down, she does not attempt to rear much. I win round three.

Blaze and I get tucked in tonight, everything is cozy and warm, except I'm slightly bothered by the horrible stink of my puppy because he spent his day rolling and chewing happily on last fall's abundance of putrid big game hides and guts. Stink or what, phew!

THURSDAY–DAY FOUR

I'm getting tired of canned, fried prem and greasy eggs for breakfast, but that's all I brought with me. A juicy steak right now would look pretty inviting. Part of me sees Fancy's rippling, muscled hind quarters as a juicy steak for a French or Belgian person who eats a lot of horsemeat, but let's try again, shall we?

I saddle up, this time I slack off the tight tie–down some to give her a bit more comfort, but still give me some control over her. She tries to fight me about two miles out, but she either won't or can't rear and suddenly I can start to enjoy such a splendid mount; her smooth gaits, and excellent style of travelling when she decides to just behave herself. She does well, and we cover a lot of beautiful northern bush country, as if we belong in whole to this wilderness we ride through. After three hours of riding, I have made a circle, bringing me back to Robert's place. She has sort of obeyed me and I consider her to be working well under the circumstances. I cool her out, then unsaddle her and turn my back for just a second.

Her teeth graze my shoulder and in the same motion she throws her head violently sideways like she has been doing since birth (often resulting in stitches to her noggin when she connects with a post or barn wall). She manages to knock my hat off, glasses off, and thank God I have my own teeth, or they would probably be lying on the ground too. What worries me isn't the fact my glasses are buried in a fresh pile of horse dung, what worries me is I thought I had won this round of the fight and she just tried to bite me. Oh well, there is always tomorrow.

FRIDAY–DAY FIVE

Everything is so peaceful out here in the woods this morning. I had a really good sleep too, because Blaze slept under the bed instead of on it. Better yet, I finally ran out of prem so I didn't have to eat it for breakfast. I saddled Fancy up in the crisp, forest–scented air and adjusted her tie–down to the correct position for any horse forced to wear one. On I get and away we go. Forty–five seconds later, she realizes, hey man, I can rear again because my nose isn't tied down as tight anymore. The battle is on again. I should, at this point, tell you that, NO, she is not barn sour. A barn sour horse is hell to ride because all they want to do is go back to their buddies at the nice comfortable barn. She couldn't care less about the other horses or the barn itself, she doesn't ever mind being ridden. Fancy just darn well wants to go in her chosen direction, not mine.

For once she concedes the round to me, and we head out. For a green horse, she sure can cover the ground and she is full of vim and vigour, never seeming to tire. We sail along for about four or five miles, finally getting to see this area of Saskatchewan's abundant wildlife, in the flesh. Scatterings of white-tailed deer leap around us in the trees and bush, bordering the cut line we are on, but my mare takes no notice of them. We pass through an area where bear have been very recently (fresh bear droppings in two spots) she snorts and trots on. A yearling moose stands motionless, as we flow past. All is going well. Here comes another gate to open. Hey this one is electric, the battery-operated charger ticking away.

I step off and reach for the rubber hand hold on it, to open it. Here is where things become interesting. Remember me telling you that I rarely have my electric fence turned on at home and how Fancy has got in the habit of grabbing the top wire in her teeth, pulling back on it, then letting go to hear it go PING, when it snaps back? I think she likes the noise it makes and finds this an amusing pastime. You guess it!! She grabs this top wire, goes straight in the air, whirls, slams into the barbed wire fence to her left, whirls again, jerks the reins out of my hand and lights out at a dead run. The way she is travelling flat out, you would think she's running the Kentucky Derby. I'm standing there, watching her disappear and thinking about the long walk home. What is this? She's turning and whistling in alarm, like a wild horse warning others of danger. Now she spots me and she's coming back to me at a fear-crazed run. She slides to a stop with her shoulder against my chest, her head over my shoulder, and I feel like just maybe I could get to like this mare all over again. I check out the eight-inch gash on her chest, where she whirled into the barbed wire, and find out that for all the blood dripping out of it, it's really only a minor cut. I lead her for half a mile, until she calms down enough for me to get back on and head out again. Altogether we cover about twelve to fourteen miles with Fancy working like an old broke horse for the last few miles. Her coming back to me like she did makes me like her a whole lot more today.

SATURDAY–DAY SIX

I awake to the rustle of a grey squirrel zipping up and down the outside wall. He peers in at me, eyes bright buttons, nose twitching, then he's gone. Waiting for the coffee to boil, I look out the kitchen window and watch a fawn nibbling daintily on the grass in the yard. Before today is over, I will see a dozen white–tailed deer, an eagle and a big old cow moose who appeared totally unafraid as we passed by. Remember how yesterday went with Fancy? The first part of the ride was torment, with the last few miles like riding an old broke horse. Well, today was just the opposite sequence. And it was a long, long ride today. Why? Because I spent a good part of it lost, that's why. How many miles I covered, I have no idea because in the brush, I could not judge distance. I know it was over fifteen, but how many over, I have no idea. Fancy, unlike yesterday's bad start and good ending, reversed things today. For all except the last three–quarters of a mile, she worked like a pro. The last short distance was a nightmare. As tired and sweaty as she was, I don't understand it, especially since she had to have known that home was just ahead of her. She reared, she attempted to buck, she even tried to throw herself on purpose. In that last little ways, she went from wet with sweat, to dripping with white lather. We made it though. I cooled her out, unsaddled her and washed her down with buckets of water and a towel. After all, them there French and Belgians like their horsemeat clean, right?

SUNDAY–DAY SEVEN

I can't believe my week is up already. It seems like I just got here, and it's time to pack it in. I don't want to go now. I've enjoyed the solitude of this quiet existence. I don't know if I want to go back to the chaotic life of phones ringing, TVs and radios blaring, and people all around me.

The wind comes up with unusual force, howling and snarl–ing. A tall, old black poplar in the yard snaps and falls off and crashes down, inches from the lodge. Then the rain starts. It looks like I couldn't have rode today anyway. After cleaning camp, I go to load Fancy. The wind is so strong the trailer is sitting there, rocking on its own. Fancy only gets in after I tell her the main ingredients of canned dogfood. Blaze looks at her and licks his chops, yummy, dinner. I end up using twice the gas getting home because of fighting the wind all the way. Well, my house is still standing. The phone is ringing even as I unlock the door. Yup, I'm home, back in the real world. I hope you enjoyed this letter Mom and Dad. Now, goodnight folks.

With thirty more days of hard riding at home, Fancy broke out rather nicely. Since she is not for sale, I don't have to worry about anyone else riding her anyway. I have to stay on my toes to handle her, even now, but she, Blaze and I will always have our wilderness holiday to remember. Thanks to Hunt Creek Lodge, on Fowler Lake.

BROKEN BONES

A masochist is someone who derives pleasure from pain or humiliation. Trust me, I'm not that weird. Some people are nothing but accidents waiting to happen. That's not my problem. I'm convinced that my problem is my heritage. I am English, Irish and Scottish. From my English bloodlines, I get that damnable pride, where you must never give up, no matter the circumstances. From the Irish, I get that streak of "So you want to fight me, okay horse, let's fight it out!" From my Scots blood comes my stubbornness, where one must ignore pain and even knowing you're going to be hurt again, keep going.

Now that I'm older, I've finally figured out how to overcome my heritage. Sell the horse. Let somebody younger handle the rank ones, the spoiled ones and the never going to amount to a hill of beans ones. Since I figured this out, I haven't broke a single bone, so it must work.

I was only thirteen years old when a horse made mincemeat out of my back. I was leading a pinto gelding past a grain auger, walking in front of him, instead of beside him, after all he was a kid's pony, so he would never hurt anybody, right? One of my brothers was sitting up on the top rail of the fence behind us and when he decided to jump down, boom, he landed on a sheet of plywood lying on the ground. The noise of his landing sent that pinto right over top of me in one lunge. As he was jumping straight into the grain auger, he placed his hind foot right in the middle of my back, and pivoted on it to miss the auger. The resulting injury has left me with a permanently painful back condition. I never led a horse improperly again, gentle or not.

When I was about fifteen years old, a friend of a friend asked me to catch his horse for him. The mare was in a small pasture, about twenty acres or so, and had evaded capture all spring. She wouldn't be lured by buckets of oats and had access to a slough for water, so she need not enter the corrals for a drink. They couldn't run her in with a truck because a deep coulee ran down the centre of the pasture, so, as soon as she saw a vehicle coming, she would play hard to get by going up and down that coulee, where no one could follow. Chasing her on horseback had basically the same results, a rider had to slow his saddle horse, to go down those steep banks, by the time he got to the bottom, she would already be up the other side, having a great time. Since her owner said he would pay a good price for her capture, I accepted the challenge. Armed with her bridle and a can of oats, I arrived at her private domain early on a Sunday morning. My plan was to walk her down, never to chase her, just keep quietly walking after her.

I was young, strong and had all day. She wasn't frightened of me in the least, but had no intention of coming for oats. So I followed her, she grazed on ahead of me, staying just out of my reach. All morning this kept on. Around and around, up and down the coulee, I followed her, walking quietly, talking quietly. By the middle of the afternoon, I had taken to kneeling down and drinking the same slough water, she did. She was tired of this new game and every minute was allowing me closer and closer, turning her ears to the sound of the rattle of the oats in the can. Finally she stopped, turned and faced me. I allowed her a bite of the oats, then slipped the bit in her mouth and the straps over her ears. She was caught. The corral was within sight but I was plumb tuckered out, so rather than walking one more step, I jumped up on her bareback. She was a well-broke mare but hadn't been ridden since early autumn before. Well broke or not, she started buck jumping, firing out with her hind legs. They threw me up onto her withers, out of position. My hold tightened on the reins, violently she threw her head back. Bang, the top of her head connected with my nose. I rode that mare to the corral, blood pouring out of my nostrils, and my nose sitting off to one side. A month later, her owner phoned to say she had escaped from the corral and did I want to earn some money catching her again. For all I know she could have grown old and died out there because I politely said no.

At sixteen years old, I managed to get hurt again. After weeks of riding broncs all summer long, getting bucked off, stepped on, kicked and bitten, I had to pull a silly stunt, sort of showing off, you might say. One of the horses I hadn't got around to working with on the ranch where I was employed was a mutton–headed little Shetland. He was probably about four or five years old and had never even felt a rope on him. Two boys and I drew straws to see who would buck him out the chute, bare–back, for something to do on a lazy afternoon. I won the short straw, and swaggered over to the chute, knowing I was showing off but loving the attention. That chute was horse–sized, not pony–sized, and the Shetland was roaring back and forth pretty good in all that space. Now, an adult cannot stay on a midget horse anyway. All the midget has to do is put his head down and off you go over top where his ears used to be when his head was up. Knowing this, I told the boys to open the gate the second I got on him, since I didn't want to fall off him while he was able to jump backwards and forwards in that big chute. I no sooner got my legs wrapped around his belly and the gate open. He didn't buck out of that chute like he was supposed to, so I could fall off in the open, instead he whirled and tried to lunge back into and over the back side of the chute. My right knee was rammed against the big steel gate hinge. I can still hear the cracking noise in my mind to this day. I will always have trouble going up and down stairs or steep inclines with what's left of my knee cap. When ever I get tired, I limp, and dancing has always been more pain than pleasure. Ponies don't have to be big to teach big lessons.

A big bay gelding of mine taught me another lesson. He was at that time my favourite saddle horse and not for sale, like all the rest were. He had been raised from birth by me and was always a pet. He had been easy to train and even though I rode him hard, he remained more of a friend than just another horse. One cold winter day, I needed a saddle horse in a hurry, so I hollered at the bay to come for his oats. He came straight to the saddling shed and dropped his head to munch on the pile of grain I had poured on the ground for him. I had grown lazy working with him, and often saddled him up without first haltering him for control. Being in a hurry, I grabbed a saddle blanket and stepping up to him, told him to whoa and threw the blanket on his back. Well, there was some ice crystals cling-ing to the hair on his back, and when that heavy pad landed on them, they went snap, crackle, pop. He spun so fast, I never had a chance to move. Wham, both his hind feet hit me at the same time. The force of the kick lifted me up and actually threw me right over top a horse–drawn cultivator parked next to the shed. I never did go riding that day, or for awhile afterwards either. Not with two broken ribs. Now I always have a halter, rope or bridle on the gentlest horse when I saddle up.

A man contacted me one day with a problem he hoped I could rectify for him. Seems he had this well–bred mare with the problem of striking with her front feet at anything or any-body who got close to her front end. This is a very dangerous habit and since I was in the business of training horses and retraining spoiled ones, I agreed to work with her. The first thing I did when she arrived at my place was hobble her front feet and scotch hobble a hind leg. Then I sacked her out. Using an old blanket, I gently slapped that mare all over with it, particu-larly the chest and front legs. She never blinked an eye as that blanket hit her back, hind legs, tail, belly, neck or head. But she would go right on the fight each time it came in contact with her chest and front legs. A horse will only resist being sacked out so long, then when they realize they are not being hurt in anyway they quit fighting. Hobbled the way she was, she wasn't doing any damage to me, only annoying herself. As I slapped her over and over on her front end, I was watching her ears and expression for signs of calming down, and missed seeing the tongue of the buckle on the leather hobbles slowly tearing through the leather with her frantic attempts to strike me and the blanket. When the hobble strap let loose, her hoof came up and connected with my hand holding the blanket. My thumb snapped like a twig. A week later, I returned her to her owner, her habit of striking cured. He was curious about the cast on my hand. Not wanting to be taken for a wimp, I explained it was just a little accident working with somebody's horse, nothing serious, but it sure interfered with my town job and riding colts for a couple of weeks. I keep my leather equipment well oiled now and check it for any beginning tears or defects before I put it on a horse.

Skip was a three–year–old mare, not very big, and needing some discipline real bad. She was spoiled rotten by her owners, and now they had hired me to break her to saddle. She had a nasty temper and figured the only thing humans were put on earth for was to give her treats and oats. I hate working with horses like her because they will hurt you and themselves at the same time, because they have no respect for humans. After a couple of days of ground work with her, she had accepted the saddle and bridle without a fight. I knew she was just sulking, though, and even though she wasn't a big horse, I was worried about just stepping up on her. I knew she had to blow sometime and get it out of her system, and had been hoping she would do it while I worked with her from the ground.

I don't normally get another rider to snub for me but Skip had me worried. I knew a young man who if mounted on one of my good geldings might be able to do the trick. He agreed to listen to my instructions as what to do and not to do, because he had never snubbed a bronc to the horse he was sitting on before. In the middle of the pen, I showed him how much rope I wanted reaching from his saddle horn to the halter I had on her under my snaffle bridle. I showed him how to take a couple of clean wraps around that horn. I told him, how once I was on her to get the gelding moving and keep him moving, in a circle to the left, since I was going to be on her, on his right. I specifically told him, she can't hurt you, but she can hurt me, so even if you think she is going to climb right into the saddle with you, DON'T unsnub that rope, just keep moving. He fancied himself a brave man who wasn't afraid of no iddy biddy little horse.

As I stepped up on her, she laid her ears back, but remained quiet while I took a deep seat and told him to move his horse out. The second she felt that halter rope tightened up, she went on the fight. This is a common happening with a snubbed horse, so what happened next caught me completely by surprise. The man snubbing for me panicked. He was in no danger whatsoever and he couldn't get those wraps of rope off his horn quickly enough. She shot straight in the air, fighting having her head tied solid, and her head was no longer tied at all. With her head unexpectedly freed, she came straight up and over backwards. Her weight drove me flat into the ground, her and the saddle on top of me. That was the third and hopefully the last time I've been knocked unconscious. The first couple of times a horse laid me out cold are hardly worth mentioning, but this one did the trick. The saddle horn drove into my ribs, breaking two of them and tearing muscle away from the bones. Once again I was laid up from my town job and finished riding for a spell. The owners of Skip figured I wasn't the right person for the job, and hired someone else to break their little darling. The next rider wasn't the right one for the job either, nor was the third. The last I heard of Skip, she was on the inside of a dog-food can, not a bad place for her in my books.

I made it through my late twenties and early thirties with nothing more than a broken toe or two from getting stepped on by horses the size of baby elephants. The popular running shoes just don't give as much protection as a pair of good leather riding boots. I was in my late thirties before my last wreck.

A man asked me to work on a long yearling stud colt for him. Seems this pretty chestnut had an aversion to being led. Seems he didn't much like his feet picked up either. Seems he liked to bite and kick a wee bit too. I found out a long time ago that if you throw a horse like this down on the ground, tie all four feet together, and leave him there for an hour or two, while sitting on his side, sacking him out by gently slapping him with a blanket, and generally doing what you want with him, he will have an attitude adjustment by the time you let him up. I long ago learned how to lay a horse down all by myself, even if I am a female and not that big either. Picking a quiet day, without anybody to bother me, I laid him down, tied him down and went to work on him. Time and time again he tried to sink his teeth into my body parts as I worked with him. Again and again he strained against the ropes binding him, attempting to kick out at me. Slowly he accepted my touching him, accepting the fact I was the boss, not him. Things went well, so I decided to release his legs and let him up, confident he had learned a good lesson in manners. Now, remember parts of me are older than my years, a bit crippled up maybe from too many rough horses over the years. I had loosened the ropes, when over the hill comes his owner, the tractor he's on, in road gear, and a large round bale of hay clutched in the green monster's bale carrier jaws, heading straight for me and that downed horse. I didn't have a hold of that yearling's head, no way to stop him from coming up off the ground when utter fear of that charging tractor overtook him. My stiff knee and beat up old bones were just too slow to carry me from my squatting position, up and out of his way. His flashing front hoof caught me high up on my cheek and on my nose. After going to my town job for six weeks with black eyes and a swollen face, I finally went to a doctor, who informed me my nose was broken again and so was my cheek bone. I really do hope that was my very last wreck be- cause I hurt all over.

I did manage to break a bone in my ankle last year, stepping out of the back end of a horse trailer, into an old badger hole hidden by long grass. No horse in spitting distance of me though, so I guess this time doesn't count.

SKIDDOR & FRIENDS

They say that a person's pets often take on the personality of his or her owner, in which case I'm in serious trouble. They may lock me up. Because I don't have a single normal pet or horse on my property. Even my quarter horse stallion is not normal. Three Kits (herein referred to by his nickname, Skiddor) is sixteen hands high, an American Quarter Horse Association stallion who is bred for the track. His pedigree is a long list of champions, his conformation excellent, his potential as a sire great. So what's the problem? I'm afraid Skiddor thinks he is a dog. A very large dog. Thank heavens he is an outside dog, not a house dog or my problems would be a lot worse.

Let's start at the beginning. Once upon a time, I began searching for a new stallion prospect. My search took me far and wide, but no horse I looked at was good enough. Then one day I found him.

Having sustained a serious leg injury as a foal, he had been kept a stallion for his potential as a sire, even though he would never be able to race. He was raised properly on a large breeding farm. His first one and a half years were normal ones. He was a normal horse.

THEN HE CAME TO LIVE WITH ME. Things started out okay. Although he enjoyed the run of a two–acre paddock, he was lonely for companionship. This is where my husky/white shepherd cross dog comes into the picture. Blaze and Skiddor were just a couple of half-grown puppies, growing up together. They played tag. They ate together (yup, Blaze took a liking to rolled oats twice a day, when Skiddor was fed, both their heads buried in the feeder at the same time). They drank together, because regardless which one went to the water trough to drink, the other one was immediately also thirsty. I can't say they slept together though, because Blaze wasn't normal. He slept on the small BBQ table on the balcony, rain, snow or shine, it didn't matter, he slept on top of that table. By the time he was grown, his legs and head hung over the sides. Looked pretty uncomfortable to me, but then I've been known to sleep in some pretty weird places, too.

Blaze taught Skiddor to chew on sticks, a lost glove, plastic toys: basically nothing was safe from them. Their favourite game of all was Tug–a–War, Blaze on one end of an empty burlap sack, Skiddor on the other. Sometimes Skiddor would even let the smaller Blaze win. Then you would see an eighty-pound dog galloping across the pasture, dragging a thousand-pound colt behind him. Honest!

One bad thing though. Blaze taught Skiddor to chase cats. No cat is safe on this place. Skiddor never lays his ears back at anything or anybody. Except cats. He will leave his feed, even other horses to chase a cat. I have seen him stretched out flat, sleeping. A cat strolls by, he grunts and groans, gets to his feet and chases the cat under the nearest building or fence. Satisfied, he goes back to his resting place, relaxes, and is soon asleep again.

Skiddor is now two and a half years old with ten wives to his credit. He has a gentle old bred mare for companionship. Blaze didn't take kindly to his buddy's interest in the opposite sex, his jealousy being so extreme that I was forced to give him away. Blaze may be gone but Skiddor still chews on anything and everything. His now six–acre pasture comes complete with enough fallen tree branches to keep him amused for hours. I have seen him pack an eight–foot branch around all afternoon, even though he steps on it and has a great deal of trouble getting it through the corral gate. No matter, he will pack them around like Blaze taught him to. Occasionally, I can't help myself and I will get an old feed sack and play a game of Tug–a–

War with him. He sometimes lets me win too. Well, at least he never learned to bark at people. Well, not normal people any–way.

Skiddor must be seeing nothing but spots before his eyes now. On a sunny afternoon, wherever he looks, spots abound, because now I have a yard full of running, barking and playing Dalmatians. These beautiful dogs, which were bred long ago to be coach dogs, following their master's carriages, have a natural instinct to hang around the horses. The mares are not pleased with their presence, but the stallion welcomes them with happy snorts and playful jumps and leaps. His performance when they go visit him leaves other people convinced that he means to harm them, as he dances around them in his pasture. He would no more harm his friends than give up mares as his other favourite pastime. He places each hoof down with extraordinary care, even after a giant leap in the air, with a mighty backwards kick which would put the Lippizan stallions of Vienna to shame. Ears half back, he snakes his head towards them, his powerful jaws, which could crush the life from their bodies should he choose to do so, remaining firmly closed. Should one of them decide to take a rest in the deep, fresh straw of his covered shed, he is apt to approach them with gentle steps and doze besides the sleeping dog, sometimes even lying down and stretching his huge frame out beside them.

Such is the life for my best friends, these dogs and horses that share my home and bring me many hours of pleasure with their antics and joyful love of being alive. What more could I ever want?

A RIDER'S DREAM

Out of the mist, a magnificent stallion emerges, surrounded by billowing clouds, his galloping hooves treading air. He races towards me, muscles rippling down his shoulders and across his chest. Wait, I look closer and begin to see the outline of a rider, seemingly lost amidst his long, flowing mane. The horse thunders on towards me, and now I can see it is a girl clinging to his back, no bridle, no saddle, just her and the stallion, not two separate beings, but a single entity.

The buzzing ring of my alarm clock yanks me from my dream, back into reality. As I dress, I think of the chores waiting to be done. There is a stallion out in my corrals, maybe he is galloping around out there, but it is impossible to tell in the heavy morning fog. His mane is long and flowing because it needs to be trimmed yet again. I know one thing for certain, until I'm certified legally insane by a whole slew of doctors, you won't catch me riding him without a bridle or saddle. My dream was nice but right after I feed the horses, there is a barn to be cleaned, something I keep forgetting to include in my fantasy dreams.

For every horse that is a dream come true to break and train, there is always one who makes my hobby of working with horses a test of both skill and patience. With Jeep, who had been allowed to get away with rearing over backwards on his rider, I worked long and hard and he still ended up a spoiled, dangerous animal, unfit for use by man. Like the pretty sorrel Arabian gelding, who had learned to bluff his inexperienced owner into believing he was a tiger in sheep's clothing. Sure I faced him down, taught him who was the real tiger in the corral. He knew better than to run at me with ears back and teeth bared. He even broke out rather nicely but when returned to his owner was soon running the man right out of the pasture again. What a waste of time and trouble on my part. Or the grey, pony–type mare who had gotten away with acting like an outlaw each time her master mounted her. She had herself so convinced that everyone could be made to jump off her when she acted up, that nothing I did would change her mind. Time and time again, I stayed on her while she threw her fits, until we were both exhausted. Then, she would behave until the next ride. I told her master the truth, she just wasn't worth the trouble. Or the pinto gelding I pur–chased at a sale as only halter broke, only to find out he was actually well broke, but had been spoiled because someone had let him get away with purposely running the rider's legs and knees into fence posts, trees, corners of buildings, even sides of vehicles. He had learnt that his rider would soon tire of his game and get off him, letting him once again get his own way. I broke him off the habit but not without both my legs and knees taking many beatings. When I resold him, he prob–ably went right back to his painful habit.

I was the fifth owner and trainer for the tall, chestnut gelding. His thoroughbred breeding was above par, he was the result of careful selective breeding for producing a hunter/jumper horse. The problem with him was he didn't want to be a well–schooled horse over those big jumps. No, he wanted to be a bucking bronc and set out at an early age to show his riders and trainers that he was mighty good at it too. He was a powerhouse of a horse, big boned and standing sixteen and three hands high. A long way up when it comes to getting bucked off. I liked the looks of him and knew if I could break him of his savage bucking, I would be able to triple my money when I resold him. It was not to be. I fancied myself a fair good rider but he had being a bronc down pat. I couldn't hold his head up with a bit in his mouth so resorted to my heaviest, rawhide bosal. When he decided to blow, hackamore or no hackamore, he would plunge his head down, giving himself the slack he needed to dump me in the dirt. Man, oh man, he could buck. I was just another owner and trainer in his life who failed to teach him a thing. I sold him to yet another trainer who had stars in his eyes over how much the fancy-looking gelding would be worth if he could take the buck out of him. The last I heard about the horse he had got his wish and had been sold to a rodeo stock contractor where he would be able to buck to his heart's content.

The truth is, I have never failed to do a proper job of breaking a horse if no else had ever messed with him. I greatly prefer to get a horse who has never been handled past maybe halter breaking. A ranch-raised horse who isn't spoiled by being loved, petted and fussed over is even better. These horses have respect for people, instead of walking all over top of a person like a thousand-pound toy poodle. Many of these horses are the ones I remember best as being a rider's dream horse.

Amigo, a palomino gelding, was as good after only one ride as other horses with thirty days' training. He simply wanted to please me with every inch of his soul. In only two weeks, I was able to sell him to a young girl who wanted to be the one to train her own horse. Even though she was young and inexperienced, Amigo was like a big kitten, accepting everything in stride. The pair of them were a team for many years, doing everything together from English dressage to western pleasure.

Smokey was only pony size, standing a bit under fourteen hands high. I wanted to train him for sale to be a gentle mount for children. He had a naturally lovable disposition and never blinked an eye as I taught him to be mounted from either side, to have and accept someone sliding off his rump or crawling under his belly and between his legs. Never once did he ever shy or try to buck during his training both with a saddle and bareback. He became the much-loved pet of a family with four children. I couldn't have bought him back for a million dollars they thought so much of him.

Jeronimo was a chestnut who maybe wasn't very big, but his heart was huge, filled with the desire to please me in anyway possible. He was born, I think, to pack a rider on his back with the greatest of care. He liked being ridden so much that once saddled up, he would become impatient should I not mount him right away. He'd start bumping me with his nose and turning his left side towards me. Once he was trained, I picked a home for him where I knew the people were kind to their horses so that he might always enjoy being ridden so much.

Pal, another palomino of mine, was also a pleasure to train. He too, actually liked being ridden. Once I was mounted on him, he would turn from being a sleepy-eyed, lazy-acting mutt into a quick-stepping, let's go, let's go horse who could pack me all day and night without ever tiring. The next morning when I went down to the corrals, he would be the first horse to amble over to the tack shed to get riding again. He went to a teenaged boy who had the experience to contain Pal's enthusiasm over getting to be ridden.

A three-year-old dun mare I purchased at a horse sale took to being ridden like a duck takes to water. In sixty days of riding, I could do anything with her. Rope off her, not that I had much luck catching anything, do spins and rollbacks without a single misplaced step, swim a river or claw our way up the side of the steepest mountain. When asked to back, she simply flew backwards until told to stop. She worked with perfect head set, on a loose rein. I liked her so much I turned down many good offers on her. The day came though, when a prominent horseman on the quarter horse show circuit would not take no for an answer. She went on to become a champion in each and every event he showed her in. Many times I have wished I could have owned dozens more just like her.

In all my years of training, I rode just about every western breed of horse in the book, with a few mongrels thrown in who could pull a plough too. Big or small, the ones I remember best are those who willingly put an effort into pleasing me, their rider.

HORSES CAN TALK

I don't have to be under the influence of something stronger than tea to see horses talking to each other. It never took a college or university degree to know what they are saying either. Years of watching and working with them has enabled me to learn and understand a great deal of their language.

I once attended a training clinic for horses and riders, where the teacher may win big at the shows and is an excellent rider, but even after all his years in the horse business he could stand to learn a thing or two about reading horse language. Had I had someone to place bets with at this two-day clinic, I might have won enough money back to pay for the clinic in the first place.

To start the first day off, he lectured us on getting to know your horse and understand him. He explained it takes months and years of working with many different horses to get as good as he was.

Then he had a two-year-old gelding brought in the arena, which was already saddled and bridled. He stepped up on that gelding without checking the cinch, bridle, or anything else. Seems to me he was there to teach us the correct way of working with young horses, and should have done an equipment check before mounting. I have done it for so many years that I automatically pre–check my equipment before getting on, even if I did the saddling myself.

While he explained to us that the gelding had three months' riding on him, he proceeded to trot him around in a circle, showing us how good the horse was progressing in his training. The first thing I noticed was after a couple of laps, the horse was cocking one ear back more than the other. He had his right ear sort of flopped over sideways and back. The trainer wasn't reading that horse's language, but I was, and the horse was trying to tell him something. The next thing I spotted was that every time the trainer picked up on those reins to stop or turn the colt, his nose would come up, out of position. The trainer would then bump his legs against the colt's sides, and use a see–saw motion on the two reins to get the colt to drop his nose back down. After about twenty minutes or so, the gelding was performing worse and worse. So the trainer stepped off him, and explained that all horses have a bad day and after all, this was the gelding's first time working with about twenty students standing around him. Before his assistant led him away, I walked up to him and moved the right stirrup aside, wondering what was his half cocked ear had meant. The cinch strap was not only twisted, but the metal tongue on the cinch ring itself was poked straight into his tender hide, making every movement of himself and his rider very painful. I reached up to his head and checked the bit; it was a good inch too loose in his mouth, no wonder he threw his head when rein pressure was applied. He had tried to communicate his discomfort to the rider in horse language but nobody listened.

The students who had brought their own horses with them were then asked to mount up and form a loose circle around the trainer. Each one in turn, he approached and attempted to correct their posture in the saddle. This girl should straighten her back, this woman had to get her heels down, and that young man needed to keep his elbows in. When he stepped up beside a ewe-necked bay gelding, I saw that horse tense up. It was plain that he was poorly started under saddle and still apt to act up. The trainer pulled the rider's foot out of the stirrup, saying they needed to be lengthened and he would do so. The bay was as tight as a fiddle string, with his ears crammed back, a sure sign of a bad temper. The trainer didn't watch the horse's language at all. When he finished with the left stirrup, he walked around the back end of that horse to work on the right stirrup. As he did so, the bay sucked his tail down and really flattened his ears. The trainer no sooner passed directly behind him and wham, he took a well aimed kick in the thigh. Ouch, that must have hurt. Had he been as good a horseman as he thought he was, he would have gotten out of the way the second he saw the bay horse clamp his tail down, a sure body language sign saying you are about to get kicked, buddy.

Like us, horses communicate verbally, with sound. We talk baby talk to our little ones, cooing and crooning, and mares talk to their young ones with soft nickers and whinnies. Rowdy men holler and shout when trying to prove how tough and manly they are. Stallions squeal their challenge to each other in much the same fashion. Friends call out to each other in greeting after being apart, horses neigh to each other, glad to be back together. When we are worried or upset, our voices betray our fears. Horses whinny with unmistakable concern. Like horses, some people snort, snuffle and blow, even if they don't realize they are doing it.

A person might get mad and kick the garbage can to let everyone know he is not pleased. A horse will paw the ground or strike out when he isn't happy about things. A child who isn't getting his own way might stomp his foot on the ground in frustration. A horse will do the same. Children sulk, horses sulk. An adult may balk at having to do something he doesn't want to do, and a horse does the same.

A hind leg cocked on a horse might mean he is only resting

that leg or if combined with half laid–back ears, it means he will kick you if he takes a notion to. A horse may shake his head because flies are bothering him, or maybe it means "leave me alone." Irritate a horse too much with inconsistent commands or push him too hard and he will voice his displeasure by wring-ing his tail.

By far, horses do most of their communicating with their ears. It is a universal language among horses, these quick flicks of ears, that always seem to be talking. People are the same worldwide, except they use their hands, since it's hard to wiggle our ears. No matter what country you may visit, even though you do not know how to speak the language, you can commu-nicate your needs through hand signals. It may take awhile in cases such as, no, I'm not hungry, no, I'm not feeling sick, yes, the reason I'm holding myself like this is I HAVE TO GO TO THE BATHROOM.

Take the time to watch this unique style of talking among horses. Say a half a dozen horses are loafing in the shade of the barn. All are at rest. A two–year–old stretches and takes a step closer to an old brown mare. She lays her ears back for a split second. The two–year–old instantly steps quickly to the side now, knowing he has disturbed the mare who might hang a licking on him if he doesn't move away. His stepping to the side has brought him into the next horse's private space. This pow-erhouse of a big gelding now has only to make a passing at-tempt at laying his ears back, and the poor two–year–old must jump out of the pack, rather than be sandwiched between two boss horses. Nothing was said verbally, but he knew what was being said. He works his way around the others until he is face to face with a yearling. He stops and pricks his ears forward, staring intently at the other. The yearling raises his head and pricks his ears forward. Suddenly these two friends come to-gether, like long–lost buddies. No big bosses here, just two friends, busy scratching each other's back.

Riding and training horses was a whole lot easier once I started learning their language of the ears. By listening to them, I learned to do a better job and perhaps got hurt less too.

I learned that a lop–eared horse isn't being taught a thing. Once a horse gets overtired or hot, he will let his ears kind of fall to the sides. You might as well get off him and start again to–morrow because he is sulking major. A horse who is listening to the rider on his back will be moving his ears back and forth constantly, one ear looking where he is going and the other ear listening to your commands. A horse who never flicks his ears towards you, but keeps them straight forward, isn't paying attention to anything but what's up ahead. He isn't learning anything either.

A hurting horse who is sore in his back or any muscle will carry his ears pointed back all the time, not flat back, just back. He may carry you another twenty miles without blowing up from the pain or discomfort, but trust me, he will remember the abuse and be harder to train the next time. Not even a stallion should conduct the ride with his ears flat back, pinned to his head. It means he is plumb mad at you or something and a danger to himself and everybody. Those pinned ears are a sure sign of dislike for being ridden or just a plain evil–tempered horse. I don't even try to fight it out with a horse like this. There is no point in it. Get rid of him or her.

Your horse will talk to you all the time if you only learn to listen. He will nicker a greeting to you each morning, perhaps only because he knows you bring feed to him, perhaps because he really does like you. If he is in distress he will tell you. If he is afraid he will tell you. If he is hungry he will let you know. Through his many channels of communication he will let you know everything.

If one horse tenses up and stares off into the distance at something, the other ones read his language and pretty soon they are all staring in the same direction, even if they don't know at what. For the heck of it, stand on a street corner some day and with great concentration stare up at the sky. Before you know it, you will have a crowd of people beside you, doing the same, and they know not what they are looking at.

HORSES CAN BE HEROES TOO

Perhaps you too have heard stories of a half–frozen rider who made it safely home by his faithful saddle horse, through a wind–driven blizzard of snow. How these horses, eyes blinded by snow, struggled against impossible odds to bring their masters home to safety. Many a lonesome cowboy in the days of old was saved by his horse in these conditions.

I remember well a story told to me by an elderly farmer who has long since passed on. Were it not for his horse, he might very well have never lived to grow to the gentle old age he did. His story was quite different from those that are often told around the kitchen table when horse people begin to reminisce. Here is his story as told to me, a story of a man's faith in his horse and the courage of that horse.

He and his family were, as he put it, dirt poor back then. They had no money, and basically lived off what could be grown or raised on their small farm. His young wife scratched rows in the dusty ground, planted potatoes, turnips and carrots, and with a bent back, hauled water from the well to make them grow. A handful of chickens gave them the occasional egg or chicken dinner. A couple of pigs rooted for food and tried to raise batches of piglets. Except for an ancient milk cow and her scrawny calf, their only other livestock was his team of horses for working the land. From sunrise to sunset, he toiled in his fields with this team. Bell was his favourite of the two horses. Long past her prime, this gentle giant gave everything she had to help pull the plough. Head down, she leaned wearily into the collar of her harness, day after day. Hitched beside her was Star, as big as Bell, young and in his prime. Star had been passed from farmer to farmer because he had a bad disposition. He was lazy and always letting poor Bell take the brunt of the hard pulling. There was no money to buy other horses and he had no choice but keep working old Bell, and hollering at Star to get up and pull his own weight in the field each day.

Spring became summer, then autumn, then winter arrived in all its mighty howling splendour. The winter before had been hard on his wife. She had suffered a difficult labour delivering their first-born child. The child was stillborn. Now her time grew near with the impending birth of their second child. Picking a clear day, he made her comfortable under quilts in the cumbersome farm sleigh used for hauling grain to town. Once again, old Bell leaned into her harness, Star snorting beside her, and they headed across country for the small town that lay many miles ahead of them. The snow was not too deep yet and they made good time, arriving by night fall.

His eldest sister welcomed them, for she would keep his wife with her and help tend to the birthing of this baby. He only planned to spend the one night and then journey back to the farm to care for the other livestock. Mother Nature had other plans. Overnight a raging prairie blizzard sprung up. For four days and nights, Mother Nature vented her anger on the land, but on the morning of the fifth day, she cooled her blowing winds and thickly falling snow. He chose this morning to head back, for the animals would be starved by now.

The going was hard, the horses up to their bellies in snow where it had drifted. Often he had to stop his team to let them rest, their hides steaming and wet in the cold of winter. Darkness came all too quickly. He still had six to eight miles to go. He pushed on, for there was no turning back now. Already the wind was picking up and heavy snow started to fall. Within minutes, he was in the centre of another blizzard. He stuck to high ground as much as he could and hoped that, having grown up on this land, he could guide the weary horses home to the safety of the barn. It was not to be.

Star was sulking and trying to drift with the wind, dragging old Bell with him. One second the heavy sleigh was upright, the next it was skidding down an embankment, the frightened horses losing their footing and falling with it. Amid the tangle of breaking wood and neighing horses, the farmer slid downward, coming to rest in a broken heap. In his confused mind, he realized where they were. My God, they were miles off course, they had fallen over the riverbank, pushed far off the way by the screaming wind. Worse, when he tried to stand, his right leg collapsed under him, broken. Pulling himself, hand over hand, he reached the tangle of horses and harness. His hands numb with cold, he loosened buckles and pulled straps free. With a great surge of power, Star lunged to his feet, no longer held down by the twisted leather and broken pole. As quickly as he rose, he drifted away into the whiteout darkness. Bell was much slower gaining her feet. Once up, she stood in total misery. The man knew that he was in more trouble than ever before in his life. To stay where he was meant death by freezing. His numb hands and broken leg made it impossible to crawl up on Bell's back. Her harness hung in disarray. How could Bell possibly get him home? With an idea born of pure desperation he repaired her harness as best he could, then he took the tail gate off the busted up wagon box, and working with determination in the darkness, he fastened the three-foot by five-foot gate to the harness ends. Wrapping his body, even his face and head, in quilts, he sat on the tail gate and hollered at old Bell to get up. With a moan the mare bent her head into the wind and began pushing her tired legs through the drifts. Thrown off balance, he laid full length on the makeshift sled and hung on.

When he first realized that his ordeal was over, he was at a rancher's place, bordering the river. He awoke to the rancher and his wife tending to his severely frostbitten limbs and twisted leg.

He was later to find out that Bell had plunged through the blizzard for about four miles to this rancher's home where she had been originally foaled at. Although she had not been there for fifteen years, she found it in the dark and cold. It was also the closest home to the site of the wreck. Bell had indeed saved his life. Bell was also dead. When the wagon-type sleigh and two horses took the fall over the riverbank, her chest was pierced by the wagon pole, which her and Star were hitched to, a deadly spear in the violent tumble they took. When she had arrived in the ranch yard, she had kept up a lonely whinny for help until they heard her. When the rancher took her to his warm barn to unharness her and feed her, only then did he see her wound. He stripped the harness from her exhausted body, and she sank down and gasped her last tortured breath.

When the farmer told me this story, over fifty-five years later, he proudly held out old Bell's bit from her bridle, saved all those years in remembrance of a horse who was truly a hero.

Saved By A Lady

I was about twelve years old, the day my mare, Lady, saved my life. The second I was off the school bus that day, I headed for the horse pasture to catch Lady. Not only did I love riding her each day, but I also knew that it was the best to get mounted as fast as possible and away from the yard, in case my mother had thought of house chores for me to do while I was in school. No respectable cowgirl wants to be stuck doing women's chores on a bright, sunny afternoon. With only a bridle on Lady, we galloped out to pasture, bareback. It was early in the year, and Dad's Hereford cows had just finished calving. We meandered along, stopping to check each cow and calf, something I loved doing, seeing each newborn happily nursing, bucking and playing.

In the distance, to the northeast, I picked up the sound of a cow bawling for her calf. From the sound of her voice I knew something was wrong. Booting Lady into a gallop, I went to find her. Rounding the base of the hill, she came into sight. Lady and I skidded to a halt. Of all Dad's cows, she was the only one I was afraid of, and I sure did not want to get too close to her. I named her 24–T, from the first three symbols of the metal registration clip in her ear. Nobody wanted to mess with 24–T. Personally I did not think she was quite right in the head. Dad had purchased her from a production sale, a well–bred heifer, but flighty. On the drive home, she had managed to jump out of the stock racks on the back of the truck and did a crash landing on her head. She was one crazy cow after that. Normally Dad would not keep a bad–tempered cow in the herd but he had paid a great deal of money for her and was determined to get as many good calves out of her as possible. Carefully I moved Lady closer to her, wondering where her calf was. She was next to the fence, and sure enough, there was her calf, on the other side of it, lying down next to some big rocks.

Nothing I couldn't handle, I would simply ride up the fence line to the nearest gate, go through it, and come back down the other side. Then Lady and I could spook the little critter back under the bottom wire to his momma. Everything went as planned until we got to the calf. The poor thing had laid down between two rocks and had got his hind leg twisted back behind one. He was trapped and unable to rise.

I really hated to get off Lady and put myself in danger from 24–T, but I could not leave the baby in such a predicament. Jumping off Lady's broad back, I left her with reins down, and moving slow as to not upset the cow anymore than she already was, I reached the calf. Reaching down, I grabbed the trapped leg and lifted it up to free it.

Everything started happening mighty fast then. The calf let out a frightened bleat and 24–T came through the three–strand barbed wire fence to his rescue. Bellowing in rage, she charged me. I had no time to move. The cow was fast, but my mare was quicker. Whirling around, she fired both her hind feet into the rib cage of the mad beast. The blow knocked the cow off course. I was paralyzed with fear and frozen to the spot, unable to move. Again the cow charged. Again Lady's heels connected with her shoulder and chest. For a split second the cow went to her knees, her nose buried in the dirt. Lady spun around and ears flat back, she squealed and attacked the cow with her teeth and front feet. The two combatants went at it again. This time the cow nailed Lady in the flank, actually lifting her up and sideways. By now I had regained my senses and was off, running as hard as I could go. I ran through the deep, freshly ploughed field until I collapsed, my oxygen–starved lungs shooting pains through my chest. By now, 24–T had figured out that her calf was up and free. She stood, head lowered, pawing and throwing dirt up over her back. Lady still stood between us, facing the cow, ears back. The cow finally called her calf to her side and turning, purposely crashed back through the pasture fence, leaving the mare alone.

Lady turned her head, looking at me, and nickered. Then, faithfully as always, she trotted to my side and rubbed her great head on my shoulder. I am convinced to this day that she knew she was saving me from serious harm, when she fought off the attacking cow.

No Known Reason

My friend Susan tells the story of tangling with a wicked–tempered cow, while riding with two friends on a government grazing lease next to her home north of Ardmore. Susan was mounted on Bo, a big thoroughbred Hanovarian cross gelding with a gentle disposition and good mind. Mike was on an American Saddlebred Tennessee Walker cross gelding named Hearty. Linda was riding her good quarter horse gelding, named Big Mike. Her husband took a lot of ribbing from people, being referred to as Little Mike whenever Big Mike was around.

They were walking along, enjoying their ride, when out of nowhere came a cow looking for a fight. She left the peacefully grazing herd for no apparent reason. None of the riders were experienced with cattle enough to know they were in real danger. Suddenly, she lowered her head and charged Mike's horse, catching him in the flank and knocking his hind legs out from under him. As the horse struggled to stay on his feet, she rammed him again. The gelding panicked and began rearing up in fear. Knowing Mike was a beginning rider and in danger of being thrown to the ground, Susan yelled at both Linda and Mike to get their horses away from the cow, into the heavy timber and make a run for the nearest gate to escape. Bravely she reined Bo in between the beast and Mike's horse. The crazed cow slammed into Bo's rib cage, knocking him down onto his side. Susan barely had time to yank her foot out of the stirrup to keep her leg from being crushed under the horse's falling weight. She stayed in the saddle as he lunged to his feet. Again and again the cow slammed into Bo, again he was knocked to the ground. Never once did Bo panic under the assault, which surely would have further endangered his rider. When Susan saw that the other riders were clear of the danger, she drove Bo ahead, away from the enraged cow.

Had Bo not have been of such brave heart, had he not stood his ground against the attack, perhaps someone could have been killed. A bovine on the attack is several hundred pounds of deadly intent.

No one knows why this cow, who was not being bothered in anyway, went on the fight, but three riders went away with a lot of newly learned respect for the supposedly docile beasts.

LOSS OF A FRIEND

We all have friends. They may be our immediate family, or the ones we cultivated over the years. They are our friends, our life-support systems that we are involved in every day, every waking moment. The people we talk with, the people who make it all right. I have many friends. They comfort me and nurture me. They are my life line.

Whiskey was my friend. There's no easy way to say goodbye. She was the best. I try to forget what she meant to me. I try to pretend now that she was just another horse. She wasn't just another horse. She was Whiskey. I miss her so much. I write this chapter of the book, late at night, all alone. Because that is when I best remember her, when my mind is clear. I remember having to say goodbye.

Throughout this book I have talked about horses. I laugh with you over their antics. I cry with you for I was there. I talk about good horses and bad horses. I talk about the beginning of life and death, the ultimate end. All good times come to an end.

All life comes to an end. Again, there is no easy way to say goodbye.

I'm a horse person. I'm intelligent. I know when the time has come. I know when my human feelings must be overridden for the sake of the animal. I know when it's time to say goodbye. So why was it so damn hard with Whiskey? I listen every day to so-called friends and horse buddies say the same thing. "You mean you had a veterinarian put her to sleep, well didn't you lose money?" "Couldn't you have sold her for meat and got seven hundred dollars or so?" Pardon my attitude, but go take a hike.

I will never know exactly what was wrong with Whiskey. But then, she never was a horse to have the usual common problems. All I know was I had my final midnight ride on her early on in November. Just me and Whiskey. She wasn't that old. Pushing twenty years old, yes, but still young. She wintered on self-fed hay, all she could eat, and a bit of grain when I went to see her every day. The water in the trough was heated and always available. Yet she grew more despondent. She was in good flesh, fat in some people's books but she suffered. I had two veterinarians look at her, sure she was is some kind of pain but they know not what it could be. There was no external evidence of founder, nor was there a reason for her to founder this late in the year, when the grass was no longer lush. She never broke into the grain bin and overate, and she was not road foundered. She did not stand like a foundered horse, with hind feet well under her body, front feet extended to take the weight off foundered front hooves. Yet she did not want to move, as if her feet were causing her extreme pain.

And I asked anyone and everyone who knew her. "Don't you think her head is getting bigger, doesn't it appear to be swollen in some way?" For the last year and half of her life, I couldn't get it out of my head that the very shape and size of her skull and face was changing. As she had always had one of the homeliest heads of any horse I owned, too large and coarse for her thor-

221

oughbred body, I couldn't put my finger on why I thought her head was growing and getting worse to look at. She had no abscessed teeth to cause this.

The two veterinarians who checked her did not think she was really foundered, and if she was, it would have to be in all four feet equally, instead of only her front feet, which is the usual case. As for examining her head, they scoffed at me.

I am a fairly competent farrier myself. I had two other good farriers check her and they ruled out founder as I had done. Yet she appeared stiffer every day, in more pain every day, moving around less and less. In desperation, I had a self-proclaimed horse chiropractor out to treat her. There is no doubt in my mind that with his gentle fingers that he found and treated certain pressure points on her body, and that on other horses it worked, but on Whiskey, it showed no improvement.

The day started out like any other day. I awoke, and as I made my first cup of coffee, like all the other days, I pulled back my kitchen curtain and looked out to the corral, my gaze finding Whiskey.

She had not moved an inch from where she had been standing the evening before. Her head hung down in desolation. It was time.

I have had to shoot three horses in my lifetime to put them out of pain. I could not do this final act for her.

Yes, I could have gotten the local vet out to do it, but I had to know once and for all what was happening to my dear old friend. It would mean hauling her sixty miles to a vet clinic that had an X-ray machine, and veterinarians specializing in equines. I gave her a shot of pain-killing Bute to make the journey easier on her. That sixty-mile trip was for me the longest stretch of highway I have ever travelled in my life.

Those two lady vets were thorough in their examination, the X-rays done with ease. The results hard to understand. Her bones in her face and skull were actually enlarging but also becoming more porous, with loss of density. The only thing listed in their journals, even close to her symptoms was known as "Big Head Disease," which strikes young, often malnourished, horses. She was neither young nor lacking in a proper diet. The coffin bones in all four feet were rotated, showing founder, but how, why? Because there was no external evidence of founder, they felt it must have been a slow gradual rotation of the coffin bones and because all four feet were affected, they said perhaps it was something wrong with her internally causing it.

I did not watch as they put her down with a quick, painless drug. I did not hold her head in my arms, one last time. I couldn't. When it was all over, I held my pain and tears inside and went home. It was weeks before I quit looking out the window, first thing in the morning to check on Whiskey. It was only then, that I cried, because saying goodbye to an old friend is never easy. Goodbye my friend.

THE
AUTHOR

Gayle Bunney was born in the town of Oyen, in southeastern Alberta. Her parents, Ralph and Rebecca Caskey, still live there, although they are long since retired from the farm. She has lived all over Alberta and northern British Columbia. She has worked with horses in such communities as Rocky Mountain House, Rimbey, Sundre, Drumheller, the Calgary area, Brooks and Bonnyville, where she raises top bred quarter horses and an array of different breeds of dogs.

She wrote this book for none other than the horses themselves. Since they cannot speak for themselves, then she will do it for them. She does not pretend to be the kind of expert about horses who went to clinics, schools or academies to be taught about them. Instead she raised, trained and rode them all, learning through the school of hard knocks. She simply has a great love and passion for them, and although there were times when she has made mistakes with them, or did not handle them correctly, she hopes that she learned from those mistakes.